The Escort

Gina Robinson

Gina Robinson
SEATTLE, WASHINGTON

Book Layout ©2013 BookDesignTemplates.com
Front Cover Design by Hot Damn Designs

The Escort/ Gina Robinson. -- 1st ed.
ISBN 978-0615823508

New York 1898

The Barge Office was choked with people. Immigrants seeking entry into the United States nervously waited their turn in ragged columns, shuffling, looking longingly out through grimy windows, hoping to catch a glimpse of Manhattan's Battery and Castle Garden. The United States waited just beyond the tired, overworked officials at the end of the line.

Angelina Allessandro glanced frantically back toward the men's examination room where Paolo, her brother-in-law and escort, had disappeared hours ago.

Where is he? Why hasn't he come out yet? Without him, she would be deported. If you didn't have a man with you, or one waiting in the building to claim you, they sent you back. A woman alone was no good in the United States.

The line pushed her relentlessly toward the officials. She pushed back, trying to delay her fate as people shoved past her. Despite her efforts, her turn came up. Paolo was nowhere in sight. Her heart raced. She forced a smile as she approached the interviewer, wondering whether he could possibly be as corrupt as the Italian officials were. Or was America truly a place of honor and freedom? Would he press for intimate favors, force himself on her, demand a quick tumble in his office perhaps? She shuddered. What if she needed to bribe him? She had no money.

The blue uniformed immigration translator looked genuinely sympathetic as he asked her something in English.

"*Non parlo inglese.*" *I don't speak English.*

That wasn't exactly true. She spoke a little.

He switched to a slow, careful southern Italian dialect. "I'm sorry, ma'am, but I must detain you. Do you have a male escort or sponsor?"

"My brother-in-law, Paolo Allessandro, came with me from Naples on board *La Brezza Marina*. But he has not come out of the men's medical examination room." Though she tried to sound calm, her voice pitched in near panic.

The official said something in English to another blue-clad worker, who disappeared into the men's room and returned a few minutes later shaking his head in the negative. He called back a single English word, one that she recognized and filled her with dread. *Trachoma, an eye disease certain to get Paolo deported.*

"He has been sent back?" Her fear gave her words a gentle, unintentionally sensual rasp. Horrified, she cleared her throat. *Don't show fear. Don't encourage the man's attention.*

"I'm sorry, ma'am. Your paperwork says that you are married. Where is your husband? Is he in the city? Can he be contacted?"

She fought down her panic. "He is in Idaho."

The official shook his head. "He's not here? In the city waiting for you?"

"No." She saw the look of pity and skepticism in his eyes and raised her chin to cover her shame. Her husband had never intended to come to the city to claim her. Paolo, his brother, was supposed to bring her to him. "He is very busy, an important man in the mines there."

The official perused her paperwork again, then gently picked up one of her hands, and turning it palm up in his, ran his free hand over it. She flinched and tried to pull it back. His grip held her firm.

"Don't be afraid. I'm only looking for calluses." His tone was kindly but his hand trembled as it held hers.

She didn't believe him. She knew when a man was attracted to her.

"What sort of work did you do in Italy?"

"I was a cook in the household of a nobleman." There, her voice was steadier now.

He shook his head. "No good. Look at you. Wide-eyed. Pretty. Innocent." He released her hand and sighed. "I'm sorry. I am. But I cannot admit you without a male protector. It's the law. You wouldn't last a day alone in the city before some pimp would have you under his protection. I have to send you back." He sounded resigned. He pointed away. "If you would please step aside."

"No. Please!" She grabbed his arm. Images of the cramped ship, hours of confinement and illness haunted her. Being sent back was almost certainly a death sentence. The ill treatment of returns was notorious among the immigrants.

"My papa's cousin Mario is here in the city." Angelina pulled a scrap of paper from her pocket. "He didn't come to meet us. We were supposed to hire a ride to his apartment. I have his address."

"Can he be summoned? Can he meet you here?"

"Yes." Angelina nodded, not at all certain that Papa's cousin *would* come for her. He had a precious commodity—a job. She had no faith he would risk his livelihood to leave in the middle of the day to rescue a young woman he'd never met. "He will come."

She said a silent prayer to her dear, departed grandmother, who was most certainly a saint, for help. *Please make Mario come for me.*

"Good." The official smiled, looking relieved by the discovery of her cousin. He hustled her toward another desk. "You can wait here until he comes for you. I shouldn't. It's against policy, but I'll send someone for him. What is the address?"

CHAPTER ONE

New York City
April 1899

Little Italy awoke with vigor as Angelina di Maria Allessandro cruised Mulberry Street on her way toward salvation and escape. Street vendors took up residence on the sidewalk and opened their carts for the day of business ahead. Shopkeepers unlocked their doors and drew up their shades to let the morning light stream in. Early customers milled about outside, waiting to be summoned in to do the day's shopping. The air was warm with the rich scent of baking bread from numerous *panetteria* scattered among the stores. The low-slung eastern sun cast long, thin shadows and lit the corner window of Perelli's *Farma-*

cia like a sparkling jewel. Single-minded of purpose, Angelina noticed none of it.

Almost by rote, she weaved her way around the growing number of pedestrians filling the street. Under the shade of store awnings, displays of every Italian delicacy imaginable beckoned. But she paid little attention to the now familiar sights. Above her, five and six-story brick buildings blocked the blue of the sky with their girth. Dishtowels hung out to dry on wrought iron balconies above street level where rows of apartments looked like so many prison cells of this great, confining place. What was it to her? Where was the beauty? She was a country girl. The smell of fresh grass in the field. The sounds of birds chirping. *That* was beauty. Not pigeons clucking in eaves.

Men perched on the backsides of wagons parked against the curb and swapped stories, hailed buddies, and eyed women. They whistled and hooted as Angelina walked by. She should have ignored them, as Mama had taught her. But she couldn't resist casting them a sidelong smile and adding a bit more sway to her walk as she hurried past.

Angelina was not a classic beauty. Not that she cared. She had a dark, exotic, Mediterranean look—full lips, a large mouth, and snapping, lively eyes that men told her distracted them from all rational thought. If her straight Roman nose was too long, they didn't seem to object. Here in New York, even a look meant to upbraid couldn't turn the men away.

As Angelina came to the next intersection, she scanned the street for Nonna Gia and the aging tables where she sold her homemade pasta. Nonna Gia should be in her usual space outside Villari's Fish Market, with her husband Papa Joe at her side. Nonna Gia's pasta was unarguably the best to be found on Mulberry Street, and she always undercut the prices of her competitors. Angelina never bought her pasta anywhere else, but today she sought the old woman out for another reason.

A gentle breeze kicked up from the direction of the waterfront, threatening to blow off the white scarf Mario had insisted Angelina wear for modesty's sake when she went out. She reached up and secured it as she looked quickly in each direction and crossed. On the other side, a short, heavy woman peddled her wares.

"*Finocchio*! Fresh *finocchio!*"

Angelina stepped around two heavy metal washtubs perched on wooden stools and filled with fennel bulbs. She had barely cleared the tubs when Nonna caught sight of her and called out.

"Angelina!" Nonna Gia hurried around to the front of the pasta table to greet her. Angelina set her shopping basket down and bent forward to let the tiny woman kiss both of her cheeks, catching the licorice scent of anise oil, Nonna's version of perfume.

"How is business this morning?" Angelina hid her excitement behind the mundane question. It was a game she and the old woman played, each putting on a poker face for the other's benefit.

"We've just opened, but it looks to be a good day. The weather is nice. It brings the people out." Nonna turned to her husband. "Papa Joe, tend to the table while I have a word with Angelina."

"Listen to this old woman!" Papa Joe threw up his hands. "She never has *just a word* with anyone. Don't keep her long. Look! The neighborhood women are already descending on us like pigeons. Here comes *Signora* Rubino." He gestured again to emphasize his point. "Nothing ever satisfies that one."

"We won't be long, Papa Joe. I promise," Angelina said.

He urged them off with a wave of his arm.

"Come. This way, Angelina. Perhaps we can have a word in private." Nonna Gia pulled her into an unused doorway a short distance from Papa Joe and the table. "So tell me, how's Mario doing these days?" The small talk was deliberate, part of their game. No good Italian conversation was complete without first inquiring about the family.

"Mario! He treats me as if I'm some small, defenseless child, one whose virtue could be snatched away by the mere glance of a strange man. Look at this scarf he makes me wear!"

Nonna Gia chuckled. "You would like to flirt with the young men perhaps?" She wagged her finger. "It's not for you. No word from your new groom, *Signor* Allessandro?"

"Nothing. Not one word." Angelina sighed, frustrated. Nonna Gia knew of her worries. What if something had happened to *Signor* Allessandro? The mines were dangerous places. What if he was angry that Paolo had been sent back? What if he blamed her? What if he no longer wanted her?

"The winter has been hard," Angelina said, covering her fears with the story she had concocted to comfort herself. "The trains have not been running and the telegraph lines have been out of service. I am sure he's been busy in the mines. Still, I worry. I must go to him as soon as possible. I would have gone already, but Mario insists that I need an escort." She threw up her hands. "I cannot live on the charity of Papa's relatives forever."

"Your man should have come for you himself, no matter what was going on in that place called Idaho. He should not have trusted his bride to his brother." Nonna Gia wagged her finger as she talked.

Angelina sighed. They'd been over this subject before.

"Why don't you stay in New York? Catch a man here. You owe that man nothing!"

"Nonna! How can you suggest such a thing? I owe him my passage. I have made a vow of honor. And we are married!"

"Married? Bah! That is nothing! It can be annulled. You have not even met the man." Nonna turned and looked out at the crowds filling the marketplace, a tiny smile toying with her lips. "But if you insist on going, I may be able to help." Nonna spoke casually, almost noncommittally, shrugging her shoulders ever so slightly. Angelina recognized the ploy to draw emphasis away from her own excitement.

"You have found someone!" Angelina hugged the older woman before she had a chance to reply.

"Yes. But before you get too excited—" Nonna spoke as one who was hugged too tightly and enjoying the attention.

Angelina released the older woman and clutched her arm. "Who? Do I know them?"

"*His* name is Antonio Domani. I call him Tonio. Please, Angelina. You hurt the arm with your grip."

Angelina released her hold. "What about his wife? What is her name?"

Nonna Gia looked sheepish. "There is no wife, just him. Will Mario approve of you going West with a single man?"

Angelina's hopes fell. "I don't know." She feared not.

"We will find out." Nonna Gia chuckled softly and gestured with her hands. "My Tonio can convince anyone of anything. You turn him loose on Mario, there will be no problem with the convincing. Let us think on the good news—Tonio is from Idaho. The Silver Valley, he calls it. He plans to return at the end of the week. The railroads are running again."

Angelina's heart raced. She forgot the rules of their game of composure and blurted out her next question. "Which town is he going to?"

"Wallace. Tonio tells me it's not far from Harrison. The bigger question is—can you convince Mario to let you go?"

"This Tonio won't take advantage of me, will he?" Angelina put a tease in her voice. She liked baiting Nonna.

Nonna laughed. "I will personally vouch for Tonio. He has been a regular customer of ours off and on for years."

Angelina shook her head. "I'll bet you have a few scoundrels among your regulars."

"Tonio is a good man, Angelina." There was an undeniable note of pride in Nonna's suddenly solemn voice.

"Then I won't have any trouble convincing Mario to let me go with him, will I? Is *Signor* Domani willing to let me travel with him? You have asked him?"

Nonna's chuckle returned. "He wants to meet you first. He prefers to travel alone. He said something about not wanting to face a week-long train ride with a frivolous woman."

Angelina frowned. She didn't like this Tonio's attitude. "He sounds like a crotchety old man."

Nonna shrugged again, concealing a grin.

"As desperate as I am, I suppose I can put up with just about anyone. Did you tell him that I only need him to escort me onto the train? Once we're onboard, he's free to do whatever he pleases. Mario will never know the difference. I can take care of myself."

"If Tonio agrees to take you, he won't desert you. I have his word." Nonna handed her a scrap of paper with an address written in a bold masculine hand. "Here is his address. Go see him."

Angelina was breathing deeply as she reached the third-floor landing of Tonio Domani's apartment building, more from excitement than exertion. She reached into her apron pocket and retrieved the crumpled address she'd hastily stuffed there before leaving Nonna. Studying it, she walked down the hall, scanning doors for the correct address.

Number 325 looked like all the other doors lining the hall. But its innocuous appearance did nothing to quiet her nerves as she stood before it. *He must take me with him.* She willed the butterflies winging wildly in her stomach to quiet, drew in a deep breath, whispered a prayer, raised her arm, and knocked.

Silence.

She waited a decent length of time. Nothing.

This was a fine mess. When would she have time to come this way next? When could she escape from Mario's protective eye again? She quickly crossed herself, amended her prayer to add that *Signor* Domani be home, and knocked again.

Still, no answer.

Frustrated, she searched for something to scribble a note on. She could tear off a piece of the address, but she had no pencil—

Either her ears deceived her or she heard something. She stopped her frantic searching and stepped closer to the door. A deep, masculine voice hummed a tune, she was certain of it. But in this apartment or the next one over? She leaned with her ear cupped against the door, straining to hear.

Without warning the door swung open, throwing her off balance, headlong into the warm, bare arms of a stranger. She stared into a naked, well-muscled chest covered with curly black hair, held close by a man who smelled pleasantly of fresh soap and shaving cream. She pulled away slowly, afraid she'd topple over again, steadying herself on the doorjamb, shaken by more than her tumble. Much more.

"I'm so sorry." She mumbled, stumbling over her words and peering cautiously up at him.

The man before her was easily over six feet tall and handsome in a way that took her breath away. Quite possibly, no, certainly, *the* most handsome Italian man she'd ever seen. And she'd seen many. The sight of him made her warm all over, almost overheated. She clenched her hand, resisting the urge to cross herself again. Surely such feelings in a married woman were a sin of the most mortal kind.

Eyes the color of coal stared down at her, bold with curiosity as he lounged in the doorway, legs posed in a casual, wide stance. Her eyes met his for the barest second. Embarrassed, she averted her gaze from his dark, piercing one. She felt the flush of her skin under his obviously appraising scrutiny and amused grin.

He seemed to enjoy her discomposure. Little bits of shaving cream dotted his face. Out of the corner of her eye she watched as he swiped at them with his towel, still staring at her, waiting for her to speak again. But her tongue froze.

"Can I help you?" he asked at last.

"I...I'm afraid I have the wrong address. I'm looking for Antonio Domani. Do you know him? Which apartment is his, if you please?"

"You found him. I'm Domani."

She stared in disbelief. This couldn't be Tonio Domani. Nonna wouldn't be foolish enough to believe Mario would allow her to travel alone with *this* man.

"Nonna Gia sent me," she began uncertainly, "I am here to talk to...you?" She couldn't keep the question from her voice. "About a trip west to Idaho. But there must be some mistake. Is there another Antonio Domani here? Your father perhaps?"

Tonio tipped his head back slightly and laughed a deep, hearty, amused laugh. "There is no other Tonio. I am the one and only. Some would say fortunately. What other misinformation did Nonna give you about me?"

"She said you were a good customer."

He seemed to like her answer. "True enough. Come on in." He stepped aside to let her pass.

The room in front of her displayed the carnage of someone in the process of moving. A stack of fully packed crates lined one wall and partially packed boxes sat everywhere. Wads of newspaper littered the room.

"Excuse me a minute while I make myself more presentable. I was just finishing my shave when you knocked." He walked to the small bedroom that adjoined the main room, pausing to call back over his shoulder. "Make yourself at home."

As Angelina walked to one of the few remaining pieces of furniture in the room, an old worn chair, a photograph in a silver frame drew her attention. It seemed strangely at odds with the disarray of the room, set carefully on a starched white doily atop a well-crafted cherry end table. A young woman smiled out of the gilded frame.

Angelina picked it up to get a closer look. The photograph had obviously been taken some years ago, but the old-fashioned style of dress did not diminish the beauty of the woman. Her thick, black hair coiled neatly on her head so as not to obscure the full view of her classic face. Large dark eyes danced above delicate high cheekbones. Her jaw was strong and firm, but surprisingly feminine, the dress she wore obviously expensive. A heavy gold cross hung against her well-shaped bosom.

The cross caught Angelina's attention. It looked similar to the one that she wore secretly tucked beneath her own high-buttoned blouse. She absently traced the outline of her own necklace with the forefinger of her free hand. The woman in the picture bore a striking resemblance to—

"My mother."

Angelina started.

Tonio reached from behind her and pulled the picture out of her hands. A little too roughly, Angelina thought. He set it back down, face to the wall.

"She's a beautiful woman." Angelina turned to face him.

"Yes, she was. Please, sit down." Tonio had donned a fresh white shirt, but had not tucked it in. As she sat, he shoved the shirttails down between his skin and the

soft denim of his pants, his movements natural and un-
abashed. The way he dressed in front of her was too
casual, too sensual. She squirmed.

"You are in the process of moving, *Signor* Domani?"

"Me? No. This apartment belonged to my uncle. He
passed away last week. His illness and subsequent death
drew me here from the mining country. I am in the
process of closing up his estate, if you can call it that.
As soon as I'm finished I'll be headed back."

It was the first string of more than a few words
Angelina had heard him speak. It put her immediately
on guard. He spoke cultured, classic Italian—the language imposed on the united Italy by the North not
more than forty years ago—not dialect. Most southerners still did not speak it, either out of ignorance or rebellion or both.

"I am sorry about your uncle."

"No need to be." His voice held an unexpectedly
hard edge. "I seem to have forgotten my few manners.
Shall we introduce ourselves? I believe we've estab-
lished that I'm Antonio Domani. Please, call me Tonio.
And you are?"

"Angelina Allessandro. Pleased to meet you."

"I assure you, the pleasure is mine." He extended his
hand.

Angelina stared at him, not at all sure what he expected.

"You're supposed to shake my hand." He took her
right hand in his warm, strong one, holding hers firmly, confidently, in a way that made her pulse race.
"Americans aren't like Italians. They are uncomforta-

ble kissing each other in greeting. Uncivilized of them, isn't it? A peck on each cheek is nothing."

She pulled her hand from his as if scorched and shifted to the corner of her chair without answering. The man made her feel too warm, too vulnerable.

He laughed, seemingly enjoying the effect he had on her. "Would you like a cup of coffee before we get down to business?" Before she could answer, Tonio stepped to the stove, poured two cups and returned to hand one to her. He pulled up a crate and sat down, wrapping his hands around the steaming mug as he stared at her intently.

His scrutiny heated the room. To mask her self-consciousness, Angelina adjusted her skirt and smoothed her apron before taking a sip of the brew.

"Tell me something, Miss Allessandro..."

"Mrs."

His eyebrows shot up. "You are already married?"

She nodded. She'd surprised him. *Good.* She was glad to have an advantage, even a small one.

"Ah. Foolish me. I thought you were on your way to meet your fiancé, not your husband. If you don't mind my asking, why doesn't the lucky bridegroom come get you himself? Most men would beat a quick path to New York to claim a bride as beautiful as you are. There are so few women in the mining country, and even fewer attractive ones. He must be a man with a great deal of self-restraint."

His easy flattery distracted her.

"He's never seen me." It just popped out. Her hand flew to her mouth as if trying to stuff the words back in. Franco had written to her that she must never tell.

Tonio's brow furrowed, followed almost instantly by a look of near amusement. "Ah, an infamous proxy wedding then. That explains it. The good man doesn't know what he's missing." He spoke softly, almost as if to himself.

Angelina remained mute, horrified she'd spilled her secret so easily.

Tonio filled the silence easily. "Who stood in for the groom?"

She didn't trust herself to speak.

Tonio answered his own question. "Some relative, no doubt. He signed his x on the dotted line for your husband, did he? You were hoping the validation of a marriage license would speed you through immigration? Fend off the licentious officials?"

She nodded. There was no sense denying it.

He studied her again, looking both sympathetic and incensed at the indignity of the immigration process at the same time. "Your husband should have gone to Italy to get you. He should never have let you travel alone. I would never let my sister—" He cut himself off. "Ah, but it's not my business."

Angelina still felt the need to defend her husband. "I wasn't alone. My escort, my husband's brother, was denied entry here in New York. Didn't Nonna tell you?"

"Ah, yes. The brother. Nonna did mention something." He paused. "So you want me to escort you to your husband so the two of you can go to the local priest and make the whole marriage right before God? You will make the marriage legal, won't you?"

Angelina couldn't decide what the correct answer was. Whether Tonio was mocking her or worried about the sanctity of her marriage. She didn't reply.

Tonio didn't press the matter. "What's your husband's name?"

"Franco Allessandro." She bit her lip. This wasn't going well, not at all as she expected. She was usually able to bend men to her will. But this man...

"Mr. Domani, Tonio, I have not heard from my husband since arriving in America and I am worried. Whatever you may think, it is not like him not to look after me. He is an old, dear friend of my papa. He would not leave me at the mercy of distant relatives if something was not wrong. I must get to him. *Soon.*"

"Don't know him," Tonio continued as if he hadn't heard her. "You're *Napolitane*, aren't you?"

Angelina nodded, uncertain where he was heading with the question, but afraid he would not like her answer. He was obviously a northern Italian, and she, a southern girl. The animosity between the northern and southern Italians was very much like that between the Yankees and Southerners that she had heard about here in America.

"I thought so." He spoke slowly, as if weighing his thoughts in an unseen balance. "My grandmother came from Calabria, which explains my black hair and southern features. I can't tell you what a disability they posed growing up in Turin as I did. You must have noticed my King Emmanuel's Italian. I've never been able to effect a southern dialect worth a—" He stopped himself from using the obvious epithet.

The Northern Italians were responsible for the poverty of her southern Italian homeland. Because of the North's economic stronghold over the South, they held all the power and wielded it fiercely, taxing the poor beyond the humane. Crops had failed in the largely agricultural economy of the South for as many years as Angelina had been alive. There were no jobs, so the young men left to find work. No jobs, no men, and therefore, no husband for a poor girl like her with no dowry.

"Mrs. Allessandro, I have my reservations about taking you with me to—"

"Please. Don't let my being from the South influence you. I will be no trouble. None at all. As soon as we are on the train, I release you of any responsibility—"

He was shaking his head and laughing. "Would Nonna have sent you to me if she'd thought I was that prejudiced? Class or being from the North or South matters less than fool's gold to me."

"Then why?"

He turned solemn. "Your husband, whatever his motive for his silence, has good reason not to want you in the Valley. At the best of times, it's a rough and tumble place. But with the labor tensions between mine owners and miners being what they are, things could explode at any time." There was a hint of humor in his tone. "It's no place for a lady."

Angelina set down her coffee with trembling hands, willing to beg this handsome man. "Please, sir, you must take me with you. Have you never been poor and wanting? In my whole life, I have had nothing but dreams of something better than poverty—land, a home of my own, a husband and children. All my hope for that is in Idaho.

"If I stay here, I have nothing but the loss of my dignity and the charity of distant relatives. Please."

Although his face remained inscrutable, his eyes flickered with sympathy. And a touch of wariness. She couldn't blame him for that. She was guarded herself. And grateful, more grateful than she liked to admit, that he didn't pity her. But on what grounds could he possibly sympathize with her? A man like him from an obviously high-class background? She held her breath. Finally, he sighed.

She knew she'd won him over even before he spoke. Her plea had not been elegant, but miraculously, she'd changed his mind.

"I won't be doing you any favors. You'll curse me in the end." He stood, indicating the interview was over. "The train leaves early on Friday. I'll pick you up at four a.m. *Sharp.*"

Relief made her almost weak. "Thank you. So much." She stood and touched his sleeve. Which was a mistake. Her heart pattered out of control and she flushed. She would have to keep her distance from this one. "Nonna says you prefer to travel alone. I won't be a frivolous female. I promise."

He said something in English too fast for her to catch. Then his laughter filled the room. "Nonna talks too damned much."

"There is just one more thing, *Signor* Domani. Another favor." The natural flirt came out in her. She used the tone and seductive little smile she put on as second nature when she was trying to get a man to do her bidding. "Nonna Gia brags you have a silver tongue. That you could convince the devil himself he needs a furnace. I'll need your help convincing my cousin Mario that you are a respectable, reliable escort for me." She clasped her hands in front of her. "That you will protect my virtue with your life. He will insist on meeting you, of course."

Again, the rapid English and the laughter. "I'm hardly respectable. But I'll talk to him."

Mario would be a fool to believe Tonio Domani was anything but a threat to her virtue. But all the same, nothing would stop her from going with him. *Nothing.*

CHAPTER TWO

A s Angelina stood inside the crowded Pennsy Railroad terminal surrounded by her small set of luggage, she glanced at Tonio.

Mario isn't a fool. How did Tonio convince him to let him escort me?

Angelina wasn't a fool, either. She'd been careful not to let Mario see her anywhere near Tonio before the trip, fearing Mario would somehow sense her involuntary attraction to the handsome Northerner. Maybe Tonio did indeed possess a silver tongue. Or maybe he simply held his liquor better than Mario. All she knew for certain was that Mario had met with Tonio at a bar and come home singing loudly, cradling an expensive bottle of Pino Grigio under his arm that could only have come from Tonio. Before toppling into bed, Mario gave his pronouncement—Angelina would go to Idaho with Tonio. End of discussion.

Tonio was occupied at a ticket window across the room. Angelina watched him purchase their tickets and lamented the necessity of an escape plan. He wore a black leather jacket with fringes that hung from the arms and tight denim pants that showcased heavily muscled legs. She could easily imagine herself tangled in the fringes, pressed thigh against thigh with him. But her conscience spoke against such fancy. She heard her father's voice in her mind, calling her his little flirt. She remembered the conversation she'd overheard between her parents.

"Angelina likes the men too much. She has too much passion and could be led astray so easily. She has no money. They will ruin her but not marry her. She will end up like her grandmama. We must see her safely married," her mother had said. Because there were no young men in Italy willing to marry her without a dowry, they had sent her to America to marry a man more than twice her age.

Whether Angelina felt married or not, she had pledged herself to her father's friend. And she was tired of living off the charity of others who had little enough for themselves. Her sense of honor chafed at taking Tonio's, and her common sense warned of the danger of being too near him. Once on board the train, she wouldn't need an escort. How dangerous could riding a train alone be? At the train depot in Jersey, she would lose him and continue on her own.

She turned back to stare out the window, fixing her gaze on the Dewar's Whiskey sign outside as it drifted in and out of view in the thick, ponderous fog. She hoped she looked serene and calm as she stood there, her mind whirling with her plan. She felt confident. She had only one small, niggling worry—Tonio was smart.

The terminal bristled with people. Two ferry runs had already been canceled due to poor visibility and high winds. People jostled past her as they moved toward the ticket lines. She reached into her pocket and pulled out a bag with the croissant she had purchased the day before at her favorite *panetteria*. She took a big bite of the confection. Its whipped chocolate filling oozed out over her lips. She turned again to monitor Tonio's progress. He was still at the window. She caught his eye as she slowly and deliberately licked the chocolate away.

He smiled and mouthed something to her, but she missed his message. Someone bumped her from behind. As she turned to look she was hit again. The croissant fell from her hand to the floor.

"*Smettila*! Stop it!" She whirled on the perpetrator. "*Imbecile*! It is ruined!" She pointed to the croissant.

The stocky man she faced spoke in a low, abasing tone. "Why don't you let me buy you a new one?" He reached to chuck her chin.

She turned away quickly and with exaggerated motions, counted her bags aloud in stilted, accented English. Her eyes darted around looking for an accomplice.

Gypsies in Naples used this ruse to steal from weary travelers.

"One, two, three—"

"You think I'm trying to steal your bags?" He moved closer to her, intentionally bumping the side of her breast with his arm. He reeked of stale sweat and cigarette smoke. "I just want to get to know you. You're such a pretty lady."

She shoved him away and let loose a string of angry Italian, gesturing dramatically as she did so. The man's eyes widened. He put his hands up in mock surrender before taking a step back.

"The lady told you to take a walk." Tonio spoke from directly behind her. She'd been so occupied she hadn't heard him approach.

The man backed off and disappeared into the crowd as spooked as if he'd seen a statue of the Virgin Mary cry.

"Boo!" Angelina whispered beneath her breath, delighted. She turned to face Tonio. "I was handling him."

"Were you?" Tonio stood with his coat cocked back to reveal the silver handle of a lethal looking stiletto sheathed in a leather case attached to his belt.

Angelina stared at the knife and then smiled at Tonio. "Nice blade."

"Sharp, too," he said. "Make your husband get you one when we reach the Silver Valley. They come in handy for all kinds of things—slicing meat, scaring off unwanted suitors..."

"You use yours for scaring off the ladies, then?" She grinned at him. "The women in this mining country of yours must be very aggressive."

He laughed. "You'd be surprised."

Angelina arched a brow to show her skepticism.

He laughed again as he took her arm. "Seriously, Angel. No one walks around the valley unarmed."

"I hate knives."

"Get over it or get a gun and learn to shoot." He grabbed a handful of bags. "Come on. The ferries are running again. They'll make the announcement in a minute. We have to hurry if we want to beat the crowd and make it on."

The humid, departing fog chilled the air on the deck of the *Cincinnati.* Angelina huddled her arms tightly against herself for warmth as she leaned against the rail and retched into the tumultuous, blue-green Hudson River below. The wind whipped at her, streaking her hair across her face and stinging her flesh, moist with the trauma of seasickness. The fifteen minute crossing stretched into thirty, then forty-five. Tonio came out from the warmth of the cabin to check on her.

"One bite of croissant." She clutched her stomach, though it had nothing left, worried she would wretch in front of him and horrified at the thought.

"Come into the cabin."

She shook her head. He removed his fringed leather jacket and hooked it over her shoulders. "Your coat is too thin for this kind of weather." Then he turned and went back to the cabin.

She watched him retreat, wondering about this small show of kindness. He intrigued her. Too bad she wouldn't have time to discover his motives. When they reached Jersey City, she'd be on her own. Her plan didn't prevent her from burrowing her nose deep into the rich leather of his coat or enjoying its body-warmed heat and the scent he left clinging to the collar. Even with waves of nausea clutching her stomach, he smelled good. Too good. She took a deep breath to slow her racing heart, hoping that Franco Allessandro would be able to set her pulse pattering as Tonio did. She would settle for half as fast.

"Have we missed our train?" Angelina asked.

Tonio, leaning across the ticket counter at the Jersey City terminal, waved her into silence and focused his attention on the clerk behind the window.

Angelina huddled close behind him, listening with interest to the conversation, memorizing as much of it as possible. But they spoke rapidly in quiet tones and she wasn't able to understand much. Still, it would be a useful conversation to have in her repertoire. If she succeeded in her plan she would need it soon. Frustrated, she took a step back and focused her attention on the schedule board posted above the ticket window. Fortunately, she could read English better than she understood the spoken language.

She scanned the board quickly. The fog had delayed them. They had missed their train by ten minutes. The next one with connections through to Chicago didn't leave for another hour, and the one after that three hours later. Perfect! She didn't want to spend the night in the station alone. Much better to be in the safety of the train. The incident in the New York depot had convinced her of that. As soon as Tonio finished at the window she'd ask him for her ticket. Then nothing could foil her plan.

Tonio stepped back from the window and grabbed her arm. "Come on," he said. "The train was delayed— it hasn't left yet. We can make it if we hurry." He grabbed their bags.

Angelina scrambled after him. "Why can't we wait for the next train?" She needed more time! Her thoughts whirled in a panic. She tried to delay him. "Let's stay in the depot, get a bite to eat. I'm hungry."

"I thought you'd sworn off food." He waited for her to pass in front of him, then placed his hand in the small of her back and nudged her along. "This way."

The boarding area was nearly empty when they reached it and the last call was being sounded. Tonio hurriedly hailed a porter, grabbed her arm, and handed her the ticket. "Take this and your traveling case and board the train. Find two seats together while I check the luggage. Damn! We're going to have to travel second class."

This turn of events was more than she'd hoped for. It was too easy! She considered not boarding the train at all, but under his watchful eye there was nothing else she could do. She lifted her skirts and climbed serenely up the loading steps, even pausing to turn and smile at him, but his attention was already focused on the man loading their luggage. *Goodbye, Tonio!*

She forced herself on with her heart racing. As soon as her feet hit the top step, she sped down the aisle toward the front of the train and the first exit she could find. People cluttered the aisle, stretching and shoving luggage under their seats.

"*Mi scusi.* Please, I must get through!" She ran with her bag held high, level with her head, dodging people both seated and not, looking back at regular intervals to see if Tonio had boarded yet.

A blast of steam from the engine sounded. Angelina felt a slight shift of forward motion as the engineer released the brake. Another puff of steam followed. The exit lay just ahead. She raced forward, and, head bowed, turned down the exit stairs. Her skirts caught. As she reached to free them a familiar voice stopped her.

"Going someplace?"

She looked up and went cold.

Tonio stood at the bottom of the stairs, blocking her way, fury snapping in his eyes. Without a word he stepped up, grabbed her arm, and pulled her along into a pair of seats. He was tall and strong. Resisting him was futile and would only cause a scene. But there was still a chance—

"I...I need to use the bathroom."

He pulled her ticket from her tight grip and pointed to a small cubicle at the back of the car. "Go right ahead."

The train lurched forward. She sat down, defeated. "Why bother to escort me? Why not just let me go? It would be much less trouble for you."

"I like trouble." He looked out across the aisle and through the window as the Jersey City depot disappeared behind them.

"Just what was your plan?" Tonio glared at her.

"I was going to get off and exchange my ticket for a later train."

"And did this idea just spring to mind, or had you planned it all along?"

There was no reason to keep the truth from him. "Originally, I planned to ask you for my ticket. Once we were seated I was going to excuse myself to use the bathroom and freshen up. Then I was going to get off the train and exchange my ticket. I figured you wouldn't notice until the train had pulled away and it was too late. But when we had to hurry to catch the train, I had to think on my feet."

"You don't give me much credit for brains." He stared hard at her, his head cocked a little to the side. "Why run?"

She shrugged, unable to admit to her attraction to him and the slight to her honor at being beholden to a stranger. "How did you know I was trying to get off?"

"I saw you through the window, scuttling down the aisle like a lady with a bee up her ass. I figured you weren't in that big a hurry to find a seat."

"Very observant."

"You don't like me much." His voice didn't give any emotion away.

"I like you fine." She liked him too much.

"But you don't trust me."

She didn't trust herself. Angelina tried not to squirm under his heavy gaze. "I'm tired of being beholden to others, that's all. I want to take care of myself."

"Is that all? Get over the notion. I promised Nonna and Mario that I would take care of you. And I will. I'm a man of my word."

She felt his gentle touch on her arm.

"Come on. Let's get something to eat. You complained you were hungry over an hour ago, or was that subterfuge, too?"

"It was, and I am. But I have a bag of food that Lucia, Mario's wife, packed for me."

"Leave it. We'll eat it later. This one's on me."

She turned to face him and was caught by his dark, devastating eyes. She stared into them a moment too long. She could be prisoner of those eyes forever. She dropped her gaze. If ever Papa had to worry over a man ruining her...

The cafe car was dark and dimly lit. Outside it had started to rain. Tonio ordered at the counter next to the grill and returned to the table with their food. Angelina felt his gaze on her as she dusted away crumbs left by the table's last occupants. When they were both seated, he took a drink of his beer and watched her intently as she took a bite of her grilled sandwich. She crinkled her nose without thinking.

"You don't like American food?"

"I do. But not this. It tastes like the grill."

"So you don't just eat bread and beans. Good southern food."

Angelina laughed. "No."

They ate in silence for a moment. She felt his gaze on her, but didn't look up to meet it. At last he spoke, "I think it's fair if I ask—why was your first escort denied entry?"

"Paolo got trachoma on the ship over."

"Paolo?"

"My husband's youngest brother. He's twenty-five, but he acts more like fifteen. I was at Mario's about a week when I ran into a man I'd met on the boat. He told me Paolo had been boasting about how he was going thwart immigration and jump ship and swim ashore."

"Did he?"

"He never showed up." She grimaced. "I doubt he did. He doesn't have the courage."

"Wise man. Some poor fool tries every year and inevitably his body washes up on the beach, beat beyond recognition." He took a sip of beer. "Your husband didn't have any qualms with sending you over with his younger brother? I mean—"

"I know what you mean, *Signor* Domani. No, he didn't. Paolo looks like a frog."

"You prefer your men handsome?" He leaned toward her. She liked the raw look she saw in his expression. He was incredibly handsome. And he knew it. She looked down and drew small circles on the table with the water that condensed beneath her glass.

"What woman doesn't? We all dream of princes."

"You're not worried that your husband is a frog, too?"

"He's twenty-five years older than I am. He's most assuredly a toad." She fought the urge to look up and see his shocked face. When he didn't answer immediately, she couldn't help herself. She lifted her gaze and looked directly at him.

He sat well back in his chair, smiling at her in obvious amusement. He drained his beer and set the empty glass on the table. "The difference between the young frog and the old toad being?"

"The toad has money and land and a kind heart."

"I see. You couldn't find a handsome man with money?"

"You must have left Italy a long time ago. And my guess is that you've never been to the South. There are no men. The crop failures have sent them all away. Nearly all the able-bodied men have emigrated to find work. Or they've been killed in wars. Southern women without dowries remain unmarried. And how can they get them when their fathers can't work?"

"There is always the convent," he said. "A wise and pristine choice."

"Filled to capacity."

"A blessing then." He leaned forward and her heart skipped a beat. "I can't picture a girl with your temperament there anyway."

Her face fell and he laughed. He'd seen her disappointment. He had been on the verge of a compliment. Or so she'd hoped.

"Men are so scarce that the rich are willing to accept any man for their daughters, even those well below their station. Had I a dowry, I would have rejected any choice of man left to me in the village."

"It appears I missed my calling," he said. "I shouldn't be here in the States breaking my back on a mining claim. I should be back in Italy, marrying some rich southerner."

"They'd as soon spit on you, Northerner."

"And you?"

She smiled her most dazzling smile at him. "I can put up with you until Idaho."

"You won't be trying to escape again?"

"Will I need to?"

He laughed and stood up, motioning toward the door with his head. "Let's get back." As they passed through the door from the dining car he leaned close and whispered in her ear. "Maybe."

The conductor came through again after dark, not to punch tickets but to sell an assortment of goods, everything from chumming boards that were placed across facing seats to form a bed, to blankets and pillows. He was followed closely by the news butcher who sold a more varied stock—candy, cigarettes, and sundries, and, of course, newspapers. Angelina watched as Tonio pivoted the two wooden bench seats to face each other and spread the chumming board and pillows between them.

"Straw," he said thumping a pillow. "You'd think for the outrageous price of two dollars and fifty cents you'd get goose down."

Oil lamps burned dimly. Rain splashed against the windows. People were settling down for the night and preparing their beds, much as Tonio was.

"Damn! I hate second class. This train borders on ancient. Thirty years if it's a day."

"Don't like traveling with the vermin?"

"Don't like sleeping on straw and planks. We'll see how you feel in the morning. First chance I get, I'm earning our way out of here. From Chicago, we'll be traveling in style. After you." He indicated the inside of the makeshift bed, next to the window.

"I'm not sleeping with you." She blurted the words out without thinking.

"Let's get our terminology straight. Sleeping with me is a much more enjoyable, intimate occasion. This is sleeping next to me, chumming—sharing space for the mutual purpose of sleep. But suit yourself; find someone else to chum with. I'm sure the conductor can find someone suitable, for another two fifty."

She quickly scanned the coach. Other than women with families, who were already snuggled together for the night, there were no single women. Two or three men still sought someone to chum with. One, a greasy looking man who spoke some Slavic tongue, eyed her and smiled hopefully.

"Move over," she finally said.

"Nothing doing. You get the window."

"Afraid I'll try to escape?"

"I don't like sleeping next to cold glass."

She slipped off her work boots and scooted next to the window. He handed the boots back to her, along with her duffel.

"Keep your boots on or they might not be here in the morning." He tossed a thin blanket over her and slid in next to her, turning his back to her. "Good night," he said, looking back over his shoulder. He rolled forward again, toward the aisle.

He was right. The bed was hard and uncomfortable and the window cold. She tried positioning her duffel between them, but that pushed her closer to the drafty window. At last she shoved it next to the window and curled around it like it was a favorite doll. Her back butted up against Tonio, whose body warmth was exceedingly tempting. She stared outside at the dark countryside passing by. With her luck and sleeping habits she'd probably wake in the morning to find herself sprawled out over Tonio like a wanton woman. It wasn't fair that he slept peacefully while she fought the temptation to roll over and cuddle behind him. Just for warmth.

She rolled back over on one elbow and stared at him. His body was taut and firm even in the relaxation of sleep. He looked like he slept at alert, ready to pounce up and use that dangerous-looking knife on anyone who dared disturb him. His hair curled up in back where it met his neck. For the first time she noticed a jagged scar that ran up the nape of his neck and into his hairline. How would a man get a scar like that? He slept with his mouth closed. A good sign. He wasn't likely to snore.

A child cried for water at the back of the coach. His mother walked past carrying a cup for her thirsty child. "I remember those newlywed days when I couldn't keep my eyes off my man." She winked and disappeared down the aisle.

Angelina dropped off her elbow and back over to face the window. She understood enough English to get the woman's gist. Her heart pounded in her ears, but her embarrassed flush quickly cooled as she huddled next to her duffel. She was tired and shaken. Fatigued beyond what she could remember. And cold. She was used to sleeping in a bed with her sisters and then with Mario's children. Loneliness and exhaustion overcame her. She crossed her arms protectively in front of her and rolled over behind Tonio.

CHAPTER THREE

Tonio sat opposite Angelina in the dining car, watching her wolf down a big breakfast. Not that watching her was hard on the eyes. He could have stared at her all day. More like it was hard on the rest of him. He was still wondering what he was doing taking her to the mining country, why her appeal about dreams and hopes had convinced him to do this mad deed. He hadn't thought he had anything noble or chivalrous left in him. He generally regarded himself as a cynic and liked it that way. But back at the apartment, she'd been so pretty, so damned vulnerable and he owed Nonna Gia one.

Nonna was going to owe him one if he ever got back to New York. What was Nonna thinking saddling him with a woman he couldn't stop brooding about? He'd vowed to himself a long time ago that he would never again mess with a woman he couldn't have. And he couldn't have this one for reasons beyond her foolish proxy marriage. She wanted a husband who could give her a home, security, children. He had one goal and one only, to make the Jupiter mine pay off so that he and his partners would be rich. In the face of security, his dream didn't seem like much to offer a woman. And he didn't intend to anyway. A woman would complicate his life.

Angelina continued to shovel it in. For all her flirtatious ways, she made no pretense of being a dainty eater. Maybe being poor all her life had taught her to eat with gusto when she could.

"Decide American food isn't so bad after all?" Tonio asked. Speaking was better than letting his thoughts run with images of what he'd like to do with her.

They'd left the rain behind overnight, somewhere between Newark and Philadelphia. Weak sunlight seeped into the dining car through grease-filmed windows. They were nearly alone in the car. Most people traveled with their own supply of food, eliminating the need to frequent the diner. Tonio hadn't bothered with packing meals and Angelina had nibbled away the snacks Lucia had packed for her.

"I can live with it." She paused with a forkful of fried potatoes poised mid-air. "When hungry enough. I prefer a brioche and a cappuccino for a first meal of the day. Breakfast should not weigh a person down; that's what midday and evening meals are for."

Angelina intrigued him. She shouldn't know about brioches. "Where did you learn about coffee and fancy pastries? I thought the peasantry had plain bread for breakfast."

"When I lived in *Signor* Costagnola's household. I can live the good life as well as you. I spent a year under the roof of one of the richest men of the region." She didn't sound as proud of the fact as she should have.

"Oh? And just what did you do for *Signor* Costagnola?" He couldn't help asking the baited question. He knew too much about noblemen's appetites and the help.

"Less than he would have liked." Her tone was flat.

Tonio felt relieved. "That being?"

"You have a dirty mind. I was a pastry chef and baker in his kitchen. I lived in the servant's quarters, but I observed the gentry closely."

"But he wanted more?"

A blush crept up her cheeks. "Why else would I leave such a position?"

Tonio felt cantankerous. Sleeping next to her on a hard board hadn't allowed him much sleep. "Being a rich man's mistress didn't appeal to you?"

She plunked her fork down and pushed her chair back.

He reached across the table and grabbed her wrist before she could fully rise. "I'm sorry. Please sit. I was out of line." He'd overstepped and he knew it. She was an innocent girl with honor, something he'd almost forgotten existed. He smiled apologetically across at her. She looked leery, but relaxed her arm in his firm grip and he released his hold. She settled back into her chair and scooted to the table.

"The women in Wallace, where I live, are jaded, their innocence long since spent. I've forgotten about youth and protected virtue. I bet you haven't even been kissed, except perhaps at *carnevale*." Thoughts of *carnevale* made him smile.

"I can see your parents parading you down the *piazza* every Sunday after mass, hoping to attract the attention of some worthy suitor, yet keeping you cloistered in their midst. And I can see the young men salivating, lascivious thoughts tucked protectively under the surface, but there nonetheless. Not daring to speak to you openly for fear of violating the code of social conduct so prized by Italian society. But later, alone with their buddies, enumerating your virtues for all their worth."

She looked uncertain as to whether he complimented or made fun of her. He did neither. "Your lips are as full and red as a dozen roses. What young man wouldn't be tempted by them? Were you old enough to be allowed out at *carnevale* last year?"

"Old enough! I'm nineteen!"

He laughed softly. "Spoken with the pride of youth. Too many more years and you'll be hiding your age. You're dying to tell me, so go ahead. Did you collect many kisses?"

"You speak openly of intimate matters. But if you must know—more than any other girl!"

His mind traveled back to the annual celebration. Masked men paraded the streets, throwing confetti and candy coated almonds at women and children, their masks affording them the protection of anonymity, giving them boldness. Young men roamed the streets seeking the girls they favored, bestowing them with chaste kisses. Girls purposefully strayed from their parents and chaperones looked the other way but only for that day. Girls went home with pockets full of candy and a sense of romance heady with kisses.

"So girls compare notes. I always imagined they did."

"And you, I suppose you've kissed many girls?"

"Many more than I should have." He pushed his plate back, suddenly full. "Tell me, what's the difference between marrying your old toad for money and taking money for favors from your rich *Signor* Costagnola? Surely he was much wealthier."

"Marriage is honorable." She sounded sure of herself.

He wished he felt her conviction about anything outside of the Jupiter.

"Honor, what is that?" He laughed derisively. "So for honor's sake you find yourself banished to the United States." Her arranged married angered him. Although it was tradition in Italy for marriages to be arranged, he'd seen the damage they wrought. He preferred the American way of choosing one's own spouse. Soon enough Angelina's innocence would be betrayed when the realities of being married to a stranger twice her age became clear to her. She was a woman with such passion. She deserved more. As it was, he intended not to go far enough to witness her disappointment.

"Only for two years."

He stared at her until she felt compelled to continue. "In two years we will have enough money to return to Italy and live comfortably. *Signor* Allessandro has promised."

"In two years he'll have to drag you back kicking and screaming, believe me."

"How can you be so confident? You act as if you know me well."

"I do. You remind me of a younger version of myself. So damned free-spirited you tried to take off on me and go it on your own. Once you get a taste of walking down the streets unaccompanied, talking to whomever you please, conducting your own business, you'll forget your longing for the shackles of the medieval life you led in Italy. American women will soon have the vote and with that—"

"I won't stay. I miss Santa Croce already. When will you return?"

"Never," he said.

She gave him a look he was sure meant to pierce the truth out of him, but he didn't waver.

He set his napkin on the table. "Stop looking at me like an angry cat. What would you have me do? Go back and marry some Northern girl? They don't have the shortage of men there that they do in the South, so I feel no guilt in that regard. Speaking of which, why didn't your Mr. Allessandro wait two years to marry, when he could go back and collect a handsome dowry from some desperate rich girl? Why send for a poor one without a dowry?"

"Mr. Allessandro is forty-four years old. He doesn't want to wait any longer to start his family. Why don't you go back?"

"I told you, I'm not the marrying kind. And if I were, it would be to an American woman. I like their sense of independence. They don't want men to rule them."

"You've forgotten, sir, that the real ruler of the home is the Italian mama."

He smiled, genuinely amused. "I haven't forgotten. I had one myself. But the woman can only cajole the man. She has no real power of her own. It's a crime for a woman to show any intelligence or initiative. When it comes down to it, if the man is strong, the woman has no say. My poor mother learned that the hard way."

"What about your family?" she asked. "Don't you miss them?"

"What's left of my family disowned me years ago."

She stared at him questioningly. "You had an uncle."

"Yes, I did." He stared back at her. "And now he's dead."

"We should return to our seats." She rose, setting her napkin on the table and brushing a few inconspicuous crumbs from her skirt.

Tonio came around to her side of the table and pulled her chair out, then leaned close to speak into her ear. She might as well know what kind of man he was.

If she kept her guard up, he might be able to stay away from her.

"I got a girl pregnant when I was nineteen, the same exalted, wise age you are now. I would have married her, but my father decided she was too far below our station to carry the Domani name. He sent me away. "

She colored, a deep obvious scarlet.

Her eyes were wide with surprise as he took her arm and guided her to the door. "After you."

The rails clattered on endlessly as the train shimmied along on its boundless route. Tonio sat beside Angelina, reading yellowed letters from a bundle he'd carried aboard in his traveling duffel. Angelina studied him from the corner of her eye. His face was a placid mask as he read, but his eyes were hard and angry.

She turned to look out the window but didn't process the scenery. Her mind was busy with other thoughts. She was more intrigued by Tonio than ever. Even as an uncomfortable silence settled between them, she wondered about him. Maybe it was true; women did prefer men with bad reputations. And his was more than a bad reputation. It was reality, spoken from his own mouth.

She sighed. All she really wanted out of life was a decent, intelligent man. One who worked hard. One who loved her beyond reason. One like her papa. There were no such men in Italy; there were hardly any men at all. And now she found herself headed to a husband she'd never met, seated beside a man who, despite her best defenses and all good sense, stirred in her strange and unsettling emotions. One whose compliments and attentions she craved when she should have berated herself for even thinking about him. The more she tried to remember that she was married to a good, kind-hearted man and must uphold the family honor, the more she was drawn to Tonio.

She'd never known a man who had affected her in any stirring way. She knew she possessed the ability to fluster them and turn their heads and she reveled in their attention, as much as was permissible under the tight constraints of the society she came from.

Life in her home village of Santa Croce had been simple, bound by tradition and social stature. Each day her father, Pasquale Di Maria, left when the sun rose to work in the fields of the rich landholders in the surrounding countryside, sometimes traveling for hours upon the family donkey to reach his destination. He was not a skilled worker, like the grafters who traveled the country carrying small black tool cases resembling doctors' bags. He was an ordinary field hand, poorly paid because of his lack of skills.

Angelina, her sisters, and mother attended to the domestic duties. Their house was a small one, located in the village with all the others packed tightly together like row houses. In front and in back of the house were narrow cobblestone streets. There were no yards, but each family had a garden plot located across the stone bridge just outside the boundaries of the village. Angelina and her sisters tended the garden where they raised lentils, peas, fava beans, tomatoes, and herbs. On a warm spring day, her sisters would walk through the streets inhaling the smells of clay, warm straw, and sweet herbs. If it rained they would splash in the puddles that pooled in the holes left by missing cobblestones.

It was down these same streets that her mother had walked her and the two sisters nearest her in age, the three considered old enough to marry, to the town square, the *chiazza*, as *piazza* was pronounced in dialect, to do the shopping or go to church on Sunday.

The church was located at the far end of the *chiazza* from her home. Simple by Italian standards, it was made of aged gray stone. Inside it had a domed ceiling, a huge statue of the Christ and the Virgin Mary, and crucifixes hung or were placed in every available nook. On the walls were paintings of the Stations of the Cross. She and her family attended mass every Sunday; not to do so was a sin and would subject one to social condemnation. Besides, it was the social event of the week.

She and her sisters dressed in their finest for these strolls to mass, hoping to attract the attention of the single young men. It was a tradition centuries old, this strolling along the streets and there were well-defined, though unwritten rules. Men walked with men, women with women, unless a man accompanied his wife. A man never spoke to a woman walking alone, or even stared at her, for she could uproot him with a glance. A woman was not greeted unless her husband was present. But the discreet, admiring sidelong glances Angelina received as she walked along behind Mama and Papa were not lost on her. And though that was as close as she was ever allowed to a single man not of her family, it had been a titillating experience. But it, and the stolen pecks on the cheek at *carnevale* last year, paled next to the maelstrom of emotion she felt as she sat next to the undeniably handsome Tonio.

He folded the letter he was reading and returned it to its faded envelope with unexpected reverence. The gentle crinkling of paper caught her attention and she turned to watch him as he replaced the bundle of letters in his duffel.

"You seemed entranced by the scenery," he said, "Anything interesting out there?"

"I wasn't really watching. I was thinking."

"About what?"

She considered for a moment before speaking. "What happened to the girl?"

"What girl?"

"The one you almost married."

"She died."

His look gave nothing away. She couldn't tell whether he was sorry or not.

"The baby?"

"He died with her, in childbirth."

"Oh! I'm sorry." She felt herself color. Perhaps she'd been too bold in asking. She looked down and played nervously with the finely crafted gold cross that hung on its long chain over her bosom, glad to be out of the avaricious city and able to display it.

"It was a long time ago. I'm not even sure I'm sorry anymore. I'd never wish them dead, but I couldn't have changed what happened. The baby was too big for her.

They would have died no matter what. That's what the midwife said."

"But you know it was a he?"

"Her mother was hysterical after she died. She insisted they take the baby. Her daughter didn't want to go to her grave pregnant and her mother had to know positively that the baby was dead and could not be saved. The baby was a boy."

"How sad." She considered the tragedy and the shame, both for the girl and the baby. Illegitimacy was not accepted. "And the poor baby went to his grave a..."

"Bastard. Are you too delicate to say it?" He seemed suddenly angry.

She'd probed too far. He stared at her as she toyed with her necklace. She dropped her hands into her lap.

"He wasn't. She married someone else. The baby was named after him and buried with his family. My father bought her a husband."

"Oh." She paused but couldn't stop herself from asking. She wanted to know everything about him. "And your father, did he disown you then?"

He saw the look on her face and frowned. "Don't get any romantic notions about me giving up my family for the love of a woman. It was rebellion on my part, pure and simple. To this day I have a hard time picturing her face. She was young and beautiful and innocent. Hell, we both were, if you can believe that." He laughed, but it was at himself and it had no humorous ring. "But to answer your question—yes, my father disowned me then. Actually, when he found out about her. But in reality, it had nothing to do with her."

"Is that why you came to the United States? To get away?"

"I came because my father cut me off without a penny and I had no way to support myself. Seems we have a common enemy in poverty, don't we?" He was looking straight ahead. His voice was bitter. "My uncle was here and he sponsored me to come over."

"Is your family very wealthy?"

"Extremely." Then he laughed, but his mood had turned and his laugh was lighter. He looked her in the eye and for a brief moment they connected.

What she saw there made her feel as if her breath had been taken from her. For an insane moment she had the strong desire to lean up and kiss him, kiss away all past hurts, make him aware of only her. It was madness. She looked down, trying to collect herself, but she couldn't completely stifle her natural urge.

"You like money?" he asked suddenly.

"I'd like to have it."

"So would I." He motioned with his head toward a group of men huddled around a pair of dice at the front of the car. "I can play craps with the best of them. What I win we'll use to travel first class from Chicago. Deal?"

The breathless feeling returned as his eyes bore into her. "Yes," she said, but she felt she would have said anything to hold his look and the marvelous trembling feeling.

He rose and stepped into the aisle. "Wish me luck."

"Good luck, Tonio." It was barely a whisper, but his name sounded good on her tongue.

She watched Tonio as he went to join the game. He stood outside the circle until the shooter passed and all bets were settled. The circle of men opened to welcome him into their midst. It was a mottled group that sat at the front of the coach near the vestibule, placing bets and tossing dice in the largest area of clear floor space available. They were immigrants mostly, like her, from all over Europe, yet they spoke a common language— English. She listened carefully from her seat only a few rows back from them. Each man had his own accent, some so heavy that at times it was a wonder that they understood each other at all.

Only Tonio spoke like an American. Even as she listened for his deep voice as he called out his bets, she marveled at his ability to wash all trace of the lilting, romantic Italian out of his words. His r's were suddenly hard, not lightly trilled and rolling like when he spoke Italian. He pronounced his a's in the harsh, flat way of the Americans. She wished she spoke English better, and she envied his casual composure as he sat well at ease among the varied crowd of men.

Tonio sat at profile to her, his left side toward her. One small, errant curl looped over his left eye giving a boyish appeal to his otherwise strong, masculine face. He sat off to the side with one long leg straight and one bent, leaning on the bent one with one elbow, using his free hand to set out his wagers in a pile in front of him. He rolled his shirtsleeves up as the shooter to his right passed him the dice, exposing powerful forearms with strong veins that stood out in a purely masculine fashion.

She marveled at the strong physical appeal of him. Everything, from the way his shirtsleeves tugged at his muscled upper arms to the way his shirt tapered into his jeans against a flat stomach, hinting of a narrow waist, spoke of masculinity. Tonio tossed the dice, rolling seven, a natural. The other players who'd faded him groaned as they tossed him their bets.

The game interested her little. She'd watched hours of it beneath the hull on the *Brezza Marina.* The only way to win consistently was to bet with the odds, but fools frequently gambled recklessly in hopes of big payoffs. She stared transfixed at Tonio until he turned and caught her at it, then she made a point of concentrating on the other players.

As the game picked up and the men were rapidly wagering and paying off, she noticed that one player skimmed coins off the top of his pile before he paid off. The game was becoming so heated that none of the others seemed to notice. He called and set out one wager, but paid another. The men were laughing and spirits seemed high. A few drank beers they'd evidently bought in the dining car. In light of the mood, no one suspected a cheat.

She watched another round to confirm her suspicions then made her way past the game to the vestibule that connected their car to the coach in front of it. She stood looking out the tiny vestibule window pretending to take in the scenery and stretch her legs. But she watched the man in question in his reflection in the glass. She stood watching the cheat, unsure how to

warn Tonio, until the conductor came through and said
something to her.

"He asked you to move out of the vestibule. If we
have to stop suddenly you'd be crushed in the folds between cars," Tonio said in Italian without looking up
from his game.

She looked at him, surprised he'd noticed her presence. Pleased he was aware of her when his attention
seemed elsewhere. It gave her the opportunity she
sought. She stepped back into the car and leaned down
to speak to him in an intentionally warm, hushed lover-
like tone.

"Thank you so much for your concern. The man
with the blond mustache cheats. He holds back part of
his wager. I've watched him enough to be sure."

"What does she say?" one of the players asked.

"She wants to know how to play."

"I'd say she wants something else. And it ain't dice. I
know looking at her makes me want something else."
The men laughed. "She going to make you quit?"

"No woman tells me what to do," Tonio said. Then
he spoke to her in English, for the men's benefit. "You
can't play, honey. This is a man's game." He switched
to Italian. "I suspected, but we don't want to cause a
scene."

"Demand payment, then scare him off with your
knife."

He laughed.

"You are wearing it?"

"I always wear it. This is penny stuff, not worth the
trouble. Go back to your seat."

"No."

The men laughed again. No was no in almost any language.

She stood up again, positioning herself directly opposite the cheater.

Tonio sighed. "She wants to watch."

The game picked up again. Angelina made no pretense about it. She watched the cheater like a hawk watches a field for mice. Under her surveillance he lost his nerve and quit, mumbling an excuse about needing a bite to eat. The game broke up quickly. She sauntered back to her seat with Tonio on her heels.

"You ruined the game."

"I watched. That's all."

"I was winning."

She shrugged. "You were letting a cheater fleece all of you."

"I was cheating, too."

She turned on him, eyes blazing, but he didn't cower.

"I had *you* in the background to rattle their nerves."

She flushed. It was a compliment of sorts. "You weren't really cheating?"

"On my honor." He crossed his heart. "I've never met anyone with such high morals!" He laughed loudly and fully.

"Then you must not associate with very nice people."

"The best in the Silver Valley."

"If that is true, then perhaps I should be worried." She turned from the aisle into her seat.

"Yes, definitely. You should be worried."

"I want to play dice tomorrow."

They'd just finished making their bed for the night. Angelina sat on her side of the chumming board, next to the window, brushing out her long hair with smooth even strokes.

"You can't. It's a man's game." Tonio watched her with interest, holding down the urge to grab the brush and attend to the task himself. He wondered what was so damned enticing about her, other than the obvious.

Her eyes flashed fury. "You won ten dollars. I can win at least that much."

"If you are going to insist on relying on a man and believing that you must have one to take care of you, then you are going to have to allow us our games, unhindered with your company." He smiled at her. He liked seeing her temper up. "Besides, everyone knows that betting is highly mathematical, based on odds, and women don't understand such things." He waited, anticipating her response.

"*Porco cane!*"

She'd insulted him by calling him a pig dog. He probably deserved it.

"I have a head for math that puts yours to shame!" She shook her brush at him.

He believed it. He'd seen her add the prices for their meals in her head, calculating the bill ahead of time and tossing in her share before the cash register was done chiming.

"It takes nerve."

"I have nerve."

"It takes money."

He had her there. He knew she had none to waste. He saw the disappointment register. His eyes traveled down from her face to where her gold necklace lay in the pillow of her bosom. It was a good excuse to stare. Her hand flew to it immediately.

"Lend me the money. I'll pay you back with my winnings."

"No."

"You aren't being fair. Part of the money you won today is mine."

"I'm being incredibly fair. That money is for train fare."

"You're afraid I'll do better than you."

"I tell you what, to prove how fair I am, we'll play a practice game to see how it goes. If you win, I'll back you with a few dollars. If the men will let you play. If I win, I get the necklace."

"No!" She shook her head emphatically. "This necklace for a few dollars? You're crazy. Name something else."

His eyes traveled to her pouting lips. "All right. A kiss." He played a dangerous game, but he had no intention of winning. She wanted to play. He'd let her, with dignity.

Her triumphant smile was not lost on him.

"I'd as soon kiss a donkey." She paused coyly, for effect, he was certain. "But I accept your deal."

"I'll stake you two dollars. The loser is the first one to go broke." He pulled two dice from his duffel. "Shall we begin?"

The game wasn't much fun with only two playing. He had a supreme run of luck, which even he had to admit to himself. Since there were only two playing the one had to fade the shooter every time. He naturaled, against all odds, five times running, bankrupting her inside of ten minutes, even though he'd meant to lose.

"That showed no skill! That was merely luck," she complained.

"Poor loser. Luck is part of the game."

"I suppose you want your kiss now." Her tone held less disgust than it should have.

From her flushed cheeks and pursed lips he could tell the idea excited her, though she tried to feign indifference.

"No, I think not. That was for effect," he said.

Her face fell, but was quickly followed by a scowl.

"When I kiss a woman, it's because she wants it as badly as I do. I don't do it on a whim of luck."

"Then you admit you were lucky tonight!"

"Maybe."

"You'll let me play tomorrow?"

She was quick on the uptake.

"Maybe." The way she stared at him made him want that kiss after all. "We'll talk about it in the morning. Sleep tight." He lay down and turned over. He felt her fuming behind him. She wasn't going to give up. He was certain of that.

CHAPTER FOUR

Twenty five dollars in coin, including a glittering gold half eagle that sent Angelina's heart pattering every time she looked at it, towered in a pile next to Tonio, who sprawled casually on the floor in the half circle of men, legs outstretched toward the side. Angelina knelt behind him, her full skirt billowed around her, leaning against his back, at times pressing forward against him, her hand resting intimately on his shoulder, in an effort to see around him and watch the play of the dice as they bounced off the wall under the window. All her previous anger at the men for not letting her play on her own was forgotten in the passion of their winning streak.

Tonio placed the bets she dictated, seemingly amused by the enthusiasm she'd gained for the game since being allowed some part in it, although she was never allowed to toss the dice. The other men seemed less amused by her presence. She used a system, betting with the odds every time. During the morning of play she'd lost only one bet, and that one on the come at even payoff. As soon as the traitorous dice had settled in their lie, her nose had wrinkled in disgust. Tonio laughed at her as he paid off and remarked that he'd never let her play poker.

The man immediately to their right was having an unusually long and lucky streak as shooter. Angelina studied him during play and concluded quickly that pure luck was responsible for his success. He recklessly placed bets with the odds well against him. Sooner or later his streak would end and it would be their turn to shoot. Angelina was betting it would be sooner. She eyed his pile of money, which was larger than theirs. With that much cash they could surely buy first class tickets from Chicago.

Somewhere in the last twenty-four hours Tonio's goal had become hers. As Tonio wooed her with his tales of first class travel, her excitement at the novelty of train travel paled. Something in her longed to experience the opulence of first class, to see how the rich lived. She felt his impatience when they pulled over to allow an express to pass, or when they were sidelined for hours loading freight. She longed to feel the rush of traveling at top speed, the way passenger-only trains were allowed. The urge to compete and win, to see a tall store of money in front of her overcame her. She could not fell it. But it did not erode her caution. With studious even betting, they would win. Tonio had noticed her addiction and mentioned that her eyes shone with a pretty gleam of avarice. She thought it was a compliment.

"Greed comes before a fall, isn't that what they say?" he'd added.

She realized then that he was insulting her. "I believe that's pride."

He laughed, well aware of the proper saying. "You let gambling fever get hold of you, you're lost. Be careful Angelina. I've seen eyes like those aplenty surrounding gambling tables, happily watching as their owners lose everything."

"Place our bet. One dollar on a natural." She let her irritation show. The game continued.

The man to their right tossed the dice. They bounced off the wall and fell back into a pair of fours. Angelina leaned close and whispered in Tonio's ear. "Place two on a gag that he won't make his point with a double four."

"No, bet right that he comes on the next roll. Same two."

She shook her head. "He's foolhardy. He'll take our bet. We're guaranteed a win. He just rolled two fours, what are the odds he'll do it again?"

"Ten to one."

He didn't need to tell her, she could figure or recall odds faster than the rest of them. She knew that he was baiting her.

"If we lose, we pay off at the same," he continued.

"He just rolled his one. The odds are with us."

"He's on a hot streak."

Angelina didn't listen. She leaned past him and scooped the half eagle out of the pile. "See, I'm preserving our original investment." Then she set two silver dollars out in front of them. Tonio called the bet, which the man accepted as Angelina had predicted. The man shooting held the dice out to her to blow on.

"Care to blow out my luck?"

She shook her head. "Tell him, I'd as soon spit on them. He hasn't a prayer of winning."

The shooter laughed and tossed with great care, aiming at the wall with exaggerated movements. The dice bounced, the first die landing a solid, stationary four immediately. The second rolled to the edge of the semicircle, nearly out of play, before settling into the second four. Angelina's mouth fell open.

"Hot damn!" the victor cried out.

She covered her mouth to stifle a scream. She couldn't look at Tonio. He must be furious. She fled to her seat. Twenty dollars, over a week's worth of wages, gone!

"With that little stroke of luck, I pass," the shooter said. He moved to hand the dice to Tonio.

"I'm out. Go on without me."

She heard his steps coming down the aisle, then felt his eyes bearing down on her from where he stood in the aisle, but she couldn't look up to meet the fury she expected to find. He reached over her and let the window down a few inches. Cool spring air swept down on her.

"You look green." His voice was calm.

"You can look at me." He settled into the seat next to her. When she still refused to look up, he gently pulled her chin round and tipped her face to meet his. "I won't hit you. Is that what you expect?"

"I'm sorry. I lost all your money."

He showed her the half eagle. It glinted gamely in the sunlight. "What did I lose? I still have my original investment."

"I'd be furious."

"That's you."

She pulled away, confused by his gentleness. "Spoken as someone who grew up with money."

"Is it harder to have had and lost, or never to have had at all?"

"It was a safe bet. The odds were against him."

"That's why they're called odds, there's always the chance—"

"He shouldn't have won."

"Angelina, you can't always bet with the odds. Sometimes you've got to go with what's in your gut."

"You knew he'd win?"

"I would have bet differently. He was hot. Where were your country superstitions to guide you when you needed them most?" His tone was light, joking. He was trying to cheer her.

"*Aristicratico!*" The word was a barely audible whisper under her breath.

"I may have come from nobility, but I'm as poor as you are. And no one gives a damn about bloodline here." He pushed up and strode off down the aisle and into the next railcar. She was vindicated that at last he was mad. But she couldn't help wondering why.

They sat in an uncomfortable silence, staring at each other over the meal that he insisted on buying with money he'd won playing craps after their big loss. He forced angry forkfuls down, followed by swigs of beer. She pushed bites around in random patterns on her plate, uneasy with his anger.

"Are you going to eat the damned food or just fork it to death?"

"I'm sorry." She took a bite of chicken to appease him.

"Look, I thought getting off the train for a meal would be a treat. We've been trapped there for days."

She took another bite. He still sounded angry.

"You thought I was gloating, buying this meal. That's it, isn't it?"

"No. Why do you insist on believing that I'm still angry? My anger passes quickly. At first, I couldn't understand why you weren't angry with me, now I can't understand why you are."

"You don't have the power to provoke me to anger."

"Don't I?"

"I don't want to hear any aristocrat crap again. I'm an American, pure and simple. The fact that I was born to a titled family is an unfortunate quirk of nature. I renounced my Italian citizenship at the first opportunity years ago. And my family sure as hell renounced me. I have no desire to ever return to the forsaken place of my birth. If you had half an ounce of brain in your head, you'd feel the same. How long is it going to take you to realize that we're on common ground here? That I'm not the enemy?"

"How long is it going to take you to realize that I love my homeland and don't share your opinion of it?"

"All right, truce." He flagged the waiter and ordered a piece of pie. When the waiter asked if the lady would like dessert also she answered for herself, ordering a slice of cake. "Where'd you learn to speak English?"

"I learned a little from my work in the signor's household and taught myself the rest in New York. Mario's boys practiced with me. Both speak a little; they must for their jobs."

"That explains your pronunciation. You weren't taught by someone who speaks it as a first language. We'll work on it. By the time we reach Idaho I'll have you speaking like a native. How much do you understand?"

"Most, if people don't speak too quickly."

"Read?"

"Enough to get by." He smiled at her, but she had the feeling he was patronizing her. "Does it surprise you that I read?"

"You think it should?"

"Peasants usually don't, and more especially, women don't. I haven't had the advantages the wealthy, or even men, have. At least they aren't looked down on for trying to learn. Papa taught me to read against my own mother's wishes. She thought it frivolous, but then, she can't see how it benefits Papa, and he is a man after all.

My parents are not well matched in that way. Mama cares nothing about learning." She sized him up.

Education was a touchy topic with her. She had a quick mind that yearned to learn, but by accident of her own birth, had been denied. If not for Papa she would have starved intellectually. "Where were you educated? The best schools? The finest Italy has to offer?" Though she didn't mean to sound adversarial, the tone was clearly present in her voice.

"The seminary," he said.

She knew he watched her reaction with immense satisfaction. His eyes danced as he stared at her. But she couldn't disguise her reaction. Her eyes went wide. A steam whistle sounded before she could press him further.

He threw a pile of money on the table and stood, coming round to pull out her chair while she sat, stunned. He helped her up by her elbow and pulled her away. "Come on. The train won't wait. I think the engineer enjoys seeing us scramble to get back." He sighed. "I was looking forward to that pie."

The depot restaurant cleared quickly, most of the clientele returned to board the soon-to-be departing train. There was a crush at the door. Tonio grabbed her hand to pull her through. She was still too stunned to pull it away.

Angelina lay on the chumming board staring up at the rounded ceiling above her. Sleep was a faint hope. Tonio sat beside her, buffing the dust off his boots as he prepared for the night. Neither one had spoken since they'd boarded. He swung his legs around and up onto the makeshift bed, then turned facing away from her in preparation for sleep.

"Tonio," she asked, "What were you doing in the seminary?"

He rolled over to face her, studying her for a moment before propping up on one elbow. "Living in exile."

She looked relieved. "You weren't studying to be a priest?"

"Angelina, you're such an innocent. What else would I be doing at the seminary?"

"Oh." Then silence as he stared at her. "Are you?"

"What? A priest? No!" He laughed and leaned into her. His face was inches from hers. "Why do you want to know? Perhaps there's something you want to confess?"

She didn't understand the look he wore. This was a serious matter. "Did you break your vows?"

"Holy Orders? I never took them. A little incident with a girl came up."

Her relief was accompanied by a surge of jealousy over the mention of the girl. She didn't like to think of him as having been so distracted by another woman that he gave up his calling to be a man of God. Yet her reaction made no sense. She surely couldn't be falling in love with such a wild and reckless man.

"Were you worried or prepared to be disgusted by traveling with one defiled?"

"Oh, Tonio! How can you joke about this? You know that if you broke your vows you'll be damned for eternity. You can't walk away from a promise with God."

"Are you so worried about the condition of my soul?"

"Yes."

He leaned even closer over her, and though she didn't understand it, his eyes lit up with some intense emotion that she couldn't name or describe. If she pursed her lips he'd come down in a kiss. Her heart pounded, but she was at a loss. She desired his kiss, and it frightened her. The way her body reacted to his nearness was unfamiliar, and exciting, but forbidden. And she had to know. The jealous beast inside her had to be sated. "Did she mean so much to you that you would give up your calling?"

He fell back from her and the mood was broken. "My calling! You misunderstand. I told you, *she* was an act of rebellion. My father was the one that sent me to the seminary. He paid the priests a donation to take me off his hands. He paraded around with his pious arrogance, happily bragging about giving a son to the Church, all the while setting up mistresses throughout the city. If the good fathers had known of his carnal life they most certainly would have refused his money, and taken me on just to save my soul.

"He drank too much and spent too much money. He taught my older brother his same whoring ways, of which my poor brother has never repented. Poor Pia. My brother's wife. He's led her a merry chase. And yet, she continues to love him, my despot of a brother.

Sometimes the evil don't get their just reward, it seems.

"No, you needn't worry about me giving up a calling. It was my father's form of punishment, that's all. There he was making bastards throughout the city and yet he blamed me for my—" He cut himself short.

"Your mother didn't stop him?"

He looked at her oddly, as if she'd missed something important he'd already told her. "She was dead. She died when I was ten, of cholera. Just like the king, the same year. Don't feel sorry for her. It was an escape.

"He would never have taken a mistress while she was alive. He enjoyed imprisoning her far too much. He kept her locked in the *palazzo*, all to himself, as if he were afraid that someone would get to her."

He mumbled something beneath his breath in English, as if he were taking an extra precaution against her understanding. She thought he said, "But then, can you ever really trust a woman?"

He continued aloud in Italian. "She was an obsession with him."

Angelina sighed. It sounded very romantic. "How very lucky for your mother to have someone adore her like that."

"She hated him," he said flatly. He'd been staring at the ceiling. He turned to look at her. "I've dispelled your girlish views. You'd like to believe that I grew up in some kind of fairytale." He looked back to the ceiling. "I suppose by your standards I did. Home was a *palazzo* with a porte-cochere and a large courtyard.

The house had a plain facade, but inside it was magnificent."

He didn't elaborate and it seemed to Angelina that he didn't like remembering. "Because I was so much younger than my brother and sister, I had the nursery all to myself. My mother spent hours there with me. It only infuriated him further. It all belongs to my brother now. Oldest takes all."

Angelina was trying hard to put the puzzled pieces of his life together. But the pieces were oddly shaped and hard to fit. "Where did you go when you left the seminary? Your father sent you away?"

"To Ethiopia, to war. Because I'd been raised since the age of ten by pacifist priests my father thought that would be the perfect place for me. And he was right. I learned many useful skills there, none of which he counted on. I learned how to use a knife and a gun. How to blow things up. And most of all how to survive.

"That was the greatest surprise of all; that I, a pampered candidate for the priesthood, would have such a strong will to live. It was the bane of his later years. I came back a well-decorated hero. He would have preferred a dead son sent home on a medic's stretcher. Then he could have bragged about my heroism to his friends, buried me, and been done with me. Too bad for him that I valued life too much."

He sat up and turned the back of his head toward her, lifting his hair to reveal the jagged scar she'd noticed before. Beneath his hairline it was wider and raised. "I got this when the enemy sneaked up behind me and tried to decapitate me. Maybe scalping was all he had on his mind. The army doctor did a bang up job of sewing it back on. Since that time, I don't sleep heavily, and I always carry my own knife." He let his hair down.

She felt nauseated.

"We'll be in Chicago tomorrow. We've got a day's layover there. We'll be staying with old friends of mine. We'd better get some sleep." He lay down and rolled over.

"Tonio?"

He didn't respond, but she knew he was listening.

"I'm sorry." She curled up behind him and listened until his breathing stilled and she was certain he was asleep. Then she gently lifted his hair and ran her finger along the scar, finally kissing it softly. That he was awake and well aware of her gesture, she never knew. Nor that he kept his hands tightly clenched in front of him, fighting desire that he hadn't felt in years.

She lay her head back down and drifted lazily to sleep. Tomorrow they'd be in Chicago. The West.

CHAPTER FIVE

They arrived in Chicago with a haughty burst of steam as the sleek, black engine pulled to a stop before the crowded platform. Angelina descended the stairs in a dissipating cloud of steam in front of Tonio, disappointed by the sprawling, populated city. The city with the reputation as the nation's most wicked seemed tame and ordinary as she'd ridden along the rail lines, scanning the sights for some remnant of the frontier town she'd dreamed of. But the city of nearly two million seemed little different than New York.

The depot was no better. She saw no wild cowboys, child thieves, crime bosses, or painted ladies strutting about. The crowd that thronged against the arriving passengers was like any other, a varied mix of the ordinary. Any vestiges that might have remained from the city's wild founding days were not evident from anything Angelina could view.

"Salvo! Sal!" Tonio yelled across her, as he waved at someone in the crowd. A short dark man waved back. Tonio moved in front of her and grabbed her hand, pulling her along as he swam through the crowd toward his friend.

"Tonio!" The two men clapped each other on the back.

"This is your friend?" Salvo said. "You didn't say anything about a girl."

Tonio grabbed Angelina by the shoulders and pulled her forward in front of him. "Salvo, meet Angelina Allessandro. Angelina, Salvo."

"Tonio, what? You getting shy in your old age? Why didn't you tell me that your *friend* was a woman? Thought I wouldn't approve?"

"You pay by the word in a telegram."

Salvo wasn't listening. He focused on Angelina.

"Pleased to meet you. I admit I was surprised when Tonio telegraphed that he was bringing a friend. I've known this man for nearly ten years now and not once has he brought someone with him when he comes to visit. But I can see why he would make an exception in the case of such a beautiful woman." Salvo's gentle southern Italian fell on Angelina's ears like sweet summer dew. She liked him immediately. He reminded her of the men back home.

"I'm escorting Angelina to her anxious groom in Idaho. She's a mail-order bride."

She flinched at the term. "I have an arranged marriage."

"Your husband must be a confident man to choose Tonio as your escort." Sal leaned close to her, as if he were about to reveal a great secret. "Our Tonio is a famed ladies' man. Don't let him seduce you."

"You insult the lady, Sal. She's made a vow of honor." His words would have been noble if not for the light mocking tone in which they were spoken.

"The groom is a friend of yours?"

"Never met him." Tonio nodded toward Angelina. "Neither has she."

The confused look on Sal's face amused him. "Then how—"

"His brother was bringing her over, but got sent back. Nonna Gia asked me to take her."

"Nonna Gia." Sal shook his head knowingly, as if there were no resisting Nonna Gia. "Nonna Gia. Well?" He held open his hands in front of him in a variation of the Italian's favorite gesture, the shoulder shrug meaning *What can you do?*

"She is up to her old tricks, Tonio. Perhaps this time you don't escape." He nodded toward Angelina. The corners of his mouth twitched in sudden amusement. "Stranger things have happened than falling in—"

"Let's get out of this crowded depot." Tonio grabbed Angelina's elbow to propel her forward. She didn't understand what Salvo found so amusing.

"The old woman won't rest, Tonio." He wagged his finger at Tonio and left to bring the carriage round.

A short woman with an ample bosom greeted the threesome at Salvo's apartment in Little Hell. Tonio looked like he was hugging a child as he reached out to greet her.

"Maria, it's so good to see you. You look beautiful, as usual." Tonio gestured toward Angelina. "I would like to introduce you to my traveling companion, Angelina Allessandro. Angelina, this is Salvo's lovely wife, Maria."

"Pleased to meet you." Angelina stepped up to greet Maria, who barely came to her shoulders. It annoyed her that Tonio's voice held such open affection as he complimented the plain woman.

"Here. Come on in everybody and have a seat. Dinner will be ready in just a minute. I have a few last minute preparations to make. I would have had it on the table, but you can't depend on the trains running on schedule. I ought to know! I've waited on Salvo enough times. It's good enough that your train arrived on the date it was scheduled. I half expected Sal to return empty handed. With the bad snows this winter, the trains have been off-schedule by days. The weather has only just cleared."

Maria scurried off to her kitchen before Angelina could offer her help. Dinner was served minutes later. Tonio shot Angelina a look warning her not to wrinkle her nose at Maria's mediocre cooking, all the while praising the woman too profusely. The three old friends talked and caught up as they ate. The conversation was lively. Angelina felt as if she were an invisible intruder attending their meal. As soon as it was over, the two men excused themselves and were off out the door, leaving the women alone with the dishes.

Maria seemed to have expected their departure. She immediately busied herself with the dishes. "So how long have you known Tonio?" Maria asked as soon as the door had closed behind the men. She seemed as curious as her husband had been.

"A little over a week." Angelina explained the situation. "Tonio was heading back and offered to escort me."

"He offered?" Maria asked, an amused tone to her voice. "He must have been quite smitten with you. Tonio travels alone."

"Smitten? I'm a married woman."

"Bah! No matter. You are mail-order. Nothing is final until the bride and groom have met. You don't know; your groom could send you back. I don't suspect a man would reject a woman with your looks, but one never knows."

Angelina wondered at the woman's dismissive attitude. Angelina seemed to be the only person who held her vows in any regard. "He was persuaded by a mutual friend," Angelina continued.

"Nonna? She's the only person in New York that I know of capable of persuading Tonio to do anything. Someday I'd like to meet that woman. She must be quite remarkable. Both Salvo and Tonio have a deep affection for her."

Maria set the last dish in the drainer and wiped the table. "I'd like to learn her secret. How does she convince two such proud, stubborn men to do the things she wants them to do? If I knew how to move Salvo, my life would be easy!" She gestured with her hands for emphasis. "Her, and that May woman from Idaho that Tonio is always talking about. How is it that some women have such pull over men?"

May? A warning shock pulsed through Angelina. Tonio had never mentioned her.

"How did you come? Through the port at Naples?"

Angelina hadn't been listening. Her mind had been occupied with the idea of May. Angelina didn't like her already. She was brought back to reality by Maria's question. But she found herself at a disadvantage. In her musings, she'd missed a vital part of what Maria had been saying. Maria moved to the living area. Angelina followed. Maria sat on a small couch and motioned Angelina into the worn chair across from her.

"Would you like something to drink? Some tea? Coffee perhaps?" Maria offered.

"No, thank you."

"I was asking about your trip to the States."

Angelina was grateful for the change of topic. She was certain that Maria had noticed her preoccupation after she'd mentioned May. "I came through Naples. I'm from a small village about fifty miles away—Santa Croce del Sannio."

"It's good to talk to someone from home, a fellow Neapolitan. I'm from Campo Basso. I, too, came through the port as a young bride."

"We're practically neighbors then. Campo Basso is just to the north of us. I don't think I'd know your people but Papa might. He travels, farming the large estates in the area."

Maria shook her head. "I have no people left there." She didn't explain further.

"How long have you and Salvo been here?"

"Sal, ten years. Me, eight."

"You didn't come together?"

"No. Salvo was supposed to work in the United States just long enough to earn enough money to support us in Italy and then come home for good. We dreamed of buying enough land to farm and support ourselves. We kept hoping that the years of famine and oppression would end, and that Salvo would strike it rich. But neither one came to pass. After two years, I could take it no more. I begged Sal to send for me."

"So you came? Through Naples?"

Maria looked at her solemnly, as if weighing a decision to speak further. "Things at the Naples port have not changed much in eight years. This I know from neighbors here that have come to join their husbands. The port officials are just as corrupt?"

"You know Italian officials. They take what they can get. I suppose that hasn't changed. Human nature remains the same." Angelina's words sounded cryptic, but she spoke of the infamous bribes it took to cut through the paperwork and get permission to sail, to bribe one's way out.

"You were single when you went through the port?" Maria asked.

"No. I was married by proxy in Naples before I left. *Signor* Allessandro sent the money to bribe an Italian judge to give us the proper marriage license, even though *Signor* Allessandro was still in Idaho. It was cheaper than what would have been required by a port official and safer for me. That's what he said. And it would speed me through American immigration. So you see, I am married." She didn't know why she felt she must defend her marital status.

"Aye, no!" Maria exclaimed. She was pale as a communion veil and her hands shook as she stared at Angelina. "Then you were a virgin when you went to the port! You poor, poor child!" She leaned forward to put her hand on Angelina's arm in sympathy. "The marriage, it is not legal. That can be voided easily enough if you don't like your groom, the foolish man! Doesn't he know what happens to young, attractive *married* women at the port?"

"Now sit here with me." Maria pointed to the empty space next to her on the couch. "What I must say, I wish no one to hear." Angelina moved to the proffered spot.

"Salvo and I were married very young, when we were both still in Italy. As you know, times were terrible in the *Mezzogiorno*, even ten years ago. We were so poor and there was no work for Salvo. He had heard about the land of opportunity, *La Merica*, and so we decided that he should go there and find work. When he had made his fortune, he would come home to me. But life doesn't always work out as planned. Salvo got a job building the railroads West, which is where he met Tonio. But the pay was meager. He did not make a fortune. I was so lonely without my Salvo that I cried every day, and after nearly two years he had saved enough money to send for me."

"With the naiveté of a wholesome bride I was ecstatic when my parents dropped me off in Naples to begin my journey. I walked into the government immigration offices full of hope and optimism. I was taken to the office of a junior official. All I can remember of him today is that he was very ugly, and he smelled of sweat. So pure was I that I did not smell the danger that awaited me. He pulled the blinds and informed me that there was a problem with my paperwork. There was only one way to fix it." She paused, hate and sorrow brimmed in the tears in her eyes. "'You are a married woman,' he said. 'You know how to please a man. Your husband will never know. You have a choice.'

"He had a couch in his office. He pushed me down onto it and shoved my skirts up before I could even answer. I tried to scream, but he covered my mouth and laughed. 'I can fix it so that you'll never leave the country,' he told me. 'Or...'

"Then he raped me. I say he raped me, though I did not fight back. As soon as he was finished, he went straight to his desk and stamped my paperwork. Then he pushed me out the door."

Maria watched her closely as she spoke.

"He smiled as I left, and told me that it had been a perfect interview. Then he wished me a pleasant trip. I nearly died with shame. I thought that I was the only one, until I boarded the ship and made friends with other young married women. Almost every one of them..." She choked on her words.

"I worried for weeks that I would be pregnant with that awful man's baby. I didn't know then that I was a barren woman. But after a few weeks at sea, the curse came and I was never so happy as that day to see the bright red flow.

"Others were not so lucky. One friend of mine got pregnant. We plied her with castor oil until the child of that evil man slid out far before its time. She nearly bled to death with the miscarriage, but she was a survivor and she lived. We all cried because the baby was lost, but it couldn't have lived."

Maria came back to the present. "I can see by the look of horror on your face that you know what I am talking about." Maria nodded her head, verifying her own assumption. When Angelina didn't answer, she continued, certain that Angelina had suffered far worse than she, because some unknown man had surely taken her virtue, her maidenhood. She patted Angelina's hand reassuringly.

"Don't worry, I will tell you what you must do. For your groom or any other man." She looked Angelina directly in the eye. "After only one time, you will still be tight. Nearly as much as a virgin. No man can tell the difference there. You must act frightened and nervous. And, this is important, in pain. Distract the man so that he will not notice that the maidenhead is broken. I don't think most men can tell anyway, but if he is distracted he surely won't notice.

"But there must be blood. It's the only sign a man really needs. He won't question further once he sees blood. This is what my mama told my sister before her wedding night. My poor sister had fallen straddling a fence and broken her maidenhead as a little girl." She lowered her voice. "You must cut yourself. The area between your legs bleeds readily. Use whatever you must, but do it quickly when he isn't watching, just after the act." She held her hand up and extended a finger. "A long sharp nail works best for this. You understand?"

"Yes." Angelina couldn't tell her that she was still a virgin. One official had tried to extort her, as Maria had described. But it did him no good. She told him up front that she didn't want to go to America. That her family was forcing her to go to an awful old man when she would just as soon stay in Italy. She would be grateful if he would deny her permission to leave. It was a bluff, but it worked. He had no power over her. He stamped her papers and shoved her out the door.

"You're a smart girl, Angelina. You've done the right thing coming here. I've never regretted my coming, only the circumstances of it. You've gotten yourself out of a hopeless situation in Italy and here to the United States where the pool of men, and hope, is much greater. And you've rid yourself of an undesirable escort to hook up with a most desirable one. Maybe you'll be smart enough to catch our Tonio. Goodness knows, he needs a woman."

Maria raised her hand to silence Angelina's protest as it formed on her lips. "Though Tonio has told me time and again that he has no interest in an Italian bride. He likes those blond, American beauties. No old country woman for him."

"Tonio imagines himself an American." Angelina said. It was not a compliment. "An American bride would not suit him." Her pride was stung at being suddenly dubbed unsuitable by the absent Tonio.

Maria smiled back knowingly, smart enough to detect wounded feminine vanity. "Tonio is an American. He renounced his Italian citizenship and became an American several years ago. Have you ever heard him speak English?"

Angelina nodded.

"He speaks like a native. I don't believe that Tonio speaks any Italian when he's in Idaho. He has come to visit us and actually forgotten the Italian word for things. And there have been times when he has interspersed English with his Italian."

"He has forgotten Italian words!" The revelation delighted Angelina. Tonio was fallible after all.

"It's understandable, when you don't speak a language for months at a time." Maria replied. "I think that Tonio would choose to forget his mother tongue altogether, if he didn't need it when he comes to visit his old friends." Maria smiled at her and returned to her original topic.

"You're truly beautiful, Angelina. A woman like you has opportunities open to you. If you get to Idaho, and don't like what you find waiting for you there, discard him. But you must watch yourself in the mining country. It's a rough place, dominated by lusty men.

"Tonio would be a good protector and provider. He's a partner in a mine. He believes it will pay off handsomely and make him rich. It just might." She leaned into Angelina again.

"Tonio is a handsome man, one desired by many but elusive. Many women would covet the chance you have with him. In all the years I've known him, he's never brought a woman with him. No matter that he claims he's doing a favor for Nonna Gia, even she couldn't convince him if he didn't want to do it. And we must ask ourselves, what benefit is there for him in this situation?" Maria paused significantly.

"A final word of warning for you. Tonio can be very seductive, but if you want to catch him, hold out." Maria winked. "Why buy what he can get for free? He's used to too much of that already." Maria glanced at the clock. "Come, let's go find the men. They've had their time alone. Why should they have all the fun? I feel the itch to toss a few dice myself. You know, I'm much luckier than my husband."

It was the first perfect day that Chicago had seen all year. Winter's white blanket had disappeared only days before under the onslaught of heavy rains and warm winds. Dirty traces of snow still clung tenaciously under the protection of the eaves and heavy shade. But the day had been sunny and the evening was pleasant. And if it was somewhat cool, the residents of Chicago's Italian enclaves didn't seem to notice. The entire neighborhood took to the streets in the age-old tradition of the evening stroll, feeling for the first time in months the gentle warmth of the low slung spring sun and reveling in the long hours of daylight.

The mood was jovial as Maria and Angelina took to the streets. Children ran and skipped ropes along sidewalks, chanting their childhood rhymes. Strong-willed grass and weeds were popping up between every sidewalk seam, lending their bright greens and delicate blossoms to the festive atmosphere. In every alley old men played *bocce*, the Italian game of lawn bowling, their shouts of joy and defeat erupting at uneven intervals.

Angelina turned to scan each alley for Tonio, but Maria walked purposefully on, stopping to chat briefly with neighbors and introduce Angelina. It was largely a southern Italian community, but each person they met spoke a slightly different dialect. Angelina found it all very familiar and pleasant. The people were much more casual than in Italy. Several men called out greetings to the two women, even though they were unaccompanied by their men. They turned the corner and Maria spoke.

"They will be at Dorso's Bar, in the back room. That's where the private games are always held. No one bothers them there."

Dorso's was a typical Italian bar, long and narrow, with a bar counter that ran the length of one wall. There were no stools at the counter. Patrons stood and paid less for their drinks as was Italian custom, because they required little service. Small tables were scattered throughout the open area. Old men sat and played cards at many, drinking either coffee or liquor, depending on their mood. They happily paid the higher prices for their fare for the privilege of resting.

Maria walked through the room toward a separate, private room at the back.

"Dorso." She nodded to the bartender.

"Maria." He did not seem surprised to see a woman in his establishment. In the mornings, before alcohol was served, many women stopped by for coffee and a brioche. The Italians did not hold the taboo against women drinking. Wine was commonly served at meals and all partook. Many women accompanied their husbands for an evening drink, though on this particular night there were no other women present.

"It's a good thing you showed up. Sal's losing. He could use a bit of your luck." He looked questioningly at Angelina.

"This is Angelina. A friend of Tonio's."

Dorso smiled and gave Angelina the up and down. "Pleasure, *signorina*. Tonio always could pick 'em."

Maria ignored his remark and marched past toward the back room, but Angelina didn't like his comment. "How many girlfriends has Tonio had in Chicago?"

Maria brushed his comment aside. "Ignore him. What does it matter?"

The betting room was cramped, with one small transom for ventilation above the door, which stood slightly ajar. A group of men huddled around a table. A large, slick man stood behind it, obviously the house's banker. The two women stood in the door, watching the game, unnoticed. The men were intent on their betting. Angelina picked Tonio out of the crowd immediately.

He was a head taller than any other man in the room. He had his jacket off, his shirtsleeves rolled up and his stiletto holstered at his waist. Her heart tripped at the sight of him. Angelina was certain that if she were a man, she would not trifle with him, but as a woman...

She felt happy and flirtatious. Her talk with Maria, while arousing jealousy, had also buoyed her confidence. Could Tonio be interested in her? For reasons beyond what she understood, she hoped so. She intended to find out this night just how deep his interest went. Just some innocent flirting. She deserved that before she went to her husband, didn't she?

Maria started to move forward to enter the room. Angelina held her back with a hand. "Let me watch a few minutes more. This game is played differently than a private game. I must watch to understand."

Maria gently pushed her hand aside. "Come. You must see the table to understand. It has special markings that show which bets are available, and it's marked with the odds."

At that moment, perhaps alerted by their feminine voices, Tonio turned and saw them. To Angelina's surprise his look was one of genuine pleasure. Something in her wished he always wore that particular expression. With the warm glow in his eyes, he was devastatingly handsome. She wanted to hold that look forever. Was it caused by their appearance or luck at the table?

"Sal, your luck has arrived," Tonio said, but his eyes were riveted on Angelina. Though many of his friends stared openly at her, he didn't introduce her, even after

she walked to the table and positioned herself at his
elbow. Without a word he pulled her in front of him, so
that she could see the table.

"What about your luck? Has it arrived, too?" she
asked.

"I'm hot tonight. Do I need more luck?"

The game resumed. The men bet with vigor. Sal
continued to lose, begging out after two more rounds.
"I'm out. I'm broke."

He and Maria looked unhappy as they stepped back.
Angelina wondered if their losses stung them or if they
regretted leaving the action of the game.

Angelina fisted and released her fingers repetitively
as she watched the banker shoot. She itched to join the
game, but she had no money to wager. She followed the
game closely, calculating the odds to herself, watching
how each man wagered, trying to determine his strate-
gy.

She watched the banker recover the dice between
bets, collect and pay out, and shoot the dice, intrigued.
She had never seen a craps table before. The game was
played differently than a private game. All bets were
made with the house.

She scrutinized Tonio's game most closely of all. But
unlike the games they played together on the train, he
didn't ask her advice. He didn't let her wager. He raked
in his winnings and kept them to himself.

A crease formed between her brows. No one but
Tonio noticed her mood. Men dropped out of the game,
cutting their losses. It grew late.

He wasn't going to let her play. He didn't trust her! He'd won enough money to let her make a small wager. Her irritation with him grew. She wouldn't ask him for the privilege. Arrogant man!

The banker looked to Tonio. "Last round for me," Tonio said. "I've kept my friends waiting too long. I owe Sal a drink. And Maria whatever she wants."

The men laughed.

Angelina scowled. He hadn't mentioned her.

"What do you think, Angel?" he said.

Angel? "Are you asking me for advice?"

"No, I'm telling you to place the bet."

She swiveled around to face him. Her stomach hummed nervously, and excitement tingled in her fingers. She hesitated on the verge of a safe bet. She knew that betting with the odds was the key to winning, but on a single bet, as she well remembered, odds were only that. Something goaded her toward recklessness. A little voice inside screamed at her to take a chance.

He leaned forward and whispered in her ear. "Listen to your gut this time."

The room seemed small and close. A tiny trickle of perspiration dripped down her back. This was her chance to redeem herself.

"He rolls craps." She pulled a silver dollar from Tonio's winnings and set it on the board, then turned to stare him down.

"The odds are seven to one against us." His eyes danced mischievously.

"Chicken?" She turned back to the table.

"Craps," Tonio told the banker as he pulled out a twenty-dollar gold piece, the house limit, and set it on the table, removing the silver dollar.

She turned back to look at him in amazement. There was a quizzical mixture of emotion in his eyes. Trust and confidence, and amusement. And something she couldn't define. If he had given her the gold piece, it couldn't have meant more. Reluctantly, she looked back at the table.

The banker shot. The dice hit the back of the table and rolled back into a pair of sixes.

Angelina screamed, delighted. She turned and hugged Tonio, still screaming and bouncing.

"One hundred and forty dollars!" she cried.

Sal and Maria watched, amused at the couple in front of them. They exchanged a sly, knowing look. Maria whispered something to Sal.

"She's quick with math," Tonio said to them. "And do you see the way her eyes dance at the thought of money?"

Tonio pried her loose and took his winnings. He laced his arm around her waist and addressed his friends. "Let's get out of here before Dorso finds out how much we took him for."

He guided her out through the door and into the alley.

CHAPTER SIX

"What does the victor want for her efforts?" Tonio asked. Gravel crunched beneath their feet as they walked through the dark alley. Little points of light filtered through pulled shades from windows on either side, lighting their way.

"Anything?" Angelina asked.

"Anything." He stopped to pound out a drum roll on a nearby garbage can.

She tugged at his arm. "Stop! You'll annoy the neighbors."

"So?"

"I'd like to get out of this alley. I feel like someone is going to jump out at us."

Tonio grabbed her hand and pulled her, laughing and running, between two buildings into the street where street lamps glowed protectively. Sal and Maria tagged along behind, too dignified to run.

"Better?"

"Much. Anyone could have robbed us back there."

"And the streets are so much safer." He laughed. "Wise choice. We must protect our winnings. But fear not, sweet lady, you'll always be safe with me." He patted his stiletto. "You forget, the darkness affords its own protection."

Maria and Sal came up behind them, calm and amused. "Next time you change the route, give us fair warning," Sal said. "What does the lady want? Has she decided?"

"I wanted out of the alley."

"No, Tonio promised you a reward; you must hold him to it," Maria said. "Or he'll be insulted, won't you, Tonio?" She held her hand to her mouth as if conveying a secret, but she made no attempt to whisper. "Remember, he said *anything*."

"In that case I know exactly what I want." She appraised Tonio. "But I don't think he can give it to me. So I'll settle for a Stella Starr hat with a Parisian gown to match," Angelina said lightly. "A dark gray walking dress with leg-o-mutton sleeves highlighted with white ribbon stripes, and matching skirt, a frilly white shirtwaist underneath, and a really fabulous evening gown of velvet."

"What color gown?"

"Deep red. No, garnet. Very low cut."

"I thought you meant something to eat, Tonio," Sal said.

"So did I, Sal." He looked at Angelina as he spoke. "The lady fancies herself a Gibson Girl. And I thought she never left Little Italy. Where did you hear about Miss Starr?"

"Oh, from people here and there. A girl can dream. I saw the fashion books, and the ladies at the train depot, the ones traveling first class." She lifted her full, dull brown skirt. "These full skirts are hardly in style for hoeing a garden, even in Italy. Someday I'll have rich, fashionable clothes. I'll look like the women of your youth." Somehow that suddenly seemed important to her.

"It's not worth the trouble. Most of them were vain and empty." He leaned close to her and whispered. "You'll never get there shackled to your old man." It was a challenge.

"Oh? And with whom could I?"

Tonio leaned close and whispered in her ear. "I'd like to see you in that dress, the garnet one."

"Perhaps you will someday. Strike it rich in your mine and buy it for me," she whispered back. He didn't seem surprised that she knew about his mine. He laughed loudly. Sal and Maria stared at them, left out of their private conversation.

"*Gelato,*" Angelina said suddenly. "I'd like ice cream."

"I'd like something stiffer," Sal said. "Maria doesn't let me drink when I gamble."

"You need a clear head to win."

"See, she takes care of me."

"It's too late, the ice cream parlor is closed," Maria said.

"The bars never close." Sal looped his arm around his wife's waist. "We can't go back to Dorso's, but Napoli is just up the street."

"Old Man Gambino still hang out there?" Tonio asked.

"Suppose so, why?"

"The lady wants new clothes. Let's go. I'll buy you a drink at Napoli, Sal."

Napoli looked very much like its competitor, Dorso's, a few blocks away. A long straight bar bordered one wall. It was not crowded nor was it empty. The foursome stood in the doorway a moment while Tonio scanned the room. His eyes settled on a table of old men, smoking and playing cards at a back table. He pressed several silver dollars in Sal's palm. "Buy yourself a drink. I'll be back in a minute."

Angelina watched Tonio approach the back table. He was still several feet away when one of the old men spotted him, called out a greeting, and stood to meet him. "Antonio!"

That was all she could hear of their conversation as she watched them kiss each other's cheeks and shake each other's hand at the same time.

"What is he up to, Sal?" she asked. Before he could answer, Tonio came forward with an old man in tow.

"Sal, you haven't gotten a drink yet? Hang onto the money; I'll buy you a bottle of the best Gambino's store has to offer."

"This is the lady you mentioned?" The old man had a handle bar mustache, well waxed and as white as the rim of hair on his head, but his eyes were deep brown and as mischievous as any youth's.

"This is Angelina. She won me a great deal of money at the table tonight. I promised her anything she wanted," Tonio said. "Gambino has agreed to open his store for us tonight."

Gambino slapped Tonio on the back. "Anything for a dollar, eh Tonio?"

Angelina overheard Sal as he leaned over and whispered to Tonio. "How'd you get Gambino to agree to this?"

"He and Sebastiano were close."

"Let's get going. This old man can't stay up all night." Gambino grabbed his coat from a peg by the door and they were off, arriving minutes later.

Gambino turned the lights on and set his keys on the counter. "We must be quiet. Mrs. Gambino is asleep upstairs. Let's not wake her. She is not a woman who wakes pleasantly."

Gambino's was a typical American Italian general store. Wheels of hard parmesan and romano cheese were displayed behind glass at the counter, little knives stuck in each block for ready cutting. Wrapped salamis and pepperonis hung behind the counter in their white, powdered paper. Crates filled with sundries stood here and there at random and at the end of each row of shelves. Bottles of wine and canned goods filled the shelves, along with bottles of olive oil. There was a large bin of polenta flour and a shelf that contained kitchen items, cheese graters, and knives. On the shelf next to the cash register were two lidded glass bins, one full of candied violets, the other filled with candied rose petals.

"You expect me to find a Stella Starr here?" Angelina asked, amused.

"Gambino, show Angelina the clothing you carry."

Gambino smiled. "Of course." He took her hand and patted it. "Back this way." He dropped her hand and led the way to the back of the store where he opened a door to a room no bigger than a closet. He switched on the light.

"Mrs. Gambino's folly. She insisted I convert the storeroom for her. We cannot compete with the big clothing stores, but a woman must have an occupation. It keeps her from pecking at me."

The room was lined with shelves stacked with shirtwaists and skirts, camisoles and hosiery. One shelf held an assortment of three or four hats. Against one wall was a rack filled with dresses and more skirts, all carefully arranged by color.

"Look at this fine selection, Angelina." Tonio stepped into the closet room and gently fingered a folded shirtwaist of inexpensive lawn. "Pick out an outfit of the best." His tone was light. Angelina was sure he made fun of the inexpensive, factory made clothing Gambino's carried. He was used to much better, but to her it was a treasure room, though not, of course, the quality she'd jested of earlier.

"If you wish to try something on to try out the size, just close the door. We won't disturb you." Gambino moved to the door and motioned Tonio to follow him. "Antonio, I must catch up with you. It has been a long time."

"I was hoping to get to watch the show. Add my opinions," Tonio said. Gambino grabbed his arm and motioned toward the front of the store with his head.

"I'll help Angelina." Maria let the men pass and moved into the room.

"Come model for us when you've decided," Tonio said in parting. He followed Gambino and shut the door behind him.

It took Angelina only minutes to make her decision. A hunter green skirt caught her eye. Maria teamed it with a white button front shirtwaist accented with thin, almost imperceptible gray lines in a fine gray plaid. It had a large bow at the neck that covered from neck to mid bosom. A small, stylish brimmed white felt hat with a tiny white bow completed the ensemble. "Signora Gambino has very good taste. What do you think, Maria?" Angelina primped in front of the full-length mirror.

"You look lovely. Wearing that you could turn the head of any man you wanted."

Angelina smiled as she untied the bow at her neck and began unbuttoning the dozens of tiny buttons that scooted up the front of the blouse. She felt light and wonderful. She'd never owned anything this pretty in her life. She was half afraid Tonio would refuse to buy it. "Let's hope I never have to get out of this in a hurry."

"You're not going to model it for Tonio?"

"No, I'll wear it on the train tomorrow."

"He'll be angry. He gave you instructions."

"Let him." Angelina smiled. "You know, I believe we picked the most expensive outfit in the store. What do you think?"

"I believe you're right."

"Let's tell Tonio that it's the only thing that fit, in case he gets stingy."

"I don't believe, Angelina, that Tonio would ever be stingy with you."

Tonio and Gambino were involved in conversation as Angelina approached from the clothes room. Tonio leaned on the counter. Gambino sat on a stool opposite him. Sal browsed through the wine and swigged from an open bottle as he looked for something more to whet his need for drink. Maria joined him. From the corner of her eye, Angelina saw him offer his wife the bottle. Tonio was too occupied to notice her approach.

"Sebastiano is dead?" Gambino said. He looked suddenly old. His brown eyes no longer sparkled. "How can that be? He was in fine health last fall, when he came through after visiting you in Idaho."

"Sebastiano was sick all winter. He caught the flu. It spread to his lungs. You know they were weak after all those years in the mines." Tonio sounded sympathetic but detached.

"He was only sixty-three. Two years younger than me."

"I'm sorry."

"Why didn't he write and tell me of this? Why didn't you wire me of his death?"

"It was only two weeks ago. I had a lot to do."

"So much to do that you couldn't wire his best friend?"

"I wanted to tell you in person. I planned all along on coming through Chicago and stopping by on my way out of town, but I found you tonight."

Angelina couldn't see Tonio's face, his back was toward her, but Gambino looked stricken.

"It wouldn't have done any good for you to lose business to go to New York for a funeral. It was very small. Just a few old friends. And me." Tonio flicked a piece of lint off his sleeve.

Gambino reached out and gently touched his arm. "What's wrong between you and Sebastiano, eh?"

"Nothing."

"Perhaps you just grieve. He was always your friend, your rock, eh?" Gambino's fingers tightened around Tonio's arm. "He loved you Antonio, never forget that. He told me himself on many occasions. He was proud of you." Gambino's eyes narrowed. Angelina thought Tonio's back stiffened. "He was worried about you. Last fall when he came."

"Sebastiano was always afraid I was going to blow myself up. Yet he, of all people, should have known my skill."

Gambino looked speculative. "Oh, he knew. It was not the Hole that worried him. It was your friends."

Tonio didn't respond.

Gambino implored him with his eyes. "Sebastiano's gone now. I must stand in his place and tell you what he would have wanted. He doesn't like Mr. Baker. He fears you are tight with the wrong people, and that you are flirting with serious trouble. Don't do their dirty work Antonio. No matter how much money they offer you or how noble you feel the cause." The younger man was not heeding his warning. Gambino speared him with a look. "Or how exciting the assignment."

Sal bumped a shelf. A bottle fell and crashed to the floor. Footsteps pattered on the second floor above them. Gambino leaned forward urgently to tell Tonio one more thing before he went for a mop. "You blow that mine up, you'll hang for it. You were his boy, Antonio. Don't disgrace him." Gambino's eyes held Tonio's. Angelina saw him clench his fist and imagined his jaw clenched as well.

"I know, damn it. I know."

"Don't blame him. They were in love." Gambino jumped down from his stool. He went for a mop and broom.

Sal and Maria bent over the mess picking up the shards of broken glass. Angelina was setting her purchases on the counter when an angry woman, clad in nightclothes, stormed down the stairs from the second story. She waved a rifle at them unsteadily; its barrel was much too long for her, the gun too heavy to manage easily.

"Stop right there." She leveled the rifle on Sal, squinting for a better view of him. "No one robs Gambino's."

"Put the rifle down, Luisa." Gambino appeared from the back of the counter with mop in hand. "No one is robbing us. I opened up for one of my favorite customers."

The woman lowered the gun to her side. She was younger than Gambino by probably thirty years. Perhaps his daughter, Angelina thought, though she looked nothing like him. She was short and heavily built with dark hair accented too strongly with henna. It glowed beneath the bulb over the stairs in an unnatural red halo. Luisa snorted. "Who deserves such treatment, Gambino?"

Tonio turned and faced the stairs. The movement caught Luisa's attention. The moment she caught sight of him her look softened. "Tonio? Oh, how nice of you to visit us. Of course we are always open for you. What brings you here?" Her tone was suddenly sweet and flirtatious. She leaned the gun against the wall and descended the last step to ground level, intentionally letting her wrapper fall open to reveal heavy breasts thinly concealed beneath a gauzy gown. Angelina, who was only steps from Tonio, walked to him and looped her arm through his in a protective gesture.

"Sebastiano is dead." It was Gambino who spoke. "Tonio came to tell me."

"I'm sorry." Her voice was smooth, holding not the slightest trace of sympathy. She glared once at Angelina but did not halt her progress toward Tonio.

"Go back upstairs, Luisa. This doesn't concern you." Gambino looked stricken.

"Why? I'm allowed to offer Tonio condolences."

"Stop acting like a tramp and go back upstairs. You're not dressed for company." Gambino's tone was authoritative.

Luisa threw Gambino a look filled with hate, but she obeyed and retreated up the steps, pausing to invite Tonio for dinner. "You will come, won't you Tonio? We'll have a special meal to honor Sebastiano."

"Go!" Gambino commanded before Tonio could respond.

Luisa thumped up the stairs and out of sight.

"You must forgive my wife." It took Angelina a moment to realize Gambino was speaking of the woman. "She is a mail-order bride. She is not happy here. It was a vain old man's attempt to recapture his youth, sending for her. How much happier I would have been with a settled woman my own age." He didn't have to sigh; the weary tone of his voice said everything.

"Give Luisa my apologies. We can't come for dinner. Our train leaves in the morning." Tonio turned to Sal. "Grab some wine, Sal, and let's be off."

Gambino cleaned the mess. Tonio settled the bill, not bothering to glance at Angelina's purchase. He seemed distracted. He paused only to confirm that Sal had enough wine for the evening.

As they were leaving, Gambino handed Tonio a brown wrapped package. "*Baccala*," he said. "Salt cod."

Tonio looked at him quizzically.

"Because you couldn't come to dinner. Top it with some tomatoes. You have those in Idaho? Enjoy it some night when you come out of the Hole hungry. And think of this old man. Don't forget me now that Sebas-

tiano is gone. You come see me." He hugged Tonio and
they left.

Sal and Tonio opened the wine as soon as they were
out Gambino's door, each swigging from their own bottle as they walked toward home. Tonio swirled his in
his mouth before swallowing, then rotated the bottle to
read the label. "Pinot grigio."

"I bought the best. It was on you."

Tonio didn't laugh.

"This reminds me of our railroad days. Late nights,
a bottle." Sal tipped his bottle back for another drink.

"We weren't drinking wine."

"Ah, but we must respect the ladies present. We had
no women on our arms then. We're better off tonight."
Sal smiled at his wife. "Much better off."

Sal reached over to nibble his wife's neck as they
strolled. She grabbed the bottle and took a large drink.
Tonio offered his bottle to Angelina, but she declined.
Her hands were full of packages. Tonio didn't offer to
help with them.

Perhaps she was the only one who noticed, but Tonio's mood had changed. His jubilant sense of victory
was gone and now his mood was somber, almost morose. His eyes were hard, and he wasn't drinking to celebrate but to forget.

The steps to Sal and Maria's apartment were dark
and dimly lit. The foursome sat at the bottom, too
wound up from the evening to go in immediately, enjoying the night air and the stars for a moment. Sal and
Maria sat a few steps behind Tonio and Angelina and

nibbled and kissed each other. Angelina stared ahead, embarrassed. Tonio opened another bottle of wine and insisted she drink. The alcohol settled pleasantly on her senses, warming her in the cool night air.

Angelina heard heavy breathing and sucking noises behind her. At last Maria excused herself and Sal, claiming they needed to make up the bed.

"We'll give them fifteen minutes," Tonio said when they'd left. "That ought to be long enough." He wasn't talking about a bed being made.

They sat in silence until the alcohol loosened her lips. Her earlier mood had not changed but was enhanced by the wine. She longed for the flirtatious intimacy of Sal and Maria.

"Tonio, do you think I'm pretty?"

"Reasonably so." He looked up at the stars visible between buildings.

She frowned. "Only reasonably?"

"I've known a great many very beautiful women in my time."

"They were no prettier than me. They merely had the clothes to show them off to advantage."

He turned to look at her and she smiled. There was a hint of amusement in his dark eyes.

"I look very pretty in the new clothes you bought. Perhaps I'll show them to you sometime." There was a pause as she considered him. He was not in a mood for conversation. "Dorso thought I was very pretty. He said you could pick 'em, so I assume I compare favorably to past women in your life. I didn't tell him I wasn't yours."

"What did you tell him?"

She smiled in answer. "Were there a great many?"

"What? Women?" He looked genuinely amused now. "Hundreds."

They sat thigh to thigh. She leaned into him. "You must be a very good kisser or perhaps very bad. Do you know I've never been kissed? Except at *carnevale*."

"I should hope not." His voice was tinged with humor, but he gave his tone the proper moral attitude.

She ran her tongue around her lips and smiled.

"Let's hope that Mr. Allessandro is an experienced kisser. That duty should be his."

He'd ruined the mood, seemingly on purpose, intent on keeping her at arm's length. But he was right. She had no business flirting when she was already married.

Curse it all! She didn't feel married. She was a young woman who hadn't had the chance to flirt. And now it seemed that opportunity was forever lost. "What a proper chaperone you are!" She started to rise. He grabbed her.

"You want embarrassment, go upstairs now. Sal and Maria won't be finished yet."

"What a vile mind you have. They're making the beds." She shook him off and stood.

He rose with her. "They're making it in the bed. It doesn't take sophistication to have understood their message, believe me."

She'd stood too fast. The world swayed and blurred before her eyes. She hadn't realized she'd drunk so much, or that the wine had affected her at all. She blinked. Tonio steadied her with a strong grip on her shoulders. "Are you all right?"

"Fine." She stared him down. His eyes were dark and unreadable.

"Good." His mouth came down on hers, hard and swift. They stood like a teepee, locked in a chaste, tongueless kiss. To her, an unsophisticated, naive girl, the kiss was reckless and wild. She stood with her hands to her sides so that all guilt at such an indiscretion would be his, her emotions reeling at such a simple act. She'd slap him when he released her. She had to, it was expected.

But suddenly the game changed as Tonio exceeded the bounds. He bent at the knees to level the difference in their heights. Without releasing her mouth he pulled her close between his thighs and pressed her against him, wrapping his arms around her so that there was no escape. The chaste kiss ended as he pried her mouth open and ran his warm, wine-tinged tongue inside.

His mouth covered hers completely and followed her head as she twisted to free herself from the passionate thrusting of his tongue. She wedged her hands between them, against his chest in an effort to push him away. At the same time he rocked against her with his pelvis. She felt him, warm and hard, pressed against her through the folds of her skirt. She tingled with unexpected pleasure and for a moment stopped her struggling. Then, more from fear than moral outrage, she twisted her mouth free.

He didn't try to recover her mouth, but bent kissing her neck, sucking and nibbling as he made his way down to the top of her breasts, which heaved with something other than indignation.

"Stop!" It was a feeble plea she didn't really mean.

One hand worked its way from her waist to her breast, cupping it with his fingers and brushing the top with his thumb. "Sweet," he said. "Sweet."

He'd gone too far. She'd gone too far. She wrenched free and ran up the steps. He called after her. "Chicken!" He was laughing. She banged into the building. Behind her, he swooped up her packages, and laughing, followed her up to the apartment.

Maria, flushed and glowing, let her in. She was already dressed in nightclothes. Tonio came in moments later looking calm and unruffled. In the corner of the one-room apartment opposite the kitchen, a single bed was made and turned down for the night.

"I'm sorry," Maria said, "we only have one bed. But won't it be fun, all of us sleeping together? Ladies in the middle, men on the edges. Get your night things, Angelina. The bathroom is just down the hall. I'll show you." Maria winked at Tonio.

Angelina grumbled as she went to get her traveling bag. Among the poor Italian peasantry where beds were a luxury, it was common practice for hosts to share the only bed in the house with guests and for everyone to sleep together. That didn't upset or surprise her. What bothered her was that she was fairly certain she wouldn't be sleeping next to Sal, and she was too distressed by Tonio to think of being near him again. She hadn't even slapped him. She grabbed her bag and stormed off after Maria.

She couldn't sleep. Behind her Sal and Maria cuddled provocatively, comfortably intimate after years of marriage. Their familiarity forced her to turn and face Tonio, who, despite her strongest mental urgings, refused to roll over and face the wall. She studied him carefully, trying to analyze what she felt for him. It wasn't love. How could it be? Had she known him long enough for that? But it was something unfamiliar and exciting and wild, and totally irreconcilable to anything she'd felt before. His breathing was slow and even. He slept as if unaffected by her presence next to him. She frowned. That hadn't been the case earlier.

She ran her hand lightly over his forearm, which rested exposed above the covers. It was so different from hers, covered with coarse hair and strong veins. She skimmed his upper arm, running lightly over the curves of his biceps, firm even in sleep. His breathing quickened. Intrigued, she ran her fingers over his cheek and lightly brushed a curl off his forehead, careful not to wake him. He breathed harder. She smiled in delight. She did have an effect on him.

She scooted down in the covers and in a bold move lightly caressed his hip, anxiously listening for his responding breathing. Men were such a curiosity. She'd never been as physically close to any man as she was to Tonio at this minute. She remembered their earlier kiss and the hardness as he pressed against her.

And her own scandalous reaction to it, the tingling between her legs. Men weren't usually hard, were they? They were soft and limp, like the statues in the *piazza*.

She balled her fist, resisting, she shouldn't do it, but she couldn't help herself. She wouldn't wake him, but she had to satisfy her curiosity and feel him. She reached carefully between his curled legs. Through the soft fabric of his pajamas she felt him and was vindicated. He was small and limp, but *she* tingled with pleasure. She ran her fingers along his outline, and suddenly it lost its limpness and grew hard and long beneath her touch. A hand shot out and grabbed her wrist. His eyes flew open and bore down on her.

"Enough is enough," he whispered.

"You had your feel of me earlier. It's only fair."

"Bitch," he said, but she had the distinct impression it was a compliment.

"Are going to let me go, or will you make a scene?"

"You'll go back to sleep and leave me alone?"

"What a turn of events," she said. He was ruffled. She heard it in his voice. She put on a contrite look. "Yes."

He released her hand. She withdrew it quickly, cuddling it against her chest. He rolled over to face the wall, pausing to turn back over to address her one final time. "Be thankful Sal and Maria are here." Even though naive, she knew what he meant.

As she stared at his back, the scene at Gambino's came to mind. She recalled clearly Gambino's statement that an older woman would have suited him better. She pictured herself in Luisa's place, flirting madly with any man that happened by, trying desperately to fill some need that an old husband would never satisfy.

Even as her face flamed at the thought, she had to admit that she could imagine Tonio touching her, and she liked the image. He was unlike any man she'd known. He was smart, and sharp-witted, and mysterious. He had a mine that was going to make him rich.

But she had made a vow of honor to *Signor* Allessandro, by all accounts a decent and hardworking man who had sacrificed a great deal to bring her to America. She could not disgrace her family by running off with another man. Not that Tonio would run off with her. He was set against marriage. But if he wanted to, she was not certain that she could resist the temptation.

Her thoughts ran too close to the scandalous. She made the sign of the cross to ward them off. God help her! After Tonio, could she ever be happy with *Signor* Allessandro?

CHAPTER SEVEN

A clock chimed the half hour. Eleven thirty p.m. After a nearly fourteen-hour delay, amid rumors of avalanches on the western tracks, they were back on the train again. Chicago was two hours behind them. Angelina felt surprisingly alert as she sat cross-legged on her sleeping berth, and examined the splendor of her surroundings. She switched on the light, a sculpted glass lamp seated in an ornate brass wall sconce, illuminating the tapestry that shielded her from the hallway just outside her berth. Thin strands of gold and green thread glowed richly in the maroon background of the curtain. Overhead the dark cherry wood ceiling was polished to the brilliance of a looking glass.

Angelina kicked off her shoes and tucked them into her duffel. Tonio's friend, a Northern Pacific Railroad clerk, had upgraded their tickets for a nominal bribe. She marveled at Tonio, he had the most amazing way of living in a style considerably above the means of the common miner he claimed to be. She wondered what he had planned for the rest of the money he'd won.

She leaned back, lost in thought. She hadn't counted on separate sleeping berths. She'd grown used to sleeping next to Tonio. She'd thought she would have a few more innocent nights to last her a lifetime. She found herself wishing that Mr. Allessandro looked something like Tonio, that he would elicit some passion in her. She didn't like to think of her husband. It brought only guilt and sadness. She would have a lifetime learning to forget Tonio and love another man.

She heard footsteps approach and watched through the gap in her curtain as Tonio jumped into his berth across the aisle. She watched until his lamp went out. Then there was nothing to do but attend to her nighttime ritual.

She pulled her blouse off over her head and loosened the strings of her camisole, revealing the tops of her full breasts, remembering Tonio's kiss upon them. She pushed them up and together, wishing Tonio's hands caressed them. Then she sighed and unpinned her hair, throwing her head back to shake her hair loose. She grabbed the bottom of her camisole. Just before she pulled it over her breasts, she turned out the light.

"Goodnight, Tonio. Sleep well," she whispered to herself, hoping he didn't sleep at all without her next to him.

Tonio swung up into his berth with the ease of someone used to riding the rails. For nearly a year while he worked his way West on the railroad crew, a rail bunk had been his only private space, if it could be called that. He stooped as he sat in the cramped space. A man of his height couldn't sit fully upright. Some things hadn't changed. He slid the privacy curtain closed and undressed, casually tossing his discarded clothes at the foot of the bed. With one fluid movement he rolled up and under the covers, switching the light off in the process.

He lay there on his back for a moment with his eyes closed, arms folded beneath his head, enjoying the comfort of a real mattress, listening to soft feminine rustlings across the aisle. He could well imagine what was being exposed hardly an arm's length away. Soft curves, gently sloping shoulders, delicately formed feminine collarbones, full breasts...

He opened his eyes and stared into the highly polished domed ceiling above his head.

"Shit!"

Just a few feet above his head Angelina was clearly reflected in the ceiling. He stared mesmerized and watched as she pulled her blouse off, loosened her camisole and brushed her hair with long fluid strokes. With each stroke her full, winsome breasts threatened to escape and bounce free of the thin fabric that bound them. The reflection was so clear that he could see the dark outline of erect nipples as she brushed. A heavy gold cross, suspended around her neck on a gold chain, glinted in the lamplight as she moved. She was about to pull the camisole off when she switched off the light and the reflection vanished.

"Damn!"

He reached up and stroked the ceiling where the image had been, as if hopeful that he could restore it, then turned on his side toward the window. He was hard and aroused and frustrated—the woman was driving him insane. He pulled the window shade open and stared mindlessly at the darkness rushing by, unable to sleep.

Tonio awoke early, his mind swimming with images of the night. Damned dreams. He thought he'd seen the last of those when he'd first known the pleasures of a real woman years ago. Now that southern peasant girl had managed to insert herself into the private world of his sleeping conscious. He eased his body, stiff from the cramped quarters, up onto an elbow and peered out of the tiny window in his compartment. It wasn't easy for a thirty-year-old man to sleep with a hard-on all night.

He glanced up at the ceiling overhead. The gentle morning light coming in through the window obscured any reflection that might have been there. Annoyingly disappointed, he pulled on his clothes and jumped down out of his berth.

As he stood in the aisle, he looked up to check the view overhead. His own slightly distorted reflection peered back at him. The curtains on either side of the aisle blocked the sloping sides of the ceiling, preserving the privacy of the inhabitants of the berths from intrusion by someone standing in the aisle.

He sighed in relief, for all his annoyance he didn't want other men to get an eyeful of the unsuspecting Angelina. Why didn't the train staff do something about these awkward invasions of privacy? Surely someone had noticed the glorious reflective qualities of the ceiling before, and complained? He certainly didn't need visions of Angelina to fuel the disturbing attraction he felt growing for her.

He shook his head as he remembered his own railroad days. For all the seeming propriety of the stewards and conductors, they probably got a big kick out of knowing that the staunch and pure ladies who could afford the berths were treating total strangers to a peep show. The ladies, if they discovered that the berths were not as private as they thought, would surely be too embarrassed to report it, opting to be more careful rather than face the humiliation. He headed for the men's room making a mental note to turn out the lights in his berth before disrobing.

He considered warning Angelina to do the same, just to avoid further frustration, but decided quickly against it. He'd lived like a monk these last few years, sequestered in the mines. Maybe he needed the stimulation.

It was nearly nine o'clock when Angelina awoke. She peeked through the tiny crack in her curtain to the berth across the aisle. The curtain was open. It was deserted. Tonio was up and roaming about the train. She dressed in her new clothes, her thoughts on him.

He was imperturbable, holding himself reined in with the tightest of grips. What would happen if someone broke through the dangerous edge of his emotions? That would be something. Tonio, in love. It would serve him right to be humbled, his heart at the mercy of a woman. She sighed, unreasonably morose at the thought that she would not be that woman.

Her dressing finished, she opened the curtains, swung her legs over the edge and peered out to check the hallway. There was no one in sight. She flipped over onto her stomach and slid off, her skirt hiking up to nearly her waist before her feet finally touched the floor. She gave her skirt a quick tug to straighten it and then headed to the ladies' room.

Tonio watched amused, concealed from her view at the far end of the hallway. He stepped into view and greeted her without commenting on how pretty she looked in her new clothes. She blushed and wondered how much he'd seen as she'd slid off the berth.

The dining car was fancier than the Pennsy's, and nearly empty, except for a few late morning coffee drinkers, one of whom started in recognition and made his way towards them as Tonio seated Angelina in a chair near the window.

"Tonio! Imagine seeing you here."

Angelina turned to look at the speaker, an immaculately dressed middle aged man with a handlebar mustache. Tonio was already on his feet shaking his hand.

"Jim, what brings you here?"

"Been back East, business for the Bunker."

"Oh?"

"Checking out smelters."

"Bunker must be doing well. Don't tell me production is so high you can't keep up."

"You know the situation as well as I do, Tonio. You haven't been away that long, have you? Baker and his men are out stirring up trouble, trying to get the Bunker and some of the other large mines to go union."

Angelina didn't understand all of the rapid fire English that was being bantered back and forth, but when she heard the name Baker, she focused on Tonio and watched him closely. Gambino had mentioned Baker as a dangerous man. She could tell from Jim's tone that he didn't like Baker either. Tonio's expression was unreadable.

"We're likely to see a repeat of '92," Jim continued. "We won't be caught unprepared this time. The Bunker has to keep the operations going or the union boys win. We'll wage our own war if we have to, to keep that from happening. You might mention that to your friend Baker next time you see him. It's a losing proposition for him, Tonio. We'll hire scabs from Mexico if we have to. The Bunker isn't afraid and the owners won't back down."

Tonio looked mildly amused. "I'm sure Baker and the rest of the boys at the Western Federation will be glad to hear that, Jim."

"You know I don't like Mr. Baker. He and his ideology convinced my most respected foreman and the best damn explosives man we've ever had to quit."

"It wasn't Baker; it was the opportunity to own my own hole. The day I walked into Cardoner's Store and Orchard offered up his shares was the most opportune day of my life."

"You, the Days, Prestons, Halls, and Dad—you're all crazy. The Bunker's got all the ore that's in that valley."

Tonio smiled in response. Jim tapped on the table and seemed to notice Angelina for the first time. Although he started, he didn't address her.

"Join me for dinner, Tonio. Seven. Bring your companion if you like." He slapped Tonio on the back and walked off.

"Who was that man? Why didn't you introduce me?" Angelina asked in Italian as Tonio seated himself again and flagged a waiter.

"It would have embarrassed him."

"Why?"

A waiter appeared to take their order before Tonio could answer. When he left Tonio deferred to another topic. "English," he said. "We must practice your English. You must be fluent before Idaho or they'll eat you alive." He smiled happily. "We can't have that, can we?"

Their seats in the traveling car were thick and plush and individually sculpted, arranged in cozy foursomes facing each other. Tonio sat beside her; the two seats across from them were empty. Tonio seemed satisfied with the accommodations now that they traveled first class. He sat, head down, absorbed in the mysterious letters that occupied him during the tedious hours of traveling. Angelina watched a woman seated forward and across the aisle facing them, fascinated.

A small card table sat in the woman's foursome. She played cards freely with any gentleman that asked. In the last hour, a single man held the place of honor, an older, heavyset man. Angelina couldn't see much more than the back of his well-tailored coat and peppered hair. She wondered if he was handsome. The woman was beautiful and fashionably turned out.

She wore a low cut gold gown with a scalloped neckline. A full, scalloped ruffle of the same hid her feet. The dress was belted with a not quite maroon, almost brown, bow. She wore a choker of matching colors with a tiny drop pearl. The whole outfit was modestly covered with a jacket of matching maroon brown with gold piping. It had a wide lapel that branched at the shoulders reminiscent of epaulettes. The wide sleeves had two gold chevrons at the wrists, further adding to the military image, but softened by the addition of gauzy ruffles along the neck and wrists. The woman's hair was swept up and topped with a gold hat embellished with three large maroon plumes. She was stunning.

"Tonio, look at that woman across from us."

The woman seemed to sense Tonio's eyes on her. She lifted her gaze from her cards and smiled at him, coyly lifting her chin to indicate that he join her. Tonio didn't respond. He looked back to Angelina. "The woman in gold?"

"Yes."

"What is it you want me to notice about her?"

"She's beautiful and confident. Her clothes are gorgeous and she plays cards freely with the men. I'd love to be like her, traveling, doing what I want, being admired."

"No, you wouldn't, Angelina." He seemed amused, but his tone held a distinct warning. "That woman is a prostitute and a card shark."

"I don't believe you. She's dressed like a lady!"

"A lady wouldn't be wearing a theater dress midday. Furthermore, ladies don't engage in cards with strange men. My bet is she'll either be kicked off at the next stop or she'll leave with a customer. I hope you're a better judge of character than what you've shown me so far. Idaho is full of crooks and scoundrels just waiting for an innocent to take advantage of."

"Yourself included?" She was irritated that he could recognize a theater gown from a day dress and for showing her to be so foolish.

The door to the car opened, letting a small surge of air and engine noise in.

"Shit!"

She frowned at him.

"That's a description of what just walked into the car." Tonio's attention was focused on a short, wiry, smartly dressed man who headed toward them.

"Tonio! Baker'll be glad to hear you're back." The man spoke to Tonio, but his eyes were on her. He stared in what amounted to a gape, his eyes raking her in a lusty mental undressing. She didn't like him and neither did Tonio. When he didn't respond the man continued, nodding to Angelina as he did, "So that's why you tore out of Idaho. You had a little piece waiting for you back East. Baker wasn't happy when you left so suddenly."

"Sebastiano died, Clell."

"What? Did he leave her to you? What a lucky old man!" He didn't offer his condolences. "You'll have a hard time keeping her to yourself, Tonio. The men won't stand for it. I hope you've got that stiletto of yours sharpened. I might give you a run for her myself. I hear the Italians are screamers. She is one of your kind, isn't she?"

"What makes you think I'm available?" Angelina's adversarial tone broke through her heavy accent.

"She speaks English, all the better!" He spoke as if she didn't exist.

"Drop it, Clell."

Finally Clell spoke to her. "I know you're not his missus. Tonio won't marry up. You get tired of him, you come see Clell. I'll show you what a real man can do." He patted Tonio on the shoulder. "Just passing through. Saw your friend Jim Burte in the car up ahead. Good work Tonio, we need someone on the inside. Come see us when you get back. We might have a big job for you."

"*Caccola*!"

"Exactly," Tonio said and laughed.

Tonio stood in the aisle outside his berth and tied his tie without aid of a mirror as he dressed for dinner. "You won't change your mind about dinner?"

It had occurred to her shortly after Clell had left that Tonio's friend Jim had also thought she was his mistress. Tonio had corrected her, "No, he thinks you're my paid companion, like the lady in gold." She'd been furious.

"Are you so desperate?"

"Every man in the mining country is."

He wasn't easy to insult.

"We have very few single women. Most of the attractive ones work at the Lux and are as hard as they come." He didn't elaborate. "Idaho isn't Italy and the sooner you get used to it the better. There are no civilized evening strolls or Sunday walks to church where parents chastely parade their eligible daughters before suitable bachelors. It's a valley full of rough, working class men. That's it. When we get there, you'd be advised to watch yourself; married or not, it isn't going to stop most of those men from making a play."

"Thank you so much for your concern. Why didn't you set your friend straight?"

He only shrugged. He had no defense. Now she steadfastly refused to meet the man, Jim, who'd assumed the worst of her, and having done so, had refused to acknowledge her.

"No, I've been insulted." Besides which, she had nothing to wear. Tonio's elaborate preparations hadn't been lost on her.

"Suit yourself."

She was angry that he didn't try to persuade her. "I'll be in my berth writing a letter home. I have no desire to run into more of your friends."

"Wise choice. You can write?"

"I can do a great many things. And I didn't need to attend fancy schools to learn them."

"*Brava,* Angelina, neither did I. The most useful things I know I learned from life." He turned and headed down the aisle, pausing to call back over his shoulder. "Enjoy your evening, and don't wait up." She had no intention of waiting up for a man who would not defend her honor. She did not understand much about Tonio, but she felt him pushing her away.

Sometime around midnight, disappointed that Tonio had not come back for her, she set her partially written letter aside and laid her head down. She would rest a minute before getting ready for bed.

The sound of metal rings sliding across a rod woke her with a start. She sat up to scream. A hand clamped over her mouth so quickly that not a peep escaped. She tried to bite down.

"Calm down, Angelina. It's me."

Tonio stared at her from the dimly lit hall. His eyes were dark and serious and he smelled like whiskey and smoke. He uncovered her mouth.

"Tonio?"

He was drunk. She didn't know how she realized it. He showed none of the common signs. With both arms now free he reached in and scooped her into his arms. He said something in English, words she didn't recognize from her lessons with Aldo and Davida. Then, with her still in his arms, he kissed her, hard and passionately. She looped her arms around his neck and kissed him back.

He released her mouth and spoke. "Angelina, I'm a bastard."

Then his mouth was on hers again and she didn't care what he meant.

CHAPTER EIGHT

A discreet cough brought an end to their embrace, reminding them that there were others in the car. Tonio set her down.

"You don't tell me anything I don't already know," Angelina whispered. She traced the outline of his mouth lightly with her fingers. He didn't smile or laugh as she expected. His look was frighteningly solemn. She dropped her hand and nervously fingered her necklace. He covered her fidgeting hand with his own.

"That may be true. I need to talk to you someplace private. The salon car should be empty at this hour."

She was too nervous to look directly at him as he seated himself next to her on the plush red velvet couch. Heavy velvet curtains framed stained glass windows. Above, the ceiling was frescoed in mosaics of gold, emerald green, crimson, sky blue, violet, and black. She felt shabby and underdressed in such opulent surroundings, but Tonio seemed at ease and unimpressed. She skimmed her fingers across a walnut end table next to her and waited for Tonio to speak. Her heart thumped wildly.

"I hurt your feelings tonight. I wanted to apologize." He ran his hand along her arm. "I know you think I'm cruel for letting everyone believe you're an easy woman. I could have told them the truth, but they wouldn't believe it. There's something between us, Angelina. Let them believe it's only lust."

He nuzzled into her neck and whispered into her ear. "There are things going on here that you don't understand. I'm caught in the middle of a dangerous battle. It's better if you don't know anything. You're safer if they think you're incidental to me."

"What battle, Tonio?" His breath in her ear sent pleasant shivers down her spine. It took all her concentration to speak. He sucked her ear lobe and her heart raced out of control. What was he talking about? She kept expecting a declaration of love, but he stopped short and pulled back.

"Damned arranged marriages." He spoke the words with the force of an epithet. His change of course caught Angelina off guard. Only the alcohol on his breath and the odd jumping of his thoughts gave away his inebriated state.

"What are you talking about?"

"I'm no good at loving people, Angelina. Less so at protecting them." He stroked her hair. "Do you hear what I'm saying? Maybe I'm as warped as the man who raised me, unable to really love."

"I don't believe that," she said.

"Believe it. Did I tell you that just before he died, my uncle told me that he, not his brother, was really my father? I was so angry with Sebastion. I broke that old man's heart because I couldn't accept the truth from the man who treated me like a son, who loved me. I am a bastard." He leaned into her.

He ran his fingers lightly through Angelina's loose hair in a tender, lover-like gesture and stared at the gold cross she nervously played with. Under his appraisal she stopped her fidgeting. "My mother had a necklace very much like that one. She never took it off, even though she owned far finer jewelry. I always wondered what happened to it after she died."

He dropped his hand from her hair and lifted the necklace from her fingers. He studied it closely for a moment, then gently set it against her bosom. "It was probably a gift from Sebastian. Likely, my father melted it down after her death.

"My father is a bastard, as you like to put it. But he is one of the best men I know. More should be like him." Angelina put her hand on Tonio's arm. She wanted to take him in her arms and comfort him but wasn't brave enough.

She held up her gold cross. "How do you think my family came to own such a valuable treasure? My grandmother gave this to me when I was small. She told me it was a gift of true love, that someday I would find a man that loved me as much as the man that gave

it to her loved her. I believed her. You could call me a
fool.

"When I was older, I found out it was a gift to her
from her lover, a wealthy landowner, a married one.
She worked for him when she was very young. She got
pregnant. His wife forced her to leave. He gave her this
necklace in parting."

He pulled her close once again. "You didn't have to
give up your family skeletons for my sake. That's the
difference between us. You give love and comfort
where you can. And me..." He leaned down as if to kiss
her. "I can't save you from this damned arranged marriage of yours."

He kissed her but it was a rough, drunken kiss,
fueled by alcohol and frustration. When he released
her, she rose shakily.

"Not like this, Tonio. Good night."

The next day, as Tonio sat next to her poring over a
long report filled with numbers, Angelina marveled at
how easily they picked their routine back up. Tonio
apologized for his behavior of the night before, stating
as obvious defense his drunkenness. She accepted with
the distinct feeling that his past was no longer open for
discussion and he hadn't told her all he'd meant to.

He'd regained control of himself easily. At breakfast, he appeared freshly shaven, without any signs of
suffering a hangover, or any genuine embarrassment
for his confessions or actions. He ate a hearty breakfast,
then spent the next two hours tutoring her in English,

both pronunciation and writing, as he had for the last several days. Then he retreated to his mining reports.

Though she was curious about them, there was no use peering surreptitiously over his shoulder to read them. They were written in technical terms in English. She recognized few of the words. Seated in his lap was a leather bound ledger. From time to time he entered numbers into its neat columns.

"What are you working on?"

He was so absorbed in his work that she had to repeat the question twice before he looked up. He continued copying numbers as he spoke. "Assay reports for the Jupiter."

"I thought you were a miner, not an accountant." She nodded toward the ledger.

"I'm a mine owner. That makes me bookkeeper, miner, slave."

"Tell me about your mine, Tonio."

"You must be bored. No one opens that topic with me willingly."

She shrugged.

"What do you want to know?"

"How you got it, what it's worth, how much money you make from it."

He laughed. "You'll be sorry you asked." He set his reports aside. "I bought in as a minority partner last winter before leaving for New York, for groceries, if you can believe that." His eyes lit up as he spoke. "I was up at Dan Cardoner's store getting supplies when Harry Orchard came in. Cardoner wouldn't sell to him without cash. He'd already exhausted Cardoner's patience with him and his credit. He offered to trade Cardoner his share in the Jupiter to clear his debt and cover what he wanted. I offered to cash Cardoner out for half of Orchard's debt and half the shares.

"I'd been looking to get in on the Jupiter, pestering the Halls to let me in, but none of the partners were selling. I turned in my resignation to the Bunker the next day and started working my claim immediately. I own enough shares to make me a rich man when we find the mother lode."

"And what makes you think you will?"

His papers rustled as he adjusted in his seat. "We've assayed out some good samples of galena—that's silver ore. And geologically speaking, we're on the right side of the valley to find the main vein."

"What does that mean?" She knew nothing about mining.

"Thousands of years ago there was a single large silver vein. Then according to the geologists, there was a great earthquake that split the land and created the valley. It split the silver vein as well.

"But it did more than just create the crevasse of the valley. The two sides of the land mass shifted several miles. You can see it as you travel through the valley. To the west all of the mines, most notoriously, the Bunker Hill and Sullivan, are all located on the south side of the valley. As you travel east, it shifts. There all of the ore has been found to the north of the valley floor.

"Burke, where our mine is located, is north of the valley, well within the range of the shift. Not a single ore sample has been found to the south in our area. When we get to Idaho, pay attention. As we travel along you'll see what I'm talking about. All of the mine tunnels will be on one side and then they abruptly shift. No one has found the north side of the mother vein yet. But the twin to the Bunker's vein has to be there. I believe we have it within our claim, and we're going to find it."

"You quit your job?"

"Going with my gut, Angelina. I know we have a winner. I felt it from the beginning. Harry Day, the primary owner, is a sharp man. He's run core samples that look promising. We're pulling galena, just not the quality and quantity we'd like to see."

"When we get to Idaho, why don't you take me to your mine and let me pan for silver? I'll find your vein."

This time he laughed loudly. "You could find my vein all right, but it wouldn't be silver. No, darling, you don't pan for silver. You blast tunnels into the ground to find it. That's my contribution. I blast tunnels. In fact, there's a good supply of my best dynamite aboard this train."

She pulled back from him. A frightening gleam sparked to life in his eyes when he mentioned blasting.

"I got it cheap from the railroad. A buddy of Sal's stole it. Sal's buddy is a shovel leaner, likes to make a buck the easy way. He had no use for it, so I got the whole pilfered lot for a fourth of what it's worth. That'll cover my share of the Jupiter' expenses for a good six months."

"We could be blown up?" She didn't mean to sound shrill.

"It's inert. It won't go off unless someone sets a spark to it. The railroad knows I'm shipping it and they've taken precautions. Imagine the irony, the railroad shipping its own stolen dynamite."

She wasn't convinced.

"I wouldn't risk your safety, would I? After all, I am the assigned guardian of your virtue. I suppose that includes your life." His light tone turned serious. "I'm careful with explosives, Angelina. If I weren't, I wouldn't be here. Dynamiting is dangerous art. Only the skilled, of whom I'm the best, survive."

"Modest?"

"Truthful."

"Now that you've quit your job, your share of mine profits supports you?"

"Hardly." He laughed. "The mine's official name is the Jupiter, but the partners refer to it as the Hole, mostly because it's a hole in the pocketbook. The ore we take out doesn't even cover expenses. Each partner has to chip in monthly or sell out to someone who can. Most everybody has another job to pay their share of the costs. May Hall cooks for the Colonel, her husband Al drives a locomotive. Gus Preston quit his job at the dairy to work full time in the mine. He pays by sweat equity. A couple of years ago he was solely responsible for all of the drilling that was done."

"And you?"

"I have a small inheritance from my uncle, I mean, my father. And I work in the tunnel."

Angelina's mind whirled with possibilities. Mining intrigued her. "What kind of expenses?"

"Supplies—food, kerosene, tools, explosives. Assaying fees. And of course labor. Which right now is running about sixty-five man days a month at the going rate of $3.50 per day. We pay union scale. Many of our partners are strong union supporters and we don't want any violence.

"There's a labor war brewing in the Valley. Small skirmishes break out from time to time. But sooner or later, it will be an all-out war. The union wants the big mines like the Bunker to pay scale. The big mine owners are refusing, paying their men much less. They won't come to a meeting of the minds without violence."

His talk frightened her. She wondered about Mr. Allessandro. Could he have been hurt in one of those skirmishes? Could he be in danger? Could Tonio?

"Idaho miners are a breed unto themselves and not a civilized one. They blew up the Frisco in ninety-two, that's what I mean by war. A Pinkerton agent was called in to root out those responsible. Since then there's been no love lost between the owners and their employees. We pay scale, but if the men get violent there's no guarantee we'll be protected. Mob mentality has a life all its own."

"So you and your partners plan to remain neutral and hope for the best. What if they blow up the big mines and leave yours alone; will it affect you?"

He smiled, pleased with her interest and acuity. "It will if they blow up the rail lines or the assay office or threaten our men."

"You really think you'll strike it rich?"

"Noah Kellogg, the old prospector whose jackass discovered the Bunker Hill and Sullivan vein, did. When we find the twin vein, we'll mine it ourselves and make much more than old Noah ever dreamed of."

"It seems to me that if an *ass*," she emphasized the word, "can find silver, then you ought to be able to."

He laughed outright at her insult and replied lightly. "Thanks for the vote of confidence."

"What happened to the jackass? Maybe he could help you, too."

"Dead."

"Too bad." She watched him pick up his papers as he prepared to return to work. "Tonio, why did you agree to take me to the mining country?"

"A woman should be allowed to pursue her dream, no matter what the consequences might be. I'm liberal-minded enough to want you to have that chance."

He adjusted the ledger in his lap.

"The mine is your dream?"

"For now, yes."

She nodded. "I believe in your gut. You will find that galena and be rich. You won't forget your old friend then, will you?"

"Angel, I'll never forget you."

To her surprise, Tonio set his ledger down and left without saying another word.

Angelina walked the entire length of the train before she found him, sitting cockeyed on the rail of the caboose. She watched him from the doorway, studying him as he poured some kind of powder from a small vial onto tiny sheets of thin paper. Then he twisted the paper closed and threw them over the rail. His eyes lit up as he watched the small, paper bombs fly overboard and hit the ground.

His profile was strong and proudly Roman. His dark hair blew in the breeze. He was so absorbed with his game that he didn't notice her. Something about his passion for it scared her. He seemed too fascinated by the power of his small creations.

"What are you doing?"

He answered without starting or turning to face her. "Entertaining myself. I wondered how long you'd stand in the door without speaking."

"I didn't think you noticed me."

"No one sneaks up on me, not since the war." A sudden updraft blew his hair up, above his collar, exposing his scar.

She shuddered at the reminder of the violence he'd suffered.

He turned to face her. "Not that I ever wouldn't notice you, Angel." His voice was warm and sultry. It was strange that his formal, educated Italian fell pleasantly on her ears.

He held out his hand to her. She accepted it and he pulled her close to him and the rail.

"Watch this." He tossed a small paper over the edge.

Angelina watched it hit the track below and explode. The noise was barely audible over the sound of the train.

"Such a small show of power, but power nonetheless," he said.

"What's the powder?"

"Gunpowder. It explodes with the force of hitting the ground, much the same way it does when the hammer of a gun hits a bullet and sends it flying."

"Where did you get it?"

"I reload all my own ammunition."

She shuddered again. He pulled her into him, thinking she was cold. "You could blow yourself up. Why don't you just buy new?"

"Reloading is cheaper and untraceable. There aren't any store owners can tell you how much ammunition I've got."

"And why is that important?"

He laughed. "It's obvious you don't come from the Valley. Baker, our union leader, advocates every union having a gun club. A man needs protection."

He wrapped his arms around her and held a paper out to her to hold. "Feel the excitement for yourself. Help me make one."

She held it firmly, enjoying the feel of his breath against her neck as he reached past her and poured the powder, then twisted the paper.

"Toss it."

She threw it over the edge. It hit a rock from the rail bed and exploded. There was a certain excitement to the act but not as much as when he turned her to face him and his lips came down on hers in a hard, passionate kiss. She pressed herself into him and clutched his shirt as she parted her lips and invited his tongue in. Just as she leaned forward to taste his mouth with her own tongue, he released her. The warm, throbbing kiss ended.

"You and I could make a good team."

"Yes." Her breathing was ragged. Tides of unexpected warmth and excitement washed through her, reaching the far recesses of her body. He toyed with a strand of her hair that had blown loose.

He looked at her expectantly, but she didn't know what he expected. "It's grown suddenly cool out here. Let's go in." She turned. He tucked his papers and vial inside his pocket and followed her in.

They spoke little for the rest of the day. What was there to say? They were attracted to each other, and it was forbidden. She would go to her husband, he to his mine. But he would never be far from her thoughts. For the rest of her life she would carry the burden of their passion and everything would pale in comparison to it.

She retired to her sleeping berth. She undressed with the light on. She pulled off her camisole and lightly tossed it at her feet. She thought she heard Tonio curse from across the aisle and wondered what had upset him.

She grabbed her brush. Her breasts stood erect and tightly budded in the cool night air of the sleeping car as she brushed her hair using long strokes. She felt glad to be free from the confines of her clothes. All the rest of her life weighed down on her too heavily. Finally, she pulled her neatly folded nightgown from the end of the bed, calmly pulling it on. Fanning her hair, she lay back on her pillow and blew Tonio a kiss before turning out the light.

The curtains across the aisle rustled. She heard the rings slide across the rod, then the thump of feet hitting the floor. Her heart thumped a loud, patterned rhythm in her ears as she waited for her own curtains to be thrown back. She stiffened and braced in anticipation, wondering what it would be like to be in his arms, here in her own berth, with sleeping people surrounding them, locked in their own private cocoon. There was dead silence.

Then she heard the rings screech across the metal rod again. And the floor wheezed as weight was lifted from it. He'd swung back into his own bed. Deflated, she slumped against her pillow. The wild, urging tingles that had assaulted her private being disappeared.

The car was stiflingly quiet. Someone coughed. She felt like screaming. Then she heard the small click of a light switch. Tonio appeared in her ceiling, shirtless, the covers pulled to just below his navel. The reflection was so startlingly clear that she could see the individual, coarse, curling hairs that clouded his chest. His black eyes flamed with passion. She couldn't be mistaken. He was like a dark, lusty dream, real and yet, not. She blinked to make sure that she was not already dreaming.

Then he winked and clicked the light off. She was seeing Tonio reflected in her ceiling. He'd seen her undress, night after night. He'd seen her half naked. She should have been furious. She should have blushed. Instead, she reached up and gently stoked the polished wood where his image had been. Then she rolled over and punched the pillow, knowing she wouldn't be able to sleep.

CHAPTER NINE

Angelina sat at a table, staring at her menu, but not seeing it. Her mind was occupied with other, more important matters. Outside her window the barren hills of eastern Montana had long since rolled by, replaced by the mountainous terrain of the Rockies. The train chugged swly up the steep grade of the eastern slope of Lookout Pass. A porter had cracked the window beside her table. The morning air became chillier by the minute, its sweet alpine scent mingling with the breakfast fragrance of the dining car. Little clumps of dirty snow, hanging tenaciously to life in the shade of sturdy evergreens, began to appear as the train made its way up the mountain.

Angelina wore the traveling outfit Tonio had bought her in Chicago. Her small white hat was pinned slightly askance shading one side of her face. The casual observer would have mistaken her expression for serenity, seeing nothing of the turmoil and apprehension that knotted her stomach. Sometime early in the afternoon the train would descend Lookout Pass and cross from Montana into Idaho, arriving in Wallace within the hour. She had just that long with Tonio. Then he would walk out of her life.

She picked up a spoon and toyed with it as she sat, then set it down and readjusted the napkin next to her plate, wondering for the hundredth time if she had the courage to live by her honor and meet her husband. Or, if she had the courage to ask to run away with Tonio. She was fairly certain he would refuse her. He'd said almost as much. So maybe it wasn't courage she sought but resignation. She played with her grandmother's necklace.

She looked up in time to see Tonio enter the room. His dark good looks caught the attention of two ladies at a table in front of her. They buzzed in quiet conference, but Angelina knew what they discussed.

"Good morning." She smiled her finest for him.

"Playing with your cross again. Soon, you'll have a different one to bear. One that may weigh more heavily around your neck than that delightful gold one." He smiled as he seated himself in the chair opposite her. "Have you ordered yet?"

A waiter appeared. Angelina ordered in the slow, correct English Tonio had trained into her in their diction lessons. Gone were nearly all traces of her accent. He smiled in approval. It buoyed her confidence to realize that she had a gift with language. Concentrating on her English soothed her. She must appear calm and assured. Tonio ordered and the waiter disappeared.

"Today is the day you meet your white knight, is it not?" Tonio asked. "Savior from spinsterhood, great protector and all that."

"I hope. If he has received Mario's wire, he will be waiting for me."

"Then it will be your wedding day as well. The old man will probably squire you right to Cataldo Mission so you can be married legally and before God. The Mission is the only Catholic Church in the Valley. He's no doubt making elaborate plans even as we speak. I hope he gives you the fairytale wedding you deserve. And let's not forget the wedding night."

"My marriage bothers you. Tonio—"

He shook his head. "Don't say it, Angel. I told you I'm not the man for you. But to answer you, it's the idea of these mail-order, arranged marriages in general that I disapprove of. Have you forgotten where I came from?

"My parents were a mail-order couple. My beautiful mother was from Milano, and of course Papa was a *Torinese.* Growing up in their home, I saw how wonderfully the arrangement can work." His voice dripped with sarcasm. "What did my lovely mother get for her end of the bargain? My ass of a father and early death. Wonderful things, those. And of course, me."

"Not all arranged marriages turn out badly." She wanted to believe that.

"For your sake, I hope that's true. But I fear, well, never mind my fears. Here." He shoved some papers her way. She'd been so preoccupied she'd been unaware he'd been carrying anything.

"What are these?"

"I've written down the address of the boarding house that I stay in when I'm in Burke. The second one is the location of the mine, the third, our mine's office, and the last one is the Halls' address in Wallace. I live with them from time to time. If you ever need me..."

I always need you, she thought.

"If you can't reach me, go to May Hall. She has a heart of gold." Tonio cocked an ear. "Sounds like our engine's having a tough time of it."

Almost as soon as Tonio spoke, the pitch of the engine whine changed to an efficient hum and their speed accelerated as the train reached a plateau.

"Is this the May that Maria told me about, the one with so much influence over you?"

The train engine whined as it continued up the steep grade.

"Is that what Maria said about May?"

"Yes, and I have been secretly jealous for some time wondering about her."

He shook his head and laughed. "Don't flirt with me, Angel. Now is not the time. Once you meet May, you'll see that she's not my type. And like others I know, she's a married woman." He took a sip of coffee. "She has a mind all her own, campaigns for the suffragettes, and takes in any stray she finds. Big hearted. Al's a lucky man." He looked straight at her.

The light dimmed and a shadow fell over the table as the train entered a tunnel. Seconds later they emerged on the other side, racing along at top speed.

Tonio reached to catch a pen from rolling off the table as the train rounded a narrow bend. With his free hand he reached to clasp hers. "Angelina, I have a proposal to make to you—"

He didn't finish his sentence. He was interrupted by a loud thud that resonated like thunder. In the instant before she understood what was happening, Angelina looked out the window to check the weather. The sky was clear. With a confused look, she turned to speak to Tonio. Then she screamed as the table slid across the floor.

A series of smaller thuds reverberated from the front of the train in rhythmic succession. The screech of metal slamming against metal roared through the rail car. People screamed as furniture slid and crashed to the front of the dining coach. Angelina's head was thrown back by the sudden jolt of the dining car smashing head-on into the coach in front of it. A loud release of air came from the accordion vestibule as it collapsed and the two heavy rail cars collided.

For a brief moment it seemed as though the dining car would remain upright and intact on the rails. Moments later the illusion was broken as a jolt from behind sent the dining coach shimmying off the tracks. It balanced upright precariously for a second and then toppled sideways into the hillside bank to the right of the car. Glass flew as rocks and trees covering the embankment shattered the windows. Angelina fought to maintain her balance as she was thrown sideways into the wall between two windows.

As suddenly as it had begun, it was over. Angelina uncovered her eyes and stared into the wreckage around her. A chair was pushed over on top of her, but she was too weak to push it off. To her right a large rock protruded through the shattered remains of a window. To her left a sad fir, snapped off a few feet up its trunk, oozed pitch and emitted its rich life's essence, its top hanging limply to the side. Everywhere at her feet were the smashed remains of white porcelain dishes and drinking glasses.

Her cheek stung and her right arm seared with pain. Coffee stained her sleeve. She stared at it, dazed. Still making no move to push the chair off, she picked up a napkin that had fallen next to her and dabbed at the stain as if she were still seated and had clumsily spilled on herself. The normal action was horribly misplaced in the wreckage that surrounded her. She winced the moment the napkin touched her sleeve. It took a minute for her to realize that her arm was burned, and the coffee stain was somehow responsible. Unable to cope, she closed her eyes.

Suddenly, the weight of the chair was lifted from her. She opened her eyes to find Tonio standing over her, his eyes dark with concern. She held her arms out to him. He lifted her gently and enfolded her in his strong embrace.

"I can't get the stain out."

"It's all right, Angel." His voice was soft and comforting. She thought she felt his lips brush the top of her hair. "We'll get you a new shirtwaist. Don't worry."

She clasped his neck as if it were life itself. "It hurts."

"What? Your arm?"

She nodded.

"I'd say it's burned. Just another bad cup of coffee."

She laughed. It brought her back to reality. She lifted her face to look at him. "You're bleeding." His cheek was bruised. A gash ran the length of his chin. Blood oozed out through the torn skin, peppered with the dark stubble of his beard. She dabbed at it with the napkin she still held.

"So are you." He took it from her and wiped at her cheek.

She felt weak and dazed and her head pounded from the bump it took when she hit the wall. She wanted nothing more than for him to hold her forever. It seemed to her that they were the only two people in the car. Somehow her mind blocked out the screams and cries of the other passengers. Tonio tried to right a chair for her to sit on in the ridiculously sloping car. He gave up and set her on the floor, but she refused to let go of him until he commanded her to so that he could scoop some snow from outside the broken window to put on her burn. He was carefully applying it when the thud of a metal rail car door slamming shut sounded out. Several people screamed, including Angelina. Tonio looked up, his eyes wide, a distant look filling them.

"Shit! The dynamite!"

Angelina's throat closed in horror as the same thought occurred to her. He scooped her up with lithe grace and strength, carrying her to the edge of the car where he kicked at an exit door on the uphill side until it swung open. He paused a moment on the edge, checking the jump, then plunged off with her still cradled in his arms. They hit the ground upright. Tonio ran toward the freight cars shouting. "Get everyone out! Evacuate! We're carrying dynamite!" He didn't think to put her down, though she could have run for herself, and she didn't think to ask him.

Mercifully, there were only two freight cars attached to the train. Tonio swung her down as he reached them, dragging her with one arm encircling her waist. The freight cars stood upright amid the tangle of cars on the tracks. Two crewmen were already unlocking them and swinging the doors opened as they reached them.

"Careful!" Tonio called out. "There's live dynamite in there." He turned to her. "Stay here and take cover if anything goes wrong." He left her rooted in place about twenty feet back from the cars. She watched as he talked to the men, then peered into the freight car. She could see his shoulders slump in relief. He jogged back to her.

"Thank God, Angelina! The crates are undamaged and the cars seem stable. We could've had a hell of an explosion on our hands."

People swarmed the rail bed and surrounding forest as the crew evacuated the train. Rumor spread quickly.

The engineer and two crew members were buried alive in an avalanche of snow. The engine was completely buried. No one else appeared to be seriously injured. Tonio threaded his way up the tracks toward the engine, pulling Angelina along with him. A crowd gathered as they curved around the bend. Tonio stopped short at the edge of the crowd and stared over the heads of the people in front of him.

"Damn."

Angelina couldn't see a thing. "What?"

He held her up under her arms to give her a peek over the crowd. The train looked as if it had never had an engine. It was just...gone. Buried in a white blanket.

"They'll suffocate it we don't get them out." Tonio's eyes had a wild, dangerous look.

A man next to him replied. "They're organizing a digging crew. They need every available man."

"Won't be enough. There's no way they'll reach them in time. I'll bet they don't have enough shovels to outfit ten men." Tonio paused, his eyes scanning the disaster. He looked as if he were making calculations. At last he spoke. "I can blast them out."

She grabbed his arm. "No! No!"

"I have to. It's their only chance." He pulled her arm away and pushed his way through the crowd to the crewmen at the crowd front who stood watch.

He returned minutes later with the fireman and several other crew members in tow. "I'll set the charge downhill from the engine. With luck we'll clear enough snow from the downhill side to reach them."

"You could set off another avalanche," the fireman argued.

"The mountain looks clear up above." Tonio nodded uphill. "I doubt that the engine was buried by an avalanche as it passed by. More likely we rounded the corner and plowed into it. Probably happened days ago. Did you notice the pack of the snow? It's hard, like it has melted and froze again. It'll be nearly impossible to dig through by hand."

"We've sent a scout group back to the last town we came through. They're going to send for the plow and a rescue train."

Tonio shook his head. "We passed the last town twenty miles back. The rescue plow will have to come from Wallace on the other side. It'll be too late, if it isn't already. Those men are either going to suffocate or die of exposure."

The fireman didn't have a choice. "Get your dynamite."

"Move the crowd back," Tonio said. "I'll set up immediately."

"How are you going to ignite the charge?"

"With a fuse."

"A long one, I hope."

"Don't worry, I can run like a son of a bitch." Tonio laughed.

Angelina stood at his elbow, staring at him as he argued with the fireman. He sounded arrogant and reckless. And she was afraid. "Please don't, Tonio."

He turned to her as if he'd just realized she was there, bent to kiss her lightly on the lips, and started forward. She grabbed his wrists to stop him as he moved away from her. She felt his pulse beating wildly and knew that his excitement was not caused by her but by the thrill of the power he was about to unleash.

"Worried?" He looked solemn for the first time, as if gauging her concern for him.

"Yes."

He seemed to like her answer. The spark returned to his eyes. "Good. Cheer me to victory. We're going to save those men."

He jogged off after the fireman, leaving her standing at the edge of the crowd, trying to sort through the tumult of her emotions. Did she love this man, or was it merely fear that set her heart at a tilt?

He was only a tiny, bent figure in the distance as she watched him from the safety of the crowd, crouched beneath the trees for protection. She couldn't take her eyes from him as she watched him light the fuse. Terrified of what she might witness, but too morbidly riveted on him to look away and give up what might be her last glimpse of him.

A small spark flamed to life. He straightened and watched it. Her whole being screamed at him to run. But he stayed for an endless, agonizing moment, making certain it would remain lit before he backed away and ran. He moved with grace, as beautiful as any athlete she'd seen. His arms pumped in time with his long strides as he sprinted across the edge of the slippery white mass. His stride picked up as he ran off the snow and onto firm ground.

The fuse grew shorter and shorter. The man grew larger and larger. Her eyes bounced between the man and the fuse. The blast went off. Snow spewed into the sky. She saw it before she heard it. A thunderous roar broke loose. He ran with his head bent, arms over the back of his head. Snow rained down on him. She pulled away from the crowd to run to him, ignoring the people that implored her to stay covered.

She landed in his arms. He was safe. He kissed her with a passion that nearly swept her away. The crowd cheered. He turned back to look over his shoulder. The snow slid away from the downhill side of the engine. It came into view, whole and intact, covered in a sheath of ice. A team of men raced toward it to rescue the men trapped inside. She heard someone shout, "They're alive! I can see them moving!" She wouldn't let him go.

"It was a brave thing you did today." Angelina leaned back against Tonio's shoulder and stared out at pinpoints of light from other campfires that dotted the rail bed and surrounding forest. They camped in privacy, well away from the others, in a secluded spot that Tonio had selected. The night was clear and surprisingly temperate. A soft, warm Chinook wind blew from the west. Tonio predicted rain by morning. A circle of towering white pines surrounded them in a chimney around the open sky above their campfire. The breeze rustled the trees creating a calming background to the day's events, occasionally carrying whispers of other voices and conversations their way.

Nearly all the passengers were forced to camp out for the night. Most of the rail cars had toppled or were unstable. The few that remained upright were reserved for the most severely injured. The three men, including the engineer, were housed in one, attended by a physician who happened to be traveling home to Seattle. They were alive, thanks to Tonio and his dynamite.

The moon rose big and full, casting its pale silvery light over their camp, blending with the golden hues of the campfire that Tonio gently coaxed. They sat together, Angelina leaning back against him, he with one arm around her, on a wool blanket spread over a soft, spongy mound of moss.

"Don't get any romantic notions of bravery and white knights about me, Angelina. I did what had to be done."

"You like blowing things up."

"I like what I do."

"I think you like it too much. It scares me." She took a deep breath. "You scare me." She didn't know why she said it.

"It's a good thing to be scared once in a while." His mouth curved in a careless smile.

She expected him to ask why he scared her, but he didn't. "You seem at home in the forest."

"I should be by now."

"Why is that?"

"Where do you think the mine is?"

She twisted back around to look him in the face. In his eyes, passion shone unveiled. Hard, intense, confusing. Intoxicating in its full magnitude. She stared at him, trembling on the verge of something too deep to understand. His next words made no sense.

"You've been given a reprieve, Angel. Use it to your full advantage." His lips fell on hers. With the smoothest of movements he pulled her into his lap, facing him as he continued with his caressing kiss. His mouth warmed hers. With one fluid movement he fell back into the soft folds of the blanket, pulling Angelina on top of him. Her skirt billowed around him as she kissed and was kissed with an intensity she'd not known was possible.

He unbuttoned her coat and slipped his hands in to caress her curves. The warmth from the fire seemed to leap into his hands as he touched her. Carelessly, sensuously he pulled her ear to his mouth and licked and kissed lazily, slowly.

His kisses traveled softly down her neck as he pulled her blouse free and unbuttoned her shirtwaist until it hung loose and open, revealing her chemise. His hands were steady as he untied the neck of her chemise.

Her breasts fell loose and free above him. He arched, pressing his hips firmly against hers. A warm masculine hardness met her.

"Make me a happy man," he whispered before taking her breast in his mouth.

"I will," she whispered. Sensuous tingles such as she'd never known shot through her, starting between her legs but ending in the remotest tips of her toes and fingers. Her breath caught and she closed her eyes so that nothing disturbed the rushing excitement that overwhelmed her. She opened her eyes, looking down to see him framed between her breasts.

He spoke, "I'm alive—"

She couldn't hear the rest clearly. It muffled as he pressed his lips between her breasts. She thought he said, "For the first time in years."

"We're both alive, Tonio."

She balanced over him, braced against the ground with her palms, her long hair loose and spilling over him along with her grandmother's necklace. He reached up and grasped her face firmly between his strong hands and looked her in the eye. "My beautiful, innocent babe. I've never wanted a woman as much as you."

He leaned up again and licked a wide circle over her naked nipples. In the cool night air they beaded into tight, dark buds of arousal. She pressed her hips tightly down against his and threw her head back.

Tonio pulled her down, kissed her, rolled them over, positioning himself in the commanding top position, bracing himself over her, the Chinook rustling his hair. He came down on top of her, kissing her open mouthed with a wild dance of flitting tongues. One hand caressed and kneaded her breast, tugged at the nipple until it pointed firm and long. He rubbed his chest against her.

Eager for the feel of his bare skin, she pushed his chest up away from her and fumbled with his buttons until his shirt fell open, still tucked into his pants. She ran her fingers over the coarse, curling hair. Brushed her fingers lightly over his nipples, then tugged at them as he had hers, then released them at his hard grunt to circle his waist with her arms and impatiently pull his shirt away from his pants with one yank.

"Too many clothes." He rolled off her, sat, and slid to her feet. "You still have your shoes on. She braced on her elbows and watched as he tugged off her ugly work shoes, then pulled off his shirt and his own boots and impatiently cast them aside. He rubbed her feet and kissed her ankles, then licked the little hollow beneath them until she shuddered.

He stood and unashamedly pulled off the rest of his clothes until he stood naked, profiled in the moon above her. The sight of him overpowered her senses. Her eyes traveled down him. She shuddered at the sight of his long, hard length. Then he straddled her on his knees, shoving her skirt up and touching her through her pantalets. Long, sweet ecstasy coursed through her.

"Please, Tonio..." She hadn't realized that pleasure could be so impatient.

He pulled her pantalets off and threw them aside. Still straddling her, he kissed the hollow of her neck. She braced on her elbows with her head thrown back.

Suddenly, he stopped. "You're a virgin. Angel, I can't take that from you."

She put a finger to his lips to silence him. "I don't expect a commitment from you, Tonio. I know what this means. I'll go to my husband. I'll fake being a virgin. Maria told me how. But today, we almost died. I want to live. I need one time with you, Tonio. Just one to last me a lifetime. Maybe then I will be able to go on."

She arched up to meet him. With one, long hard thrust he was in her. The physical jolt pushed her back on the blanket, rubbing her elbows across it. A scream of pleasure and pain escaped her.

Tonio paused long enough to cover her mouth with his hand. "Quiet, love, they'll hear us."

Then they arched together in unison. Without thinking, she grabbed handfuls of the blanket to steady herself, but the attempt was futile. The blanket scooted and bunched beneath their rhythmic motion until her legs rested in the moist moss beneath it. The pleasure built with the pain until she screamed out in final completion, the sound muffled in Tonio's hand. Seconds later he shuddered and stiffened, grunting something unintelligible into her ear. Then he relaxed on top of her.

He whispered English words into her ear, but dazed with the enormity of what they'd just done, she couldn't bother trying to understand them.

He lay on top of her, still inside for a long time. The fire crackled beside them, and it took her a moment to realize that the side of her body away from it felt as warm and comfortable as the side that faced it. Finally, he pulled away from her and rolled off.

Her legs trembled, unused to mating, reminding her of his presence. She sighed, trying to capture the moment for eternity. Something warm and sticky oozed between her legs. *Blood*, she thought.

Finally he spoke. "Your marriage is so illegal, you probably don't need one, but if you want an annulment, I will help get one." He kissed her lightly. "May can help you find a job. Probably hire you on to do the baking for the Colonel. May's one good cook but a lousy baker. Colonel probably be glad to have you."

He ran his fingers over her cheek. "Angel, I'm in the middle of something you don't understand. To involve yourself with me would be too dangerous. I can't promise you anything—"

"Tonio, nothing has changed." She reached for her camisole and began dressing. "I have broken my vow of honor for this time only. But the disgrace of breaking my vow to marry *Signor* Allessandro would be too great for my family to bear. I have no way to pay him back for my passage. I will go to him."

"Angel—"

She pulled on her shirtwaist and buttoned it with trembling fingers. "Don't say it, Tonio." She stood, searching for her discarded pantalets.

Tonio tossed them to her and pulled his own pants back on.

When they had finished dressing, she turned to him, not knowing what to say. At last, she pulled the heavy gold cross over her head. She was as big a fool as her grandmother. She kneeled by Tonio, took his hand, and dropped the necklace into it. "I don't need this anymore. I have found what I was looking for. You take it."

"I can't take this. It's your heirloom. It's too valuable."

She kissed his cheek. "Then keep it safe for me, in case I ever need it." She stood and grabbed her bags.

"Where are you going?"

"To the camp. I can't stay here. There will be too much talk. *Signor* Allessandro will not like it. Goodbye, Tonio." It took all of her will to walk away. She kept her back straight and proud, but her spirit sagged and tears blinded her as she headed toward camp.

CHAPTER TEN

A ngelina sat in what must have been one of the oldest trains the Northern Pacific ran. Light green paint peeled off the walls and the seats were nothing more than thinly disguised planks which bruised her backside, but what was that compared to her heart?

The car shuddered and swayed from side to side as it crept along, as if being hit by a strong side wind that alternately changed direction much like the wayward course of her own emotions. The injured sat everywhere, bandaged and bruised, looking pained and uncomfortable, like battle weary soldiers. She fit right in, though most could not see that her heart suffered more than her person. The smell of rubbing alcohol permeated the air, perfume of the wounded and anesthetic to the senses but not enough to numb her completely.

Angelina found herself amazingly wakeful. Calm. Numb. She allowed her thoughts to wander, trying not to think about Tonio, but every path seemed to lead back to him. To the passion and the ecstasy of being one with him. To the feel of his kiss on her lips that would have to last forever. She tried to push the thoughts away, fearing she would fall into an abyss of depression and self-recrimination, neither of which she could afford as the train rushed her to meet the man she had betrayed.

She leaned her head against the window. She'd made it through a night as long and cold as her empty heart and survived. Tonio had chosen to stay behind, along with a group of men, to help the railroad rescue the buried engine. Thank goodness. Seeing him would have been too painful.

She'd risen early and bathed in snow fed water so cold that as soon as she'd waded in her ankles went numb. She would have tumbled into the water, enticed by the idea of being numb all over, but some shred of logic kept her still. Instead, she splashed her legs and body with the icy water, scrubbing with a rag to re-move the crusted blood, retreating from the water as soon as her toilet was complete. She dried with another piece of rag and tossed it far away under a clump of bushes where she would never have to see it again. Then she dressed quickly and wound her hair into a prim knot.

At last she sat on the bank and remembered Maria's instructions on acting the virgin. She pulled her bag close and tucked her bloodied pantalets inside. She would use them as proof the morning after her wedding night. She could arrange a switch.

As she sat on the train lost in her thoughts, time raced by. Before she knew it, the Northern Pacific Flyer released a mighty puff of steam and pulled into Wallace's depot, nestled snugly against the mountainside on the outskirts of town. Behind it loomed nothing but raw wilderness climbing the stiff slope up the mountains bracketing the Valley.

Angelina peered out the window at blankets of evergreens. High above, clouds pockmarked the sky's bright spring blue. Rain threatened. The Silver Valley looked anything but silver.

By reputation Wallace was the heart of the North Idaho mining community. The bustling town packed itself tightly into the valley floor sandwiched between two steep mountainous hills on either side. The South Fork of the Coeur d'Alene River flowed east to west on the northern side of the valley, further limiting the availability of suitable building land, creating a northern boundary and an even more compact space for the ambitious, growing town. The railroad depot was on Sixth Street, the only outpost north of the river.

Angelina was on the wrong side of the train to see the passenger platform where scores of people waited to greet the weary travelers. The view from her window showed nothing more than towering evergreens with small buttercups cuddled in their shade. She gathered her things together and checked her appearance as the train came to a final stop. The gash on her face swelled red and angry against her skin. She hoped that Mr. Allessandro would not be put off by the way she looked. Maybe he would take pity and treat her kindly.

"Wallace!" the conductor called out in that tone of voice that only conductors used.

The townspeople had gathered to welcome the wounded and the heroes. They cheered as railroad men and volunteers carried injured passengers off the train. Apparently, a train full of wounded crash survivors was an event almost akin to a President's visit. The cheering continued as the less seriously injured detrained. By the time Angelina reached the platform the crowd began dispersing.

She carried a bag in each hand and surveyed the depot for signs of Mr. Allessandro, rehearsing her greeting to him, trying to recall every detail of how Papa had described him. She saw no one matching his description, no one who appeared to be waiting for her, although the man from the train, the one Tonio had called Clell, watched her with narrow, sharp eyes and lewd interest that sent a chill down her back. She stood to the side until, except for Clell, who openly stared at her, the depot was almost entirely deserted. Still no Mr. Allessandro.

Do not panic, she told herself. True, she was alone in a wild town and something must have happened to Mr. Allessandro to delay him. But there was no use imagining the worst. She must remain calm.

She walked to the window to get a view of Wallace, hoping that her husband would come riding up like a knight to save her. No husband in sight but to her relief, right across the street was a building with a sign advertising it as a ladies' boarding house. She had only a few dollars left but surely she could afford a night or two there. By the time her money ran out, either Tonio would be back in town or Mr. Allessandro would show up.

A tap on her shoulder gave Angelina a start.

"Tonio desert you, did he? You look lost. Let old Clell help."

Angelina spun to find herself face to face with him. He stood no taller than she did, but he looked every ounce tightly coiled muscle ready to spring. Though his words were benign, his gaze undressed her. Before she could upbraid him, they were interrupted.

"Leave her alone, Clell. She's not one of your harpies." A woman spoke.

"I was just offering my assistance like a gentleman."

"Mighty kind of you, I'm sure. But I'll take over now."

A plain, heavy-set woman with a kindly expression and lively, snapping eyes came toward her. The woman wore her hair twisted up on her head in an unattractive knot with tight pin curls bracketing her face that did little to soften her double chin and manly features. Yet the woman inspired confidence. She dismissed Clell with a wave of her hand.

Clell reluctantly tipped his hat and moved off.

"So what can I do for you?" the woman asked. "No one showed up to meet you, is that the problem?"

Angelina spilled her troubles. "I have just arrived from New York. I came from Italy to join my husband here. He was supposed to meet me at the depot. But I do not see him anywhere."

The woman nodded. "I see."

Angelina couldn't tell whether skepticism or pity ruled the woman's emotions. But unlike the immigration official in New York, this woman had no power to send her back. "Maybe," Angelina continued, "with the train wreck and being off schedule, he did not know when to come."

The woman looked kindly but doubtful. "The whole town seemed to know when to show up, honey. Is he from around Wallace or does he live in one of the smaller mining camps?"

"He is a miner at the Bunker Hill mine. His name is Franco Allessandro." Angelina hoped that the woman might know him, but she shook her head.

"Doesn't ring a bell."

Angelina pointed at the building across the street. "Do they have very good accommodations at the ladies' boarding house?"

That's when the woman laughed. "Oh, honey, I see you are new to the area. You can't stay there. That's a house of ill repute. The poor creatures who work there need our help, not a house guest."

Angelina felt foolish and overwhelmed, suddenly young and very homesick. Almost certainly she would unwittingly get herself into trouble.

"Come," the woman said. "Stay with me. I'll turn up that husband of yours. My husband works for the railroad. He knows just about everybody around here."

Angelina hesitated.

The woman extended her hand. "May Hall."

"May Hall! Oh, thank goodness!" Angelina had never felt such relief.

"Didn't know I was all *that* famous." May laughed.

Angelina reached out to shake her hand. "Angelina Allessandro. We have a mutual friend, Tonio Domani."

May seemed taken aback. "Tonio?"

"Yes, he escorted me from New York." Angelina told May her story. "So I am afraid that something is wrong. There must be a reason why my husband has not come to meet me or why he has been silent this winter."

May nodded. "Well now, you really do have to come stay with us. Otherwise, Tonio would never forgive us. Once we get you settled and rested, we can check at the Bunker. They may know something about your husband. But don't get your hopes up. Lately, with the trouble brewing, miners have been transitory creatures. Coming and going and showing up irregularly for their shifts. Here, let me carry one of those for you." May grabbed one of Angelina's bags. "It's a fair walk to the house."

May's home turned out to be a modest house located on Pine Street between two undistinguished neighbors. After the walk through town and up the hill, Angelina vowed that she had never felt more relief at the sight of a dwelling. Hipped roof. Second story bay window above an inset porch. Gabled ells at front and side—so very quaint and welcoming.

"Be it ever so humble," May said as she led the way inside and set Angelina's bags down. "This way. Let me get you something to eat. You must be famished."

May's kitchen was as warm and homey as one would expect from the street view of her house. She put a pot of coffee on to boil then set out a plate of muffins and sliced breads, fresh butter and jam. Angelina found that she had an appetite she thought she'd lost.

May watched her eat. "You can stay in Tonio's room until we find that husband of yours. Tonio won't mind. I have half a notion he'll be itching to get to the Hole and his room up in Burke. Town isn't a safe place for the likes of him right now anyway. There are those that would like to use his talents for extreme measures." May frowned.

Angelina felt too tired and overwhelmed to ask what May meant. They made small talk until Angelina finished eating, then May showed her upstairs to a small bedroom. "You just lie down and have yourself a good rest. There'll be plenty of time to go looking for your husband when you're up to it."

Angelina thanked her. As May pulled the door closed, Angelina collapsed onto Tonio's bed, disappointed that it smelled only of freshly washed linens, not him. In fact, nothing about the sparse furnishings of the room gave any indication that Tonio had made it home. But it was his, May had said so, which gave Angelina some comfort as she pulled off her shoes and cuddled up to sleep.

Tonio got off the train in Wallace with the intention of heading straight to the Halls for a shower and meal, but he changed course as he walked down Sixth Street. The town hummed with activity.

It feels good to be back, he thought, striding along.

This town suited him. Its wild, boisterous nature matched his. The town itself aspired to greatness and wealth. What better place for a man with his ambitions? No one thought less of him for being an immigrant, a foreigner. The town's citizens ran the gamut from the whores at the Lux building, to the mining elite in their comfortable two-story homes. It was hard not to fit in with such a varied crowd. But one man would be looking for him. Tonio had no intention of talking to Ed Baker. Better to get something to eat and head out on the last train to Burke before Baker realized Tonio was back.

Tonio turned into the Fuller House. The large, partially stuccoed brick building was the finest hotel in the region and served the best food east of Spokane in its plush dining room. A day of scant rations and heavy work digging out the train engine left him with an almost bottomless appetite. And a desire to satiate it with the best food available. He was the son of a wealthy Italian aristocrat, he was used to the best or so many believed. They didn't know about the modest fare he ate during his years in the monastery, his wartime in Ethiopia, the years he barely survived as a miner in South America, or his years on the railroad crew...

As Tonio walked into the dining room, Colonel Steward Fuller, the colorful owner of the establishment, looked up from his cup of coffee. "Tonio!" he called out. "You're back. How was New York?"

"Excellent, as usual, Colonel."

"You didn't run into any of the Fuller clan while you were back there, did you?"

"Colonel, you know better. I run with a different crowd. A decidedly foreign crowd in Little Italy. We're all blackguards you know. We have nothing to do with the elite of the upper city."

The Colonel smiled. He claimed Mayflower ancestry and great military renown, maintaining that many of his relatives remained in the East as the upper crust of society.

"Well, son, it's good to have you back just the same."

"Have you seen Nokes?" Tonio asked.

"Should be here anytime." The Colonel signaled to a waitress who escorted Tonio to the best table in the house.

Moments later, Nokes walked in and spied him. "Tonio, you son of a bitch, you're back!" he called out as he made his way to the table and seated himself opposite his friend. "How was my hometown?"

Charles "Charley" Nokes was from a wealthy New York family.

"Same as always." Tonio signaled a waitress and they ordered.

The waitress drifted off to the kitchen. Charley's eyes followed the girl until she disappeared. "I must be getting desperate; that girl is definitely not a looker, but she is single. We bachelors have a sorry plight; what we need out here is more women."

"You could go back to New York. I'm sure there are plenty of society beauties out there just dying for your return."

"Go to hell, Tonio. The last thing I'm going to do is go back and rot in some stuffy old bank."

"Tell me what's gone on in my absence, Nokes. Anyone strike it rich?"

Nokes shook his head. "No, but the miners are ready for blood, my boy. Word is they will strike, but first, they'll give the mine owners something to think about."

Several hours later, completely briefed by Nokes, Tonio caught the last train to Burke, determined to stay out of trouble by avoiding the union chiefs, determined to forget Angelina by working night and day in the Hole. He clenched his fist until his knuckles bulged white. He had the nearly uncontrollable urge to blow something up. To have the satisfaction of witnessing the utter surge of power and total destruction, anything to relieve the frustration at not being able to have Angelina. Anything to blot out the thoughts of her with another man, an older man who did not deserve her.

May's husband, Al Hall, turned out to be a thin, kind man. May seemed inordinately fond and proud of him. "Al's an engineer for the railroad." May's smile reflected her love for him.

"You'll get to recognize Al's train when it drives through town soon enough. He's modified his whistle to have a sound all its own and he toots in his own distinctive way." May gave Al a pat on the arm as he drove them to Bunker Hill Mine offices the day after Angelina's arrival.

The mine offices were located in the town of Kellogg, a few miles west of Wallace. The sun shone and a mild breeze blew in from the west as they pulled up to the office. Al waited with the horses as May led the way into the office. May, bold and friendly, quickly found a clerk willing to help them, explained the situation and inquired about Mr. Allessandro.

"Allessandro, you say? Let me check the log book." The clerk disappeared into a back room. When he returned, he brought another man with him, introducing him as his boss.

The man extended his hand. "Mrs. Allessandro, I'm Jacob White, personnel manager for the Bunker. Won't you step into my office where we can talk in private?"

Angelina turned to May.

"Mrs. Allessandro is new to this country, Mr. White. I'm here to look out for her interests and help her understand the situation. I'd like to come in with her."

Mr. White ushered them into his office and shut the door. Angelina's heart pounded in her ears. Something was wrong, terribly wrong. Mr. White seemed too somber, gave her the kind of solicitous attention that always comes before bad news. Angelina and May took chairs opposite the desk from Mr. White, who cleared his throat several times before speaking.

"Mrs. Allessandro," the throat clear, "I hate to be the one to deliver bad news when you have evidently

just arrived. But you seem unaware of your husband's
condition." More throat clearing. "He's dead, ma'am.
I'm sorry. I don't know how to break it gently."

"Dead?" The word seemed to echo off the walls. Only in Angelina's worst fears had Mr. Allessandro ever
been *dead.*

"Killed in a mining accident?" May's tone issued a
challenge.

"No, ma'am. He collapsed on the job. Bad heart, the
doctor said. We summoned help immediately. There
wasn't anything our doctor, or any doctor, could have
done." Mr. White cleared his throat again. "He was
owed two weeks' pay. I'm glad you've come to claim it.
Had no idea who to send it to. Let me count it out for
you."

Sunshine streamed into the tiny one room log cabin
that served as the on-site offices of the Jupiter mine as
Tonio walked in. Gus Preston, former dairyman, now
one of the partners, sat behind a decidedly unofficial-
looking desk, a sheaf of tunnel diagrams and supply
orders spread in front of him.

"Tonio! Welcome back!"

"Gus, good to see you. Where the heck is Harry?"

Gus shook his head. "In Boise ruling the state. Legislature's in session."

Tonio nodded. He'd have felt a lot better if Harry
had been running the mine instead of hanging out with
that bunch of yahoos in Boise who made nonsensical
laws for the common man. Harry claimed having him in
the Legislature gave them some representation.

Harry Scott was a bright, intelligent man with a receding hairline. Reared in an entrepreneurial, politically active household, the huge task of turning a small hand worked hole in the ground into a major mining facility left him undaunted. His vision kept the venture going. Conversely, Gus was a digger, a worker, not a visionary.

"Heard you had a little excitement," Gus said.

Tonio smiled at the understatement. "You could say that."

Gus arched an eyebrow and smiled back. "Lucky no one was killed. Sorry about your uncle. Got everything taken care of, I trust?"

"All closed up and taken care of. What's been up in my absence?"

"We started working a second level, an adit on the Firefly claim." He shuffled through the papers on his desk, finally pulling out a diagram of the new tunnel.

"A new level. We're a big time operation now?" Tonio jested, trying to contain his excitement. "Have we hit ore?"

"Not yet. We've barely begun to tunnel. It's good you're back. We really need an explosives expert right now."

"That reminds me. I brought a present back with me." Tonio stepped outside the door and returned with a large crate.

"Explosives?"

"The best. Got a good deal on them from a railroad friend of mine in Chicago. High grade nitroglycerin with an excellent dope for a nice clean blow. Same stuff the railroad uses to blast mountain tunnels. The rest of the shipment is back in Burke."

"Not too near the tracks, I trust?" Gus teased.

"As far off the tracks as that one-street town allows. Might be a faster way to get our tunnel, though. The amount of dynamite I bought could take away half the hillside." Tonio laughed.

The tiny town of Burke was something of an anomaly as far as towns go. Built in a narrow canyon, there was barely room for the one street and the businesses that lined it. The town existed solely to support the Hecla mine and consisted of those businesses that best suited the Hecla—a refining mill and two train depots. No mine could operate without the use of the railroad to haul ore. Since there had not been room for both a main street and a set of railroad tracks, the railroad tracks ran straight down the middle of the street. The space for the town was so small that when the town merchants heard the whistle, they lifted their awnings to prevent sparks from the passing train from setting them on fire.

"You know," Tonio commented, "We could use a better road up here. I had to haul this crate on my back."

Gus sighed. "Yeah, that and several thousand dollars. And while we're wishing, a better social climate for orderly mine development."

"H.L. still having problems?" Tonio asked.

H.L. Scott was Harry's father and the current county commissioner, as well as a Jupiter partner. He'd made a controversial decision the previous October that seemed to favor the unions. Sentiment ran to two extremes. The mining unions applauded the decision, but many politicians and mine owners were up in arms. Consequently government bureaucracy stalled. Permits were hard to come by. And confident that they had an official on their side, the unions openly rebelled against the owners.

"H.L.'s got his problems. But he'll overcome them. You've heard the latest slogan coming from Baker and the Western Federation of Miners. *Every union should have a rifle club.*"

Tonio nodded in affirmation. All the Jupiter partners were torn. Ed Baker, President of the Federation, was a friend of Harry Scott's. But Harry didn't advocate violence.

Gus tossed Tonio a key. "When you bring up the rest of the dynamite, you'd better lock it up. No use courting trouble. We've always dealt fairly with the union, but when men's tempers flare, you never know what they'll do."

Angelina felt shaky and cold, clammy to the core as Al helped her up into the carriage. Neither May nor Angelina had spoken since leaving the Bunker offices. Angelina was stunned into muteness, unable to decide if this new turn was more blessing or curse or curse or blessing. She would not have to live with an old man she did not love. She was free. Free to do what? She was stranded in a foreign country without enough money to go home. And her parents were far too poor to give her any help. Her head felt like a child's spinning top. She must find Tonio. He would know what to do. May had other ideas.

"Al, drive us directly to the Colonel's. Angelina needs a job and I need help in the kitchen." She turned to Angelina. "You did say you could cook?"

Angelina nodded. "I apprenticed in a very fine household doing mostly baking."

"Baking is good. Keeps a woman in shape. Don't care much for it myself. I could use an assistant. You can make bread?"

"Yes, with a very hard crust, the best kind. And all kinds of desserts. *Profiterole* and *panna cote* and—"

"Good." May sounded firm. "Miners down bread like they drink beer—almost too fast to keep up with." Clearly, May had no intention of letting Angelina wallow in pity and despair.

"Do you think I can earn enough money for passage home?"

May gave her an incredulous look. "Home, child? Where there are no men and the convents are full? You don't want to go back there. Here in Idaho we have the vote. Women have rights. You have rights. A woman on her own can do just fine, thank you very much. You'll work with me. We'll win the vote for our sisters all over the country. We'll be heroes, you and me. Famous.

"You can be our poster girl. Oppressed foreign woman comes to the States to an arranged marriage only to be left widowed and on her own. But she overcomes tragedy and becomes a successful businesswoman. You keep dreaming of that, Angelina. Just keep dreaming." May looked like she was dreaming herself.

"Someday that mine will pay off and..." May patted Angelina's hand. "We'll just see if we can't get you in on that deal."

"I need to talk to Tonio." Angelina wanted the feel of his arms around her. The future was open now but would Tonio want her?

"Of course, you do," May said. "But there's time for all that later. When things settle down a bit. Now's not the time to be getting yourself mixed up in the dangers." She winked at Angelina. "Trust old May. Things will work out in the end."

They pulled up in front of the Fuller House. Less than half an hour later, Angelina had a job and went directly to work in the Colonel's kitchen.

When she arrived home at May's, exhausted after baking bread and pies all day, a bag of hard candy waited for her tied with a pink ribbon with a note attached. Her heart leapt. Tonio!

The note was typed and said, "Be my sweet little piece." It was not signed. And it was not from Tonio; this she knew. Tonio didn't play games.

The words, sweet little piece, seemed insulting and made her vaguely uneasy. How did anyone know where she lived? This made her nervous, too, like a bird being stalked by a cat, watched unawares.

She took the candy outside and questioned several children who played in their yard several houses down. No one had seen whoever delivered the candy.

"For your trouble." Angelina gave it to the children, ruffling their hair. "Do not eat too much at once or you will get sick." She was sick already.

Tonio worked sixteen hours a day in the Hole, as long as the sun lasted, not that it mattered in the depths of the mine. Time was measured there by the cadence of water dripping off dark rock walls. May days were warm and dry in North Idaho. At ground level temperatures reached into the seventies. Beneath the surface in the depths of the mine shafts, the air was cool and moist. Tonio labored with his shirt unbuttoned, hanging open. The humidity caused a man to break a sweat easily. Ground water dripped on him from the walls, mingling with the sweat that poured off him to pool in half circles beneath his arms. By day's end he was completely soaked.

At the end of each day he emerged into the twilight to shed his clothes and bathe in a nearby stream. He camped just outside the entrance to the mine in the shade of a large cedar, which was much more convenient than his room at the boardinghouse in town.

The idea of finding the mother lode and making a fortune consumed Tonio and made a convenient diversion from his tortured thoughts of Angelina. He'd always worked hard, would have worked seven days a week. But Harry Scott, who managed the mine, insisted he take a day off every now and then.

Harry insisted because Tonio's job was more a matter of mind and nerve than of manual labor. The explosives expert had to be alert and well rested to avoid mistakes. A slip on his part could cost lives or at the very least the accidental destruction of a valuable tunnel. Tonio planned where to set the charges, how much dynamite to use, and more often than not, he set the blast off himself. The best dynamiters were those who had learned the craft early in life, while they were still young enough to feel invincible. A skilled dynamiter could not be made of a novice much past the age of twenty-five, an age at which they had matured enough to recognize their own mortality and had become too careful. Fear immobilized the older man.

At thirty, Tonio had been practicing the art for eleven years, since learning how to blow up Ethiopian troops while serving in the Italian army. He further perfected his skill dynamiting for the railroad. He was practiced enough to be confident, mature enough to be cautious.

Tonio left his campsite late Saturday afternoon in time to drop his dirty laundry off with the laundress before she closed. Then he met Charley Nokes for a drink at one of the local bars. Charley kept him apprised of the comings and goings of the town. The news was most often unsettling.

The Western Federation of Miners had representatives in town stirring up trouble. Tensions mounted daily. Fist fights broke out. The two friends spent hours discussing the situation, each one speculating when new violence would erupt and what could be done that wasn't being done to abate the situation. Both men agreed that this was only the tip of the trouble.

"The Colonel's got a new girl working at the Fuller." Charley always had news of a new female face around town.

"I thought with the impending strike business had slowed. Did one of his waitresses quit?" Tonio took another swig of beer.

"Nope. This girl is helping May in the kitchen, living with her, too. Comely gal. Newly widowed. Foreign—Italian like you. Name sounds like Angel."

"Angelina?" Tonio nearly dropped his beer.

"That's it! Sad tale. Came out to meet her husband only to find out that he died of a bad heart a couple of months ago. Lots of hard luck here in the Valley."

Tonio gave a slight nod. His head spun with the implications. Angelina was free, but was he? He didn't need any connections that would give the thugs in the union a hold on him.

Nokes made the shape of an hourglass with his hands. "Dark hair and eyes. Fine, a very fine woman. Even though she hides back in the kitchen, she's been attracting all sorts of attention. I've thought about throwing my own hat in the ring." Nokes chuckled. "What would my old man think if I brought home a sensuous, feisty little Italian bride?"

"You don't have a chance in hell with her, Nokes. That woman is mine."

ranco Allessandro is dead. My husband is dead.
As Angelina lay in her bed at the Halls', exhausted by a good day's work, the thought reverberated through her mind so loudly it was almost
audible.

Mr. Allessandro had promised her land, a homestead
of one hundred and sixty acres near a town called Harrison. He owned it outright, so he had boasted to Papa.
Was it hers now? Was her marriage legal enough for
her to claim it? Could she sell it, live on it, farm it?
Who would know?

She had to find out, but first she had to see Tonio,
ached to see Tonio. Word had gotten round to Al that
Tonio was back and holed up at the Hole, working sun-
up to sundown. What did it mean that he hadn't come

to see her? She wondered if he knew that Mr. Allessandro was dead. Probably not. How would he? She
would see him. She would tell him and hope for the
best.

The next morning, Angelina convinced Al to let her
ride with him in the engine of his train to Burke. He
dropped her off in the one-road town where his friend
and partner, Gus Preston, took her to the mine. The
sun baked the hills made for an unusually warm spring
day.

When they got to the mine, Gus handed Angelina a
floppy felt hat. "You'll need to wear this. It'll keep your
head dry. It's wet underground."

Gus surveyed her as she pulled the hat on. He
seemed uneasy about a woman going down into the
mine. May was a partner but she kept books, Al had
told her. She didn't go traipsing down the hole.

"It's dirty and wet down there," Gus said. "People
who aren't used to it feel claustrophobic at first."

"Claustrophobic?" There were still many words she
didn't know.

"Fearful of small spaces."

She nodded.

He continued. "It's cool in the shafts near the surface, but it gets increasingly warmer the deeper you go.
For your safety we won't go down far. I've sent Lou
ahead to send Tonio up. Are you ready?"

The mineshaft was exactly as Gus described it. Water dripped off the gray rock walls and echoed down
the shafts, bland and unexciting. Nothing spoke of rich
deposits of sparkling silver.

The tunnel was tall enough for her to walk upright through, but smaller tunnels shot off in various directions. Underground, she lost her bearings and was thankful for Gus's guidance. The tunnel floor was uneven and potholed and littered with shafts of rock.

"Core samples," Gus said. "We drill into the mine wall and pull out rock samples to send to the assayer. He tells us what we've got and if it's worth drilling farther in that direction."

He stooped and picked one up to show her. "See this one? It's all light-colored stone. You could see better in the daylight." He held it closer to the lamp he held. "Nothing in this sample but layers of stone, no galena. You can see the striation, layers of different kinds of rock and clay. A geologist could tell you exactly how the land was formed from a sample like this."

He continued walking, leaving Angelina vaguely depressed. Where was the galena Tonio sought?

"Will you strike it rich, Gus? Will you find your mother lode?"

He didn't pause for a second. "Absolutely."

"You sound confident."

"If I wasn't I wouldn't be in this venture. We'll find it. It's only a matter of time."

They turned a small bend and descended farther. Angelina spotted Tonio just before Gus pointed. "There he is. Tonio! You have a visitor."

Her breath caught in her throat. Would he be happy to see her?

"Angelina," Tonio said.

She couldn't read his tone. "Tonio."

"I'll leave you two. I've got business up above. Give the lady a good tour, Tonio. Mrs. Allessandro, it was a pleasure." Gus tipped his hat and disappeared up the tunnel.

Tonio wiped the sweat from his brow with the tail of his shirt. Another man would have been embarrassed by being caught half-naked and sweating. Not Tonio. "Angelina? What in...what brings you here? I hadn't expected to—"

"See me again?" She stepped closer to him.

Even in the dim light of the mineshaft, Angelina could discern the dark, piercing appraisal of his gaze. His shirt hung open, exposing a hard chest. Sweat glistened between the well-defined muscles of his chest and slid off his hard belly, creating a perfect curl of hair at his belly button. As always, she trembled slightly, felt the potent magnetic pull he had on her. Pleasure at the sight of him hummed through her. She could not help liking the disquieting effect he had on her.

"I came with news." She resisted the urge to touch him, wanting desperately not to cry, longing to throw herself into the comfort of his arms. Yet he remained restrained, cautious, wary of her presence. But then he thought her married. "You aren't curious?"

"I'm listening."

Angelina heard water dripping off rock and the thudding of her pulse in her ears. Now at the moment of confession, her mouth went dry. She both needed and feared his reaction. "As it turns out, life has provided another irony. When we first met, I was a bride who had not met her bridegroom. And now it seems that I am a widow who never met her husband. Through an entire marriage, I did not know him, never saw him." She might have laughed. It all seemed so ludicrous, so vaguely funny.

She didn't know what, exactly, she expected of Tonio's reaction. Certainly not the rock silent, unflinching stance he maintained.

"How?"

She wondered that he could speak in such a deep monosyllable, so low it seemed part of the depths where they stood.

"He died at the mine, of a bad heart. No one knows more than that. The mine manager gave me his last two weeks of pay. And that is it. I am a free woman."

He appeared unmoved by her presence. "Are we ever really free?" His question seemed rhetorical.

Inside Angelina felt the panic swell. Had all that they experienced been merely lust? Would he abandon her here in a land where she had freedom but no idea how to exercise it? No support, no family? A cold sweat trickled down her back between her shoulder blades. Underneath Gus's floppy hat, she felt flushed and fearful and suddenly claustrophobic, as if she had just remembered that she was supposed to be. Or maybe it was only the close proximity to the inscrutable Tonio.

She touched his damp sleeve. "I need your help. Please." She didn't like to plead, especially not on the verge of tears. "I wouldn't ask but—"

"Anything, Angel, anything," he said.

She wanted to collapse in his arms, but his offer seemed to have nothing to do with that. "Mr. Allessandro said that he owned land in a place called Harrison. I need help finding out if this is true and if it is now mine."

He nodded, thoughtful. "I have a friend, a lawyer, who keeps an office in Harrison part time. I'll give you his address and contact him for you if you like. John will know what to do."

She nodded, uncertain what to do next, paralyzed by his reticence, determined not to make a further fool out of herself.

He held out his hand to her. "Come. Let me show you the mine." He took her gently by her elbow. "I'll show you where I'm working today."

"Gus explained about the galena. Tonio, show me the silver."

Without speaking, he led her down a small, dark tunnel just off the main one she'd come down. He stopped suddenly near a pile of rock. "Here's our galena." He picked a rock up off the pile.

She eyed it cautiously. "It doesn't look like anything. It doesn't shine or sparkle. How do you know it's silver?"

"This isn't a gold mine, Angelina. Silver doesn't shine until it's smelted and polished." He held the rock up sideways to the lamp he carried, revealing a gentle sheen on the rock face. "Do you see the glisten of metal?"

He didn't wait for an answer but pressed the rock into her hand. "Feel the weight of it—that's our ore." His eyes shone with excitement.

The rock was heavy in her hand, much heavier than she expected from such a small sample.

"That isn't a high grade rock. We've got better. Come, see what I've been working on." He led her to the wall and pointed to a small round hole.

"We're going to blast this tunnel deeper. This is where I'm going to insert the dynamite." He picked up a hand drill, a long corkscrew shaped tool, and pushed it into the hole until it would go no farther. Then he grabbed a sledgehammer.

"Hold the drill, Angelina. I'll swing the hammer. After each swing, rotate the drill slightly."

She looked straight into his eyes and saw an intense excitement she'd never seen before. She faltered. "Me? I couldn't."

"Come on." His voice became smooth and sensual, softly cajoling. "What better way to see how a mine works than to do a bit of the work? We'll drill the hole and set off the blast. I swear, you've never had such fun."

He guided her hand to the drill, stroking her palm intimately with his finger as he did so. She hung on tremulously. He released her hand, stepped back, and picked up his sledgehammer. "Hold on tight and hold it steady. We don't want our hole to be crooked."

She gripped the drill tightly, shying away from the swing of the hammer, hoping his aim ran true.

Evidently seeing her discomfort, he laughed and called out. "Trust me, Angelina. I won't hit you." He cocked the hammer and swung.

The chink of the hammer hitting the drill reverberated through the tunnel and sent shock waves down her arm.

"Turn!" he yelled. "Don't look so frightened." He swung again.

After the first few strokes, she calmed, but her fingers remained white as she clutched the drill. They worked as a fluid team. Swing, strike, turn. She watched in awe as his muscles tensed and rippled with each powerful stroke.

All too soon he stopped and backed the drill out. "That's deep enough. Now the fun begins."

She flexed her stiff fingers and stretched her arm, which still pounded with the vibrations of the sledgehammer hitting the drill. Tonio made last minute calculations.

"What are we going to do next?" She was almost afraid to find out.

"Set the blast. Get back up the tunnel and wait for me around the first bend." He sounded calm but a sharp edge of excitement tinged his voice.

She stalled, uncertain. "Is this dangerous?"

"Not if you know what you're doing." He grabbed her gently by the shoulders and pointed her toward the tunnel. "Now go. Up the tunnel and around the first bend. Flatten yourself against the wall and stay there. Wait for me. Do not under any circumstances move from that spot. I'll join you in a moment. And I guarantee you the biggest rush of your life."

She did as Tonio bid, and waited for what seemed like an eternity, growing more apprehensive as she waited, listening to water drip off the rock walls. Finally, she determined that something must have gone wrong. She stepped cautiously out into the middle of the tunnel and then headed back in what she hoped was the right direction to find Tonio. "Tonio, is everything all right?"

She rounded the bend in time to see Tonio detonate the charge. He started as he looked up and saw her standing there. He mouthed a curse as he sprang to his feet and ran toward her. She froze like a startled deer.

"Run, Angel, run!" he yelled.

Her feet remained grounded. He ran toward her at a furious pace. Without losing a step, he grabbed her around the waist and pulled her to the ground, covering her with himself and cupping her ears protectively with his hands.

The next moment everything blurred. A mighty roar reverberated through the tunnel, followed by a cloud of dust. Small pebbles and debris rained from the tunnel ceiling and walls.

Tonio turned her face to his and in the height of the explosion covered her mouth with his in a deep, lunging kiss. His hands left her ears as he caressed her gently and intimately, fondling her breasts, exploring her curves.

She felt as though she were exploding. For a moment she thought he was killing them both and this was his way of saying goodbye. Her fear heightened the excitement.

He was whispering something in her ear. She strained to hear but couldn't in the noise, knowing he spoke by the gentle breath in her ear. The next moment it was over. The dust settled and Tonio pulled away, leaving her breathless and wanting.

Her ears rang but not as loud as her heart, which soared with the thought that she hadn't lost him after all. She sat on the tunnel floor covered with dust, not caring at all. He stood and dusted himself off before offering her his hand and pulling her roughly to her feet. He spoke loudly, above the din in her ears. "You nearly got us killed, Angelina. I told you to stay in the tunnel."

The words meant to sting brought only delight. He cared. For some reason he fought to remain aloof but the tenor of his words betrayed the true alignment of his heart.

But he wasn't through with her. "Don't look at me like I'm some kind of hero. Gus is going to have my head for this. He has a high regard for women and safe mining practices."

"Who's going to tell him?"

"Look at yourself. No one has to tell him."

"I'll tell him I fell and that you saved me. It's the truth, after all."

He reached over and pulled her close to him so fast it took her by complete surprise. He spoke directly into her face. "You're free now, but I'm not. Not with the Valley being a virtual powder keg on the verge of exploding. Maybe not ever." He took her chin in his hand.

"I have nothing to offer a wife—no fortune, just hard work and dreams. Not much more than a jaded heart and a life of hard work. I can't ask you to make that sacrifice, Angel. You'd be best off taking what money you have and heading back to New York. Surely there you can find a replacement husband worthy of you."

She stared at him open mouthed. "At least you have a dream. That's more than I've ever had. I never expected wealth. I was raised to accept a life of hard work." He couldn't be pushing her away. She wouldn't let him.

"But you should be able to expect your husband to keep you safe, not put you in danger." He spoke cryptically, dancing around the edge of truth.

"I don't want to go back to New York." She didn't want to leave him. "May says a woman in Idaho can do just about anything that she wants. I have a job with the Colonel at the Fuller House that's as good as any that I could get in New York. And in case you haven't noticed, there are plenty of men here who are looking for wives." Her hurt forced out the last words. Why couldn't he see that she didn't care for anything but him? She'd face any danger for a life with him.

He grabbed her arm and pulled her up the tunnel. "The tour's over."

At surface level, birds chirped and the sun continued to shine despite the sad state of Angelina's heart. Tonio took her to a campsite not far from the opening of the mine.

"There is something that I want to give you before you go." He rifled through one of his bags.

Angelina thought that he meant to give her necklace back. She missed it. She wanted it. But she wanted Tonio, too. He was the man of her heart. Why couldn't he see that?

Tonio pulled out his stiletto, which gleamed in the sunlight. "Ever used a knife?"

She shuddered, surprised and repulsed. She hated knives, not kitchen knives, only deadly weapon knives. "No, and I don't intend to. Why would I need such a thing?"

"For protection. If you're going to stay in Wallace for even another day, I'm going to insist that you learn how to protect yourself."

He grabbed her hand and thrust the stiletto into it. With his hand firmly over hers, he demonstrated a few thrusts into the open air. His nearness distracted her. But the look in his eyes, when she dared to look away from the knife and at him, was deadly, not longing as she'd hoped.

"Have you ever knifed anyone?" she asked.

"What do you think? I was a soldier at war, Angelina. I did far worse just to survive."

"But I am not at war. Why would I need a knife?"

"Because you don't know how to use a gun and I don't have time to teach you. Anyone can use a knife. You're a beautiful young woman. This is rough country."

Their hands were still locked together with the knife between them. Angelina did not wish to part. "I don't want this knife."

"You're damn well going to have it." He handed her a leather pouch. "And the holster, too. Wear it strapped under your bodice or your skirt. Keep it where you can reach it if you should need it."

"I told you, I don't need it."

"I hope not." He took her by the arm. "I'll give you a ride to Burke."

"This is your stiletto, Tonio. What will you do without it?"

"Fortunately, I know how to use a gun."

She stopped him. "You still have my necklace?"

Tonio paused. "Yes. How thoughtless of me—you probably want it back."

She shook her head. "No. I want you to keep it for me. Keep it somewhere safe. For now, I will safeguard your stiletto and you will protect my necklace."

"Deal," he said. "You know that you could sell that necklace and have your passage home? It's your ticket out of here and back into the bosom of your family."

"I know, but I would never sell my grandma's treasure. That is not what she intended."

He didn't argue. "It's your decision. If you ever change your mind and want it back, all you have to do is ask."

She lifted her chin, trying to look braver than she felt. "If I ever go back to Italy, be assured that I will."

As he caught her elbow to lead her toward town, she said. "I have not given up on you yet." And she meant it. She didn't mean to give up—ever.

John Lawlor jumped to his feet and rounded his desk to meet Tonio at the doorway, slapping him heartily on the back. "If it isn't my friend the Italian.

Come in, Tonio. What a surprise. I didn't think you had business in Harrison. What's so important that it's gotten you out of the Hole and brought you to our little town?"

Tonio surveyed the office. "Don't you do any work around here? Where are all of your clients?"

He pointed to a chair. "I don't entertain many here at my Harrison office. Most of my work is in Spokane. I come here for peace and quiet so I can get my thinking and paperwork done. Are you going to answer my question? What brings you here?"

"A lady."

John winked. "I should have guessed."

"It's not what you think. She's a married lady or widowed or some damn thing. I was charged in New York with bringing her out here to meet her husband and look out for her well-being."

"Oh?"

Tonio explained the situation.

John rubbed his chin. "Finding out about the property should be easy enough—a talk with the clerk at the courthouse. The legality of the marriage..." John stroked his chin. "Never consummated?"

Tonio nodded. "Like I said, she never met him."

"I'm sworn to uphold the law, so I shouldn't even be asking this—who knows that she never consummated the marriage?"

Tonio didn't miss a beat. "The Halls and me."

Lawlor nodded. "The groom have any next of kin, anyone who could contest?"

Tonio shook his head. "Don't know. You'd have to ask Angel."

"I'll do just that. Send her by, Tonio, send her by. It may be that all this is moot. Legally speaking, I wouldn't want to cheat a legitimate heir out of an inheritance. On the other hand, why should the state confiscate what this fellow worked so hard to provide for his bride, mail-order or not. His intention was clearly to provide for her."

"I'll do just that, John. Thanks." Tonio glanced at the clock. "I have to get going if I'm going to catch the train back to Burke. Keep me posted of any progress and send the bills to me in Burke."

The town of Harrison sprawled neatly on the shore of Lake Coeur d'Alene. In less than a dozen years it had sprung to life as a thriving lumber town boasting a population near a thousand. As she stood at the rail of the *Georgie Oakes*, Angelina counted three lumber mills lining the town's lakeside edge. It had been so nice of the Colonel to give her the day off and arrange passage to Harrison with his friend, the captain of the boat.

The hum and buzz of saws drifted out from shore as the *Georgie Oakes* negotiated its way cautiously through the log booms that stretched into the lake to the waiting stall at the Harrison ferry dock. A gentle breeze carried the scent of freshly cut pines and firs out over the water and the town. Bright, freshly milled lumber was stacked neatly in lumberyards filled to capacity, making a wholesome picture.

As the captain helped Angelina down the gang-plank, the newness and activity of the town dazzled her. The main street, a wide unpaved dirt road, ran through town, mimicking the shape of the lake. It was not smooth or flat, but hilled and banked, following the natural terrain of the land. Lumber mills and boat docks filled the lake side of the road.

On the opposite side of the street, the town's main businesses bustled. Plank sidewalks ran the length of the street on either side, as if the town had all the lumber it could ever want. Boards were spread across dirt streets to protect pedestrians from mud and dust. Several streets wound their way off the main street and up the hill into a residential district. Every structure in town was made of carefully milled lumber boards.

To Angelina, the town could have been made of gold and been no more impressive. Timber was scarce in Italy and as such was prized and used sparingly. Here the abundance of its use seemed almost obscene. The town stood as a proud tribute to its main industry and to the hope that she owned land somewhere up one of the hillsides. With land she would not be poor. She would sell it and buy a house in Wallace. Tonio would not have to worry that he had nothing to offer her. She would have something to offer him.

She pulled a crumpled piece of paper from her pocket and followed the directions to her lawyer's office. Her lawyer—the term both frightened and excited her.

A sign hanging from a lamppost marked John Lawlor's office, which was as easy to find as Tonio had assured her. His secretary led her into his office, where Angelina took a seat. A few minutes later, John Lawlor entered.

Angelina liked him on sight. A man in his late forties or early fifties with slightly stooping shoulders and a gray mustache, he reminded her of Papa. He had an infectious smile and a kindly manner of speaking meant to put clients at ease, she supposed. At least, she relaxed.

"Mr. Lawlor," she said, "your name suits your profession."

"Yes, with a name like Lawlor, what else could I be except a lawyer?"

She told him her story as he listened and asked questions, nodding, stroking his chin. Finally he said, "Tonio was in to see me earlier this week and gave me a briefing. I need to ask you a few pertinent questions."

"Yes, *signor.*"

"Did Mr. Allessandro have any children?"

"No."

"Parents still alive?"

"No."

"Brothers or sisters?"

"He had two brothers. One passed away many years ago. The other," Angelina paused. She did not like to think about Paolo. Although his disappearance had not been her fault, she felt that she had somehow brought tragedy to the Allessandro family.

"His younger brother Paolo was my escort to the United States. He got an eye disease and was to be deported. They would not let him enter the country. Later I heard that he boasted that he was going to jump overboard and try to swim to shore.

"It is a dangerous swim, *Signor* Lawlor. I was in New York for months afterward. If he had jumped and lived, he would have contacted me. Someone would have heard from him."

"Has he contacted his family or anyone in Italy?"

"I don't know. I have not heard from them since I left New York."

John Lawlor patted her hand. "I'm sorry."

She nodded.

"You were married in Italy?"

"Yes, by proxy. It's done all the time in Italy," Angelina said, though she wasn't certain it was legal, even there.

"And no one besides you, Tonio, and the Halls know that the marriage was never consummated?"

"And Paolo."

John Lawlor frowned slightly. "Then unless Paolo turns up to make a claim on the inheritance, I don't foresee any problems. Would you like to see your land?"

Angelina's pulse raced. "My land? Is it that easy?"

"I don't see why not." He extended his hand to her. "We'll take my carriage. It's a fine day for a drive."

"Mr. Lawlor, I must ask one more favor. The man at the mine told me only that my husband was dead, nothing more. I would like, that is, if it is possible, to know where he is buried. I would like to visit the man who has given me this gift and honor his memory."

Her lawyer nodded. "I took the liberty of looking into that for you. He's buried in the town cemetery overlooking the lake. It's a nice spot. I think anyone would like it, especially someone who loved this town. When I inquired about Mr. Allessandro, I was told that he was a quiet, hardworking man who kept to himself mostly. He worked in the mine in Kellogg, so he was not around here much. But the few who knew him seemed to like him and were sorry about his passing."

Angelina squeezed Mr. Lawlor's arm. "Thank you. I will write of that to my father, who was his friend years ago, and to my village for the people there will want to know."

Angelina's property was outside of town on a hillside overlooking a gentle valley. The trees grew thick and the underbrush lush. John drove her to a tiny cabin. "This would have been your home. Would you like to go in?"

She didn't want to, but John thought it necessary, that there might be something of value that she should have. It was sparsely furnished. The man had not had much. But it was evident that he had been preparing it for her arrival. He had begun to construct a little pantry and it was evident that he had put new glass in the windows. They found little. Nothing she wanted except for a few dollars that the lawyer insisted she take.

Then they walked the property. John Lawlor pointed out the property lines and identified trees for her. Most of her land was on a hot hillside, but it was still lovely property. She asked Mr. Lawlor what price it might fetch.

"Oh, you don't want to sell it. You haven't been pay-ing attention. All those trees—timber will be quite val-uable in several years' time. Probably worth more than the land itself. Wait until it's large enough to harvest and bring a good price. Then if you still want to sell the land, do it. Right now you've got a few small stands ready to be cut. Log those off now."

"I have no idea how to sell timber," she said, think-ing of the money she could use to set up a home for Tonio and her and overcome his objections of poverty.

"Ah, but I do. Give me power of attorney and I will take care of it for you for a very reasonable fee."

On the way back to his office, they stopped by the cemetery and Angelina placed a spray of wild roses on her husband's grave, feeling like an interloper in his final peace, a bit like she had stolen something from him, knowing that she had never loved him.

"I'm sorry," she said to the mound of dirt over him, to the clouds that drifted in the deep blue above. "But thank you. Thank you so much for what you've given me." A great burden eased from her.

Then John Lawlor took her arm and led her to his carriage. He took her to the train depot, for she had to take the train home.

"*Signor* Lawlor, one final question of you—could I become an American citizen, do you think?" The idea popped into her head from nowhere. Tonio was a citi-zen. She wanted to be, too.

"I think you'd make a fine American woman. Ameri-ca is good place for women and becoming much better. The ladies will have the vote nationwide in not many more years. A bright young woman could do well here. But you'd have to live here for at least five years, the minimum before applying for citizenship. And you'd have to take the naturalization test."

Five years! Well, she had time to consider that.

"Thank you, Mr. Lawlor."

He nodded. "It may take as much as a month or two to arrange the sale of the timber. I'll keep in touch."

She thanked him again as her train pulled into the station.

CHAPTER TWELVE

A ngelina had not been herself since her visit with Tonio up at the Hole. Silent. Trying to put a bright face on things. Working harder than ever. But May sensed that beneath it all lay the treacherous companions of panic, fear, and depression. What had Tonio done and said to make Angelina act so sullen? May meant to straighten that boy out. She could hardly stand seeing Angelina in such a state.

With the job at the Fuller, trying to get her assets from her late husband, and dealing with the timber mess, all in a foreign tongue in a foreign country, the girl had waded in over her head. May helped as best she could. But better yet, she saw an opportunity to force Tonio into close proximity with the girl, something he seemed hell-bent on avoiding.

Try and hide, Toni, she thought. *You can't outfox me!*

May smiled to herself. She'd never fancied herself a matchmaker. She didn't have many hopes that she'd be much good at it. But in this case, she had to try. While she understood Tonio's motives for keeping his distance, if he didn't keep his hat in the ring, so to speak, he could lose the girl altogether.

There were too many bachelors in the valley for a girl of Angelina's looks to go unnoticed. No, the men had seen her and sniffing around all too frequently for May's tastes, including that weasel Clell, who seemed more determined than ever to court Angel now that it was common knowledge she was a widow. May could only discourage them so long. She wasn't cut out to be a guardian of chastity and Tonio's interests. Angelina had been turning down all offers so far, but who knew how long she'd keep that up?

Clell's attentions worried May most of all. He was a dangerous and powerful man. She had half a thought that he was behind the anonymous gifts Angelina had been receiving, though she kept that to herself knowing how Angelina disliked the man. The gifts had been little things so far but always came with a typed note full of innuendo.

With all that in mind, May headed to Burke to catch up with Tonio. She found him in his camp at the mouth of the Hole.

"May, what brings you to the wilderness?" He seemed happy to see her.

"Mail call." She tossed him a letter from Nonna Gia, his friend back in New York. And another from someone in Chicago.

Then she handed him a box that she'd made up for him. "And something decent to eat. Someone's got to see that you don't starve to death up here."

Tonio laughed.

May shook her head. "I bet you gave your mama the dickens of trouble."

They chatted for a bit while May schemed to bring up the main reason for her visit. She brought up the topic of Angelina at the first opportunity. "Tonio, I don't like the thought of you toying with that little girl."

"She may be young but she's no girl, May." He stared at the box before him for a moment before lifting the lid.

"I thought you were supposed to be her chaperone. Seems to me she could use a little help right now, what with all the legal matters of dealing with her husband's death and all."

Tonio sighed happily as he saw the food she'd packed for him. He seemed too intent on it to care much about her scolding.

"I sent her to John Lawlor for help, even talked to him myself on her behalf."

"I call that scant help, Tonio, scant help indeed."

He shrugged. "She won't go back to Italy. I offered her a way back and she refused. If she wants to stay here, she has to learn to fend for herself.

"She could be a fine, independent woman if she tried. Problem is she's too young to know it yet. Being raised in that antiquated system in Italy teaches a woman she's of no use except as a man's servant. Training like that practically has to be bred out. There's no way she's going to survive out West unless she develops her own sense of self-worth and independence. I'm only encouraging her. She reminds me a little bit of you."

May set her hands on her broad hips. She was a sturdy woman. She had never been expected to behave in the silly, giddy way pretty women were supposed to act. Her broad features and heavy chin gave her a serious, almost mannish appearance, causing men to treat her more like one of their own than the hallowed creature, woman.

"That's fine talk, but you can't impress me any by trying to appeal to my suffragette tendencies." May paused for effect, acting as if she were considering whether or not to speak her mind when she knew perfectly well what to say next.

"I hesitate to bring this up, but that young woman is causing quite a stir over at the Fuller. Got her share of admirers." She watched Tonio carefully for a reaction and although he acted nonchalant, she knew him well enough to realize that his stoicism suggested she'd piqued his interest.

"She's turned down half a dozen proposals of marriage already. Every other single male in town is working up the courage to propose, weighing his own odds of success, I imagine. I've had my hands full shooing them off. Reason I mention it is, well, isn't the shooing supposed to be your job as chaperone?"

Tonio laughed. "I expect I've left her in your competent hands, May."

"Yeah, well, some of them aren't shooing as easily as they might." She made another pregnant pause. "Clell's been hanging around, dining at the Fuller every day that Angelina works, waiting for her to get off shift. Pestering her."

She'd hit her target. A frown passed quickly over Tonio's face and his eyes went steely at the mention of Clell. "I'll ask Nokes to keep an eye on her."

"Good idea," May said, "but there's one more problem we've got. On top of all the obvious ones, Angelina's got a secret admirer. He's been sending anonymous gifts—candy, flowers, the like. You wait too long, he may turn her head and you'll be left out in the cold. I expect, you being a full blooded male and all, that you aren't immune to her charms."

It took him a second to answer. May thought, or maybe hoped, he looked jealous for all his pretending not to be.

"May! What are you saying?" Tonio shook his head from side to side and clucked his tongue in mock chagrin. "Her recently widowed. And me! I was almost a priest!"

"Almost only counts in horseshoes and dynamiting."

"There's some that would argue with you about the dynamiting. It's a precise craft."

"You're acting a little too coy. That girl means something to you, so much so that it scares you."

Tonio ignored her statement as he pulled a cookie out of the box. He cocked a brow in such a comical fashion that May laughed. "Cookies?"

"Angelina's."

"She sent me cookies?"

"Got your hopes up, didn't I?" May had him. She knew she had him. "I packed those for you."

He tossed May a *biscotti*, then took a bite of one himself. "Delicious. The girl can cook."

"All the more reason to defend your territory." May wasn't about to let him squirm away.

He took another bite of cookie and sighed. "This would be best with a nice glass of wine to dunk it in."

"Tell that to the bartender."

He sighed. "All right, I give up. What do you want me to do?"

"For starters, how about taking a look at that girl's property and timber?"

"John is handling that."

May nodded. "Yes, that may be so. But Angelina's been fretting on it. You may trust him, but he's a stranger to her and a lawyer, not a logger. What does he know about trees and the timber business? Your assessment wouldn't hurt."

He paused mid bite, obviously considering her suggestion. "Okay, sounds reasonable. And?"

"And what?"

"You can't be finished with me yet."

May laughed. "You treat her nicely, Tonio." With her piece said, May took her leave, hopeful that Tonio and Angelina would work things out.

Angelina's arms ached from kneading bread dough in the Colonel's kitchen. She'd resorted to mumbling complaints in Italian. Hot. Tired. And the stupid bread dough would not cooperate.

"Come on, Angelina. You spoke better English the last time we met. Have you forgotten everything I've taught you?"

The deep resonant voice stopped her in her tracks. The plate froze in hand as she looked up.

"Tonio," she said in a breathy whisper to herself before she'd recovered from the shock.

He lounged in the doorway of the Fuller's kitchen in a pose only he could effect. He wore a blinding white shirt unbuttoned at the neck, his fringed black jacket held loosely over his shoulder on two fingers. The sight of him took her breath away.

Unlike the handsome, compliant man that she had imagined in his absence, in the flesh he was a presence to be reckoned with. Her legs struggled to hold her up. She locked her knees and looked him straight in the eye. She couldn't believe he'd come back. Joy flooded over her.

"Tonio? I didn't think I'd see you again for a while. Last I heard, you were working night and day in that hole."

He left the doorway to lean across her worktable and speak intimately to her. "I came to thank you for the cookies."

"You didn't need to make a trip to town for that. May told me you enjoyed them."

"A personal thank you is always best."

His presence filled the kitchen, the air she breathed, her very being. The kitchen and the problem bread dough faded into a nebulous background of nonexistence as she locked eyes with him for a period of time that was distinctly longer than appropriate for mere friends.

"What really brings you to town, Tonio?" Angelina asked.

"Why, you of course, my dear. I would have been remiss in my duties if I'd not checked up on you to make sure all is well. Nonna Gia is surely expecting some kind of report. You haven't written her yourself, have you?"

Angelina blushed. No, she'd not written Nonna Gia, or her family or anyone else for that matter. She'd been too caught up in her own problems to feel up to writing. She wanted to reassure everyone that she was fine. But she wasn't convinced of that herself yet.

Angelina's blush intensified as Tonio continued in a confidential tone. "I know you haven't written Nonna Gia. I would have caught hell by now. As it is, I got a letter from Nonna just the other day inquiring about you. Seems you left no forwarding address."

Angelina was disappointed. Had he come merely because of Nonna Gia's bidding? She should have written Nonna long ago and saved Tonio the trip. Of course people would want word of her, if only to know she had arrived safely.

"You are right to remind me of my responsibilities. I was waiting until I had good news to tell them. I have been afraid to confess that I am now a widow. My parents will worry and perhaps insist that I find a way to come home." She gave him an intimate smile, hoping to remind him that she was still in pursuit.

"I will write Nonna Gia and my family today. I promise."

"Good," Tonio replied. "There is one bit of news Nonna wanted me to pass along. Your late husband's family hasn't heard from his brother Paolo. He didn't return to Italy on the ship. Your cousin Mario has been checking with the police about him. A body washed up in the harbor. A young man of Paolo's age and general description. It was badly decomposed. There's no way to know for sure whether or not it was him. But it seems likely."

Angelina gasped and crossed herself, overcome with guilt that she was partly relieved. Paolo wouldn't be a problem for her now. "Poor Paolo. May he rest in peace."

Tonio nodded sympathetically. "You look hot and tired. Is there any chance the Colonel will let you take the afternoon off? Since I've come to town, I may as well help you get a few matters settled.

"May tells me that you are concerned about your timber, that you would like a second opinion about it. For what it's worth, I would be happy to offer mine.

"And then there's the matter of banking that money when it arrives. I was hoping to help you open a bank account."

She could have collapsed into his arms with relief. He kept a good face, a great lover's poker face, but in the end he had come to town to help her. He might fight it, but she felt certain that he loved her.

"Let me turn this dough out to rise. May can put it in the oven for me later. Just let me tell the Colonel that I'm leaving."

"Excellent. We'll go by the bank first and then catch a train to Harrison so that I can see the infamous timber for myself."

"You're sure my money is safe?" Angelina said as she and Tonio emerged from the formal atmosphere of the bank into the bright sunshine.

"Safer than in your cookie jar or under a rock," Tonio said. It was the first opportunity he had to see her in full daylight since arriving. He enjoyed the sight of her too much for his own good.

"Your few dollars are perfectly safe. Bankers wouldn't stay in business if they didn't protect their clients' money."

He didn't tell her that just six years ago, during the depression of '93, many banks did indeed go bankrupt and close their doors. He doubted Angelina even knew of such things as bank failures. She was probably more worried about a hold up.

"You know their big vault is secure."

"It's not the safety of their vault that concerns me," Angelina said. "No one in my family has ever had a bank account. Papa never trusted them, not that he ever had any money to save."

There wasn't any self-pity in her voice. It was merely a statement of fact.

"Banks fail," she continued. "At least with an honest robbery there is some chance of recovery."

He looked back at her and smiled, pleasantly surprised by her knowledge. At times it was almost possible to forget that she was a peasant. "How would your Papa know about such things?"

"Don't put on your patrician airs with me, Antonio Domani." Her words would have been sharp if she hadn't been smiling and had a teasing lilt to her voice. Her voice—he could have listened to her speak all day. He was a besotted fool.

"My Papa may not have money to invest," she said, "but he is intelligent, and well-versed in a wide variety of subjects."

"And yet, he doesn't trust banks? My family has done quite well by them for hundreds of years."

"And look where that's gotten you. Here you are breaking your back on a mine claim. I don't see much difference between you and Papa at the moment. Your high born ancestors would be horrified."

"My brother in Italy is quite a wealthy man. My only crime is being the second born son." He tried to remain unruffled, though it still galled him that his worthless brother should have all the amenities in life while Tonio had to struggle.

"Don't worry about your money, Angel. It's nice and safe now." He took her arm. "Let's catch our train before it gets too late for the trip."

The dirt road up Bell Canyon to Angelina's property was already dry and dusty in early May. Angelina imagined it would be a mud hole in early spring. Tiny baby tobacco spitting grasshoppers sang as they flew out of the road in front of Tonio and Angelina.

Tonio led the way to a cool, shady spot off the top of the bluff at the upper end of her property. Tonio carried a lunch box that Angelina had packed back at the Fuller, and Angelina a jug of cool water she had dipped from the spring near the house.

"These nasty hills. They radiate the heat."

"Basalt rock is your culprit. These hills abound with it."

"There, just ahead is our shade," Angelina said.

Minutes later they settled in the cool shadow of a large white pine and dined on the quick lunch Angelina had put together. She couldn't keep her eyes off him.

She wondered if he felt her scrutiny, or her joy at being out with him. She had missed him. She was surely a foolish woman to harbor such feelings, but they were too strong to ignore.

She felt as if she could never get enough of staring at his dark, handsome features, the lock of hair that curled over his left eye. Her body reacted to his nearness. She remembered the mountain meadow, and although it was inappropriate, longed for more lovemaking with him. But he kept his distance. And she knew he was right. She could not be with him again until they married. If only she could convince him to marry her.

She felt privately envious of Tonio as he lounged insouciantly in the sparse grass. His carefree, arrogant attitude was almost insolent in the face of fate. Without realizing it directly, she'd come to admire the Northern arrogance that she'd chided him for before. If she could effect that same confidence...

Tonio stared at her as she sat straight-backed against a tree and fought off her desires. Her hair spilled out of its once tidy bun. A tiny droplet of perspiration trickled down her neck and between her breasts. Her face was moist with the heat, her clothes sticky from the walk up the hot hill.

She tried to unobtrusively pull the damp sleeve of her blouse from her skin so that the small breeze could cool her. "What are you staring at?" She spoke in lilting Italian hoping to draw a compliment from him; though goodness knew why he should with the way she looked.

"You. I've walked you too hard this morning. Are you feeling all right?"

Perspiration dripped down her neck. She unbuttoned her blouse a few buttons, parted the fabric, and fanned herself, inhaling deeply, at the same time throwing her shoulders back to emphasize her bust. It was a girlish trick but effective. Tonio's eyes raked over her, resting a moment too long on the curves she meant to show him. And despite the fact that he remained solemn, she was pleased.

At first, she didn't understand his sudden sober mood, then the implication hit her. He worried that she might be with child, his child.

"You have no reason to worry," she said.

He seemed relieved. He looked away guiltily. "Good."

Embarrassed, she changed the subject. "Look at this land. You don't have to be a farmer's daughter to see that it is worth nothing once the timber is logged. Who would buy such a hot old rock hillside?

"You can't farm it; even the meadows that are already cleared are no good. I fear that my late husband was the only fool big enough to purchase such land! I may be stuck with it for good."

"I wouldn't say worth nothing. Land is always worth something." He rose suddenly and began examining the trees around them.

She watched him, feeling sad that the forest must be logged. Italy's forests had been destroyed long ago, replaced in the south of her homeland with malarial swamps.

Tonio snapped a twig off a tree. "You don't have to rape the wilderness like the old time Italians did to the land of our birth. There are ways to log responsibly, to replace the trees."

He gestured up toward the trees overhead. "Problem is, most of your timber's small. Must have been a forest fire through here less than thirty, thirty-five years ago that burned the forest nearly to the ground.

"If you had the time to give these trees a few more years then you would have yourself a *very* valuable harvest. But you don't have time because you need the money, and because of that." He pointed to a small stand of trees off to their right.

"What?"

"See those trees? The tops of some are already brown, others are brown to the ground, dead—pine blister rust. If you walk up close and examine the bark, you'll see it looks blistered and off color. It'll kill your trees, every last one.

"You're going to have to log those out whether you want to or not or the disease will spread to the rest of the stand. The wood's still good for lumber. A reputable mill will give you a decent price.

"I'll talk to John about hiring a logger to take out the diseased and some of the surrounding trees right away. The sooner, the better. While he's at it, I'll ask him to have them clear the underbrush. It's a breeding ground for the disease. Blister rust only thrives where wild gooseberries grow in conjunction with the pines."

Angelina felt a sudden rush of fear. She believed Mr. Lawlor would get the matter of her ownership straightened out, but now she had the new worry of this tree disease. "And if I don't?"

"The disease spreads and the entire stand becomes infected and dies. The first spark, bolt of lightning, what have you, that touches those and they act like kindling to start one hell of a forest fire, in which case you'll have more to worry about than losing your lumber. Your late husband should have taken care of it long ago, when he noticed the first tree. As it is, you're going to lose most of that stand now."

She looked around at the beautiful forest surrounding them. "Mr. Allessandro must have been very busy at the mine to let his forest get in such bad shape."

"Or his heart was in bad shape and that slowed him down," Tonio observed.

A bad heart could do that, Angelina thought to herself. Or a broken heart. When would Tonio see that he could fix both their hearts with a few simple words? *Will you marry me* would do it.

CHAPTER THIRTEEN

allace in late spring of 1899 was a hotbed of emotion and tension. The Silver Valley was embroiled in a labor dispute waiting to explode. Minor skirmishes had broken out between scabs and union miners, but so far only fists had been involved and no one had been killed. The Bunker Hill and Sullivan Mine still refused to pay union scale wages and the leaders of the Western Federation of Miners were furious. They waged a class war of ever increasing violence fueled by their militant leader, Ed Baker. Baker, who'd been imprisoned for his role in the violence of '92, was cynical about the miners' chances of ever obtaining justice.

Since '92 the Bunker had refused to hire any union labor. Anyone suspected of being a union sympathizer was promptly fired. So a Bunker employee was caught between fear of losing his job and fear of violence at the hands of union members from other mines.

The union was equally leery. New members were carefully scrutinized and only members of longstanding were allowed into meetings.

Angelina grew tired of the talk of violence around town. She had her own concerns, her own worries and plans, and she didn't intend to make the miners' problems her own.

"I had a brilliant idea the other day, May." Angelina sat in the sunny warmth of May's kitchen drinking coffee. "Have I not been a pastry chef in a fine household in Italy? Can I not bake exquisitely? Are the miners not lonely, hungry men? I have decided to sell baked goods to the miners as they come off shift from the mine. The Colonel has agreed to let me use the ovens during the idle times at the hotel.

"Just think—hundreds of hungry men filing out past us in our strategically located stand. They'll buy more cookies than we'll be able to supply. I'm going to go to Jim Burte at the Bunker and see if he can help me get permission from the Bunker management to set up right on the outskirts of their grounds. Or maybe I'll ask Tonio to get permission for me. He's a friend of his. Tonio introduced us on the train."

Angelina continued with her train of thought. "I'll put on my Italian accent and smile just so. I'll flirt but only in an innocent, friendly way. The men love that. We'll sell all the more cookies."

"The Colonel has offered to let us buy supplies through him at wholesale. All he wants for his help is a small percent of the profits. We can't lose."

"We?" May asked distractedly. She focused on something outside the window.

"I thought you'd want to be involved. It's a wonderful way to earn extra money to put into the Hole. I've figured it out. With only a few hours extra work each day we should easily be able to clear three to four dollars profit. The Colonel says we can begin tomorrow—"

"It appears we have company," May said. Someone came up the front walk. She smiled and rose from her chair to greet him at the door. Angelina was staring into her coffee cup, making mental calculations so intently that she didn't notice May get up.

"Hello, May!" Tonio's voice boomed, interrupting her thoughts.

Tonio stood just inside the doorway wearing his typical attire—jeans, white shirt, and his black fringed jacket. Her heart stopped. What was he doing back in town? She had the feeling that this wasn't a chance visit.

"Come on in and have some coffee, Tonio." May poured him a cup before he could answer. She set a box of candy in front of him. "Have a sweet, Tonio. Angelina's secret admirer sent this over just yesterday. Seems he's made it his goal in life to keep us in sugar."

Angelina blushed. All the gifts this secret admirer sent made her uncomfortable. She never touched the candy, giving it away to neighborhood children when she could. The attention from an unknown man seemed almost sinister, like she was being watched from afar. It had her looking over her shoulder when she should have felt safe. She mentioned none of this to Tonio.

Tonio cast her a quick look and took a seat at the table, his expression unreadable. "If that's his only intent, it seems honorable enough."

Angelina changed the subject. "What interrupts your work and brings you to town?" Angelina took a sip of her tepid coffee, trying to sound casual while her heart tripped over the fact that Tonio sat across from her.

"I get time off for good behavior now and again. And it's in my best interests to come to town from time to time and catch up on the news."

"Speaking of news, Angelina and I are thinking of starting a new business," May said. "We're going into the baking business." May winked at Angelina. "We're trying to put up as much money as possible before war breaks out here in the valley and work will be hard to come by."

"Yes, Tonio, exactly that," Angelina said. "I've had the best idea. I'm going to sell cookies to the miners." She quickly outlined her plan for him. "Now if you'll just go to your friend Jim and get permission for me to sell at the Bunker—"

"Absolutely not!" He fairly roared. "The Bunker is the last place I want you to be. The Bunker is a powder keg waiting to be lit. I forbid you to go!"

His vehemence stunned Angelina. "Forbid me? You can't forbid me. What gives you the right to forbid me?"

"I'm your chaperone."

"Not anymore."

"You're a single woman again. Nonna Gia and your family would expect that I would resume my duties and look out for your welfare."

"No! I'm not going to let you be an overbearing male and tell me what to do. This is the United States of America and I can do what I want!" She set her jaw and looked at him calmly. "I'm staying."

"A week or two with May and she's turned into a cussed suffragette already," Tonio mumbled.

"You can mumble all you want, but I'm not leaving."

"Fine, stay. But stay away from the mines. Get the Colonel to sell your damned cookies at the hotel then, but stay out of the mines."

"Why should I? Do you know something I don't?"

He stood to face her. "Evidently."

"Maybe you're jealous." She tried to tease. "Worried that now that I'm free I'll take up with some handsome miner?"

He gave her a sardonic grin. "I'm leaving now. But if I find out you've been up at the Bunker, I'll be back to turn your shapely fanny over my knee and give it a good paddling." He pointed at May. "You, too, stay away." As he opened the door and stood in the door-way, her next words assaulted him.

"You just try it, Antonio Domani! You pride yourself on being an American, but you're becoming an old Italian bore! The minute I start asserting my rights and using my own brain to better myself you revert to your dominant male behavior," she called out after him.

He stopped in his tracks and to her amazement smiled as he turned to look at her. "Italian bore?" He was suddenly clearly amused at the irony of the situation. For reasons she couldn't understand he was pleased with her.

"What else would you call it?"

"All right, my American lass. I'll talk to Jim for you. But you must promise me that if you ever get a warning about trouble at the mine, you'll stay away until things have cooled off."

She nodded as he disappeared out the door and down the front walk, chuckling to himself as he went. He was still laughing softly as she watched him disappear down the tree-lined street.

The kitchen at the Fuller was hot and sticky by midday. Angelina came in early to do the baking and was glad to be finished before the real heat of the day struck. She hung up her damp apron, and wiped the perspiration from her brow with her sleeve. May had arrived to replace her and she'd finished the dishes and was ready to leave. This was the part of the day she dreaded. That horrible Clell hung around too often waiting for her, just outside the door, pestering her to have dinner with him or take a stroll, making deliberate innuendos. She had not been able to discourage him.

On this particular afternoon, she checked out the windows to make sure he wasn't around before stepping out into the bright sunshine. But she hadn't gone two steps when he appeared from the bank across the street, evidently wise to her plan to avoid him.

"Angelina." He tipped his hat, which only gave her a better view of the lust in his eyes. "It is a *pleasure* to see you."

She nodded curtly and kept walking. He joined stride with her.

"Lovely day."

She nodded, still walking.

"Lovely day to have dinner with me," he added.

"I might say, 'Too lovely a day to have dinner with you, Mr. Clell.' I thought I had made my wishes known before. I do not desire your attentions."

He darted in front of her, blocking her path. "Oh, come now, Angelina. I make a very fine suitor. I assume you've enjoyed the gifts I've been sending you. See how attentive I can be?"

"They're from you? I should have known. No other man would insult me with such notes." She tried to get past him again.

He grabbed her arm. "I wouldn't throw my offer back so quickly if I were you." He paused for effect, to heighten the threat in his tone. "Tonio's obviously deserted you. A woman as pretty as you, in a town like this, would do well to have a protector. I can offer you that."

Though it stung, she ignored his jibe about Tonio. "I can protect myself, thank you."

His gaze raked over her. "I can protect you better and offer you a good time in the bargain. I promise." He spoke with innuendo in his voice that sent a shud-

der of repulsion through her. He ran his hand along her
arm.

She shook him off and glared.

"I'm a powerful man in this town and I get what I
want. What I want right now is you." He reached out
and stroked her cheek. "Those who defy me usually re-
gret it."

Angelina's heart raced with fear as she pulled away.
"Is that a threat, Mr. Clell?"

"That's a promise."

Fortunately, Charley Nokes stepped out of the
Fuller and headed their direction, calling out a greeting.

Clell backed off. "I will have you. That's a certain-
ty." He tipped his hat and walked off with an angry me-
ter to his gait.

Nokes' gaze flitted between her and Clell. "Giving
you a bad time, Mrs. Allessandro?"

She nodded. She liked Nokes. He was Tonio's friend.

"Let me walk you home," he said.

"I'd be grateful."

He offered her his arm and began an amiable banter,
but she noticed he kept his gun hand at ready.

Pale yellow washed the kitchen as the sun prepared
to drop out of sight over the western horizon. It was
nearly eight o'clock at night. Angelina still wasn't used
to the long spring days in Idaho. She sat at the table
with the day's take neatly stacked in front of her. She'd
finished logging them in her accounting ledger and her
eyes shone with satisfaction, as they always did when

she counted her earnings. "We did good today, May. We cleared just over three-fifty."

"Would that it was three hundred and fifty," May said.

Angelina was optimistic. "Just think, May. We made as much as a union scale miner makes in a day. And we didn't have to get all dirty and grimy, breaking our backs in another man's mine to do it."

The images of the miners emerging from their shifts flooded Angelina's mind. Each day, with the precision of an army in drill, the shifts at the mine changed. The day shift emerged like moles, covered with grime and sweat, squinting into the sun, as the second shift made their way up the gulch and climbed the hill to the mine.

There was only one route; the narrow gulch precluded any other. Tonio had commented that it would be easy enough for the union to blockade it, should violence erupt. But Angelina counted it a blessing. The men had to pass by her with her baskets of freshly baked treats.

Angelina was drawn to the Bunker as it was by far the largest mine in the region and hence employed the largest number of men. Bunker management bragged about the two hundred and fifty thousand dollar concentrator, the largest and most expensive one in the world. Angelina couldn't begin to imagine a sum of money as large as that.

For now she was content with the profits her cookies and baked goods brought. Her cookies sold so quickly that she gave up trying to sell at any of the other sizable mines in the area. She went only once a day

at shift change and in minutes quickly sold out her
stock.

She'd never imagined it would be so easy. It had not
been easy the first day. The sight of the masses of filthy
men had been overwhelming. Each day when she came
home it took time for the images of soot stained fingers
dropping coins into her hand to recede. Some of the
hands were cracked and bleeding, others stained and
smelling strongly of leather. The more bold men took
the opportunity to touch her hand as they dropped a
coin in her palm.

She smiled at each man and offered a small encouragement, always thanking him for his business. She
used her foreign accent on them to such effect that
they were overwhelmed by her charm. After a few days
she suspected that they bought cookies almost more for
her smiles and small flirtations than for her culinary
talents. That fact didn't bother her at all. She brought
a small bit of sunshine to their day she reasoned.

"You need a ride to the mine tomorrow, Angelina?"
Al Hall asked as he sat sipping his evening coffee.
May's husband was as quiet and unassuming as May
was colorful and outgoing. He ran his train by the
Bunker several times a day and often allowed Angelina
to hitch a ride. It saved on passenger fare.

Angelina was about to reply when the kitchen door
swung open. Al waved Tonio in. He had a duffel bag
slung over his shoulder. "Al, May, Angelina." He nodded at each one in turn. "You don't mind if I take up
residence in the small room upstairs do you?" he asked
as May brought him a cup of coffee.

"'Course not, Tonio," May said. "But I thought you'd be working up at the Hole. What brings you down?"

"There's rumor of a big strike that is to take place soon. Heard gossip that nearly two hundred men will be walking out. Could be a dangerous time."

"It'd be safer up at the Hole then, Tonio."

"It would be for some of us." Angelina could feel his eyes on her. "How goes the cookie business? I've just come from the Fuller House where I was treated to one of your baked goods. So you're selling to the Colonel now as well?"

May interrupted before Angelina could answer. "It was a stroke of genius, Angelina's genius. We bake a few extra for the Colonel in exchange for the use of his ovens and we call them the famous Fuller House cookies. It's advertising for him and us. Our cookies are selling like hotcakes, but I do believe the suitors Angelina is reeling in are surpassing our sales."

"So Charley Nokes tells me."

"Could be that an interested man ought to put his bid in for Angelina's time before it gets all booked up or permanently taken," May said. When Tonio didn't answer she continued. "I was talking to you, Mister Tonio."

He smiled. "I wasn't aware that I was an interested man."

"And I wasn't aware that I would take him for a suitor," Angelina shot back.

May nudged Al, motioning for him to leave the room with her. "I think it's time we turned in," she said, her motive for leaving the room all too obvious. Tonio stopped them.

"I was hoping to have a word alone with Al."

May shrugged and the two men left the room, retreating to the parlor where they could be heard speaking in urgent, hushed tones.

May spoke as if reading Angelina's thoughts. "He's got something on his mind. Don't worry; he'll come around one of these days."

Angelina nodded but she wasn't so sure.

Later that night Angelina rose from her bed and tiptoed out into the hall. She couldn't sleep thinking of Tonio sleeping in the room next to hers, his breathing deep and even, his body warm and hard. She shuddered remembering the delight of sleeping next to him on the train ride west. It was an image she should have banished.

Tonio's room was empty. Voices rose from the living room. He and Al were still up discussing something with heated interest. Something about dynamite and concentrators and the Frisco Mill.

"They store enough powder at the Frisco to blow up the whole Valley," Tonio was saying. "And it's unguarded, there for the taking. I could make toothpicks out of their concentrator with less."

Al mumbled something in return. Angelina strained to hear his reply. Tonio was talking again. "Baker wanted an armed labor force and that's what he's got, a bloody army. The Bunker may give in and pay scale, but they'll never recognize the union."

Mining matters! That's all he thinks about, Angelina thought with disgust. Well, at least it wasn't other women. She tiptoed back to bed. She needed to do something to get his attention, but what? She fell asleep wondering and scheming.

Angelina was up and in the kitchen early the next morning banging pans around as she prepared to cook one of those big American breakfasts Tonio loved. The clatter woke May up.

"Aren't you up with the chickens!" May's voice startled her. "I thought you didn't go in for big breakfasts?"

"I thought I'd give you a break and cook for the men, May."

"What men?"

"Al and Tonio."

"They aren't here. They left already."

"Already? Where would they be going so early?"

"Al had an early run to make and Tonio said he had errands to run."

"Errands? What kind of errands could he have so early?" Couldn't the man stay home and let her pamper him for one morning? How was she supposed to woo him into wedded bliss if he kept running off?

"Don't know. Tonio's business is his own. You ought to know that by now."

Angelina put the pans away. May never ate much breakfast. "May, I need the kitchen today, do you mind?"

"Not at all. I suppose you'd like Al and me to eat out at the hotel."

Angelina smiled. "You're quick, May."

"Not really. The way to a man's heart is through his stomach, am I right?"

"Be here for dinner, but if you could take an evening stroll before dessert? I don't want to be too obvious."

"Say no more." May headed back to bed.

Tonio wasn't back for dinner. His loss, Angelina thought as she wiped the last dish dry and stacked it in the cupboard. And after all of the work she'd done! The back door slammed open and shut. She turned to find him standing behind her just inside the doorway, an appraising look on his face.

"It appears I've missed dinner."

She leaned back against the sink, dish towel still in hand, and faced him defiantly. "Yes. I hope you had the sense to have a meal elsewhere."

She turned back to the sink. Why couldn't she be nice to him like her mama had taught her? Men fell in love with nice women, not shrews. "It's a shame you missed it. It was my turn to cook." She heard him re-move his jacket and toss it over a chair back. "My meals are always excellent."

"Then it would seem that a man couldn't lose around here. May is a very fine cook herself. I'll have to remember to be home in time for dinner tomorrow. Where are May and Al?"

"Walking off their meal." She softened and put on a delicate smile as she turned to face him. She caught him off guard. There in his eyes was the gentle, long-ing look that so confused and enraptured her. It was gone in an instant as always, but it left her encouraged.

"I saved you some dessert. Let me get you some cof-fee to go with it."

"No, Angel, I need something stronger than coffee tonight." He reached into his coat hanging on the chair and pulled a flask of rum from the pocket. "Get two glasses and join me."

"Ladies never drink anything stronger than wine." She set two shot glasses, one full of water, two plates, two forks, and a small platter of chocolate covered pas-tries in front of him and then sat in the place next to him at the table.

"*Profiterole!*" His tone was appreciative. "You must have spent all day in the kitchen. Did you even go to the Bunker today?"

"Yes, certainly. But business wasn't good. There were little yellow notices posted all over town encour-aging the men to join the union. *Immediately,* the fly-ers said. Many of the men seemed upset by them."

Tonio's look was suddenly dark. "Yes, I saw them. Be careful, Angel. Be very careful." Then he reached over and drank the water in a single swallow.

"Hey! That was mine!"

He smiled wickedly as he poured two glasses of rum. "I never drink alone. Bottoms up!" He finished his and poured another. Angelina didn't lift her glass.

"You've made my favorite dessert." He was scooping a pile of the tiny puffs onto his plate. "Did you know?" He put his fork down and reached out and took her hand in his, then gently pressed her glass into it. "Drink with me. Just one drink. It's good."

She looked uncertain.

"You're in a dark mood tonight, Tonio. Wanting others to drink with you."

"We're in dark times, Angel."

"Has something happened?" Angelina knew that the tense relations between the union and the Bunker had the partners worried. What would a strike do to the operation of the Hole? Would the inevitable violence spread to small operations such as theirs?

"Something and nothing. Humor me. Drink just one glass and I'll leave you alone."

He persisted. She lifted the glass and downed it all at once; her eyes watered but she refused to sputter or choke. What would one glass matter? It took many drinks to get drunk. He pulled her chair close to his.

"I hope you're not looking for a drunken companion tonight, Tonio." Her head was already beginning to buzz with the alcohol. Rum was much stronger than she supposed. Tonio looked amused as he enjoyed his dessert.

"These are very good, Angelina. Soft and round and creamy." His voice was low and sensuous as he devoured the tiny cream puff pastries filled with custard and drizzled with chocolate. Angelina watched him with wide eyes. He was incredibly handsome and she said so.

"Thank you, Angelina. You've never told me that before. Has the alcohol loosened your tongue?"

"I've only had one drink."

"Then I'm truly flattered."

She smiled back at him. He seemed to enjoy her rapt attention.

He poured her another drink. "To the best baker in the Valley!"

She drank half her shot.

"Perhaps you should have something to eat with that." He offered her a small pastry from between his fingers. She leaned over brazenly and bit into it. The cream filling gushed out as she took a bite and oozed onto his finger. He popped the remaining piece in his mouth and made a show of licking his finger. The last of the light faded, the room went dark.

Angelina's head sang with the effects of the rum. Her inhibitions waned. She offered him a small round *profiterole* from between her fingers. He held her wrist tenderly as he took it in a single bite sucking her fingers in with the pastry and caressing them with his tongue. He sucked her fingers back into his mouth. She flushed as he sucked first one finger and then the next finally turning her hand over and licking her palm, before sealing it with a kiss.

"But you will always bake for me, *coccola*?" He caressed the Italian word. He lifted her wrist to his lips, kissing the pulse that leapt beneath his touch.

Darling! He'd called her darling! Her heart thudded wildly. She stared desperately into his eyes and could find no mocking there. He must be drunk. "For you, yes."

"Do you know what *profiterole* reminds me of?" He turned her chair to face his and pulled her gently to his lap. With one hand he removed the pins that held her bun in place, freeing her hair to tumble wildly over her shoulders. He held her wrist firmly in his other hand. He released it as he circled her waist with his arms and nuzzled into her freshly scented hair to find her ear and whisper softly.

"A woman's bosom. *Profiterole* are exactly like a woman's bosom—soft, creamy, and ever so inviting." He ran his hand under her chin and tilted her face to his.

She leaned into him as his mouth came down on hers. Her head spun with excitement. He stood and pulled her with him, his mouth never leaving hers. She crushed against him thrusting her own tongue boldly into his mouth, her fingers finding their way into his thick dark hair.

He pulled away slightly and cupped her face in his hands. "*Sei la mio coccola. Sei il mio tesoro d'oro belissima. Sono—*"

The kitchen door swung open and the electric lights flashed on. Angelina lurched against Tonio, blinded and confused. A man she didn't recognize stood highlighted in the doorway.

"Tonio. Baker wants to see you right away."

"Tell Baker to teach his henchmen some manners. You ever heard of knocking?"

"Are you coming or not?"

"Not. Baker can wait until morning."

"Mr. Baker insisted I bring you to him immediately." The man pulled his coat back slightly to reveal a revolver.

Tonio remained calm. "Scare tactics don't impress me."

The man didn't move. "Mr. Baker requests your presence, I comply."

Tonio muttered under his breath. "I'm sorry, Angelina. I have to go. Tell May I'll be back late." He grabbed his coat and followed the man, leaving Angelina to stand stunned in the center of the kitchen, shaken and frightened.

"You are my darling," he'd been saying. "You are my beautiful golden treasure. I am—" And he was cut off. I am what? she wondered.

"*Porco cane*!" she uttered under her breath. It was easier to curse than dwell on her fear. Mr. Baker was a pig dog! A very dangerous pig dog if he employed such henchmen. She cleared the dishes, but they shook in her hands. She gave up on washing them, worried she would shatter them as fear for Tonio's safety rattled her nerves. She had to find Al and May. Fortunately, at that moment the back door opened and May and Al appeared.

"One of Ed Baker's men insisted Tonio go with him to see Mr. Baker," Angelina blurted out, explaining the situation and the threat with the gun.

"We know," May said, putting her hand on Angelina's shoulder. "Al and I saw them. Don't worry. Tonio can take care of himself."

Al nodded his agreement. "Ed would be a fool to harm a partner in the Jupiter. We've made sure to keep our noses clean."

"Come. I'll make you a cup of tea. We could all use one." May turned to put a kettle on.

May and Al's calm attitude eased Angelina's worries only so far. She remembered Tonio's warnings of the dangers of the Valley and wished he'd taken his own advice and stayed away.

"Tonio, I don't know what's got you so worked up about this Bunker business," May said.

She, Angelina, and Tonio were seated around her kitchen table the following afternoon. For Angelina's part, she was filled with relief that Tonio had returned unharmed from his meeting with Baker.

"It's not like we're going to be affected much. We already employ only union help and we pay them scale. If there's a strike and our two union men join in, well, we can work without them. It won't slow us down much. Harry will have to go work his share instead of hiring it out and the rest of you fellows just work harder. Business as usual."

Angelina watched the two of them closely. Something was going on beneath the surface that she couldn't quite grasp.

"May, I don't think you realize the scope of the problem. You remember the strike of ninety two."

"Everyone who lived here does. Most of the mines were closed for quite a spell."

Tonio didn't answer directly. He poked at his eggs with his fork. "The Bunker didn't reopen until the men passed around a petition stating that they'd work below scale until market conditions improved."

"And the men have worked in good faith and not broken their end of the bargain." May pounded the table. "They should all join the union, Tonio, and force the Bunker to comply. It's a bunch of pigheaded fools who won't join. The union's goal is to help them out. If everyone belonged we'd give management the what-for."

"The men signed an agreement stating they'd work below scale until two ounces of silver and one hundred pounds of lead sold for six dollars. It hasn't reached that yet. Management hasn't broken their promise either."

May looked annoyed. "I thought you were a union man, Tonio. You know as well as I do that an agreement could have been reached based on the price of lead alone. The Bunker's practically depleted its silver. It's a lead mine now. Even Manager Bradley said so back during the big debate over the free coinage of silver. He came right out and said he was mining lead.

"The Bunker's increased its daily output by nearly $1650 dollars while increasing payroll by only two to three hundred dollars per day. They can afford to pay. All the other mines do."

"Even still, Bunker management has not broken their end of the agreement."

"Not yet but I've heard it said that the managers don't intend to keep their promises if prices do rise."

"You've been talking to Baker."

"I've been reading the papers. It's you who's been to see Baker."

Tonio stared thoughtfully out the window. "You'll remember there was violence in ninety two."

"That shouldn't concern us. A small operation like ours, why would we be a target?"

From where she sat Angelina couldn't see Tonio's face, but May could. "Could be we have something they want," he said.

May's mouth dropped open in dismay as understanding dawned. "No, Tonio! Ed Baker is our friend. Why he's courting Harry's sister, Eleanor! Besides, we all support the union."

"But how far will we go with our support?"

"Maybe it won't come to that."

"It's coming, May. And soon. The union's asked Manager Burbidge for two concessions. He may increase wages to scale, but he'll never recognize the union."

May was still staring hard at Tonio when Angelina chimed in. "What do they want, Tonio? Surely it can't be much. Let's just give them—"

May silenced her with a look.

"You'll do what's right, Tonio," May said. Tonio pushed his plate back and rose to leave. May patted him on the arm. As he reached the door he turned back to look at Angelina.

"Stay away from the mines, Angel. It's no place for a woman. It's no place for anyone." He grabbed his coat and disappeared out the door.

CHAPTER FOURTEEN

Tonio hung his black fringed jacket over the chair back and stood gazing out the window to the bustle of Cedar Street below. The temporary offices of the Western Federation of Miners occupied the second floor of the building, above the offices of one of the few lawyers in town. Sparsely furnished, the room had all the necessities—desk, chairs, table, bulletin board. Baker was late.

Probably intentionally, Tonio thought. Baker liked the element of control. Everything was a power game with him. The door opened and Ed Baker strolled in.

"Good morning, Tonio. Have a seat." Nearly forty, Ed Baker was a tall, slender man with a receding hairline and a conservative mustache. His appearance belied nothing of his radical nature. Born in County

Donegal, he spoke with the slightest of Irish brogues. He had lived in the States for nearly twenty years.

"I prefer to stand, Ed."

Baker nodded. "Coming to my meeting on short notice the other night proved your loyalty to the cause, even if you were slow to leave your lady friend. Have you considered my proposal?"

"Yes."

The two men stared at each other coldly.

"Good, then I'll make the final arrangements. We have not always been pleased with your association with the Bunker management, the likes of Jim Burte. But now it may prove useful to our purposes."

Baker's personal assistant, Clell, closed the door as the meeting between the two continued. He sat at a small desk in the adjoining room doing nothing more than eavesdropping and waiting for his boss's next instructions, so Tonio imagined.

"Bunker Hill management has not been listening to us." Baker swiveled in his chair. "The time has come to get their attention. Blowing up something near and dear to them ought to do the trick. You're the best damned explosives guy in region. If anyone can do the job for us, you can."

"I sympathize with the union's plight." Tonio had to step carefully with his words. A trip of the tongue could set Baker off. "You know that, Baker. That's part of the reason I left the Bunker and went into business for myself. Me, and the gang at the Hole, treat our men with respect. We pay a fair wage and look after safety concerns. Half the time we're down the hole ourselves.

We're miners and mine owners. Surely you can appreciate the bind that puts us in?

"We don't want any trouble. We've decided to remain neutral in this fight for the sake of our business, as well as to preserve Harry and H.L.'s political careers."

Tonio hoped that Baker's friendship with Harry and the other Days would allow him to respect Tonio's decision and not take it personally. No one wanted to experience Baker's wrath.

"I can't get involved without jeopardizing our own concerns. You'll have to find someone else."

Tonio stood. By refusing the task, he'd put himself on dangerous ground, but he wasn't going to do anything criminal. He used his skill to mine legitimately, not destroy other people's property.

Without spinning around to look at him, Baker called out for his assistant. "Clell! Show Mr. Domani out."

Baker faced the windows. He looked back over his shoulder as Tonio left. "Make no mistake. It's still war."

Small and wiry, Clell was not the kind of bouncer one would expect the union leader to employ, except that every ounce of him was muscle. Tonio had never liked him. He liked him less now. Clell's small eyes leapt with malice as he showed Tonio the door.

He leaned close and looked up at the much taller Tonio. "Watch your backside. A word of the plan leaks out..." He smiled significantly as he opened the door and stepped back to allow Tonio to pass by.

Tonio stepped out into the street and the cool morning air, shivering slightly as he left the warmth of the building. "Bastard!" he said under his breath.

He doubted Baker knew of his assistant's violent nature. Baker was an honest man as far as he could tell, radical only where laborers' rights were concerned.

Angelina was about to turn the corner off Cedar Street when she spotted Tonio coming out of a building farther up the street. He stood in his shirtsleeves on the boardwalk for a moment, then suddenly turned to reenter the building he'd just emerged from. He should have worn a coat. It was too chilly to be out without a coat, though the day held the promise of warmth.

"Tonio!" She wanted to catch him before he got away. He turned in her direction. "Tonio!" She was breathless with excitement as she approached him. "What a beautiful day, don't you think? Look at the lilacs, they'll be blooming soon."

"Angelina, what are you doing here? Shouldn't you be locked in the kitchen baking at this time of day?" He looked genuinely pleased to see her.

She took his arm and smiled. "I've just come from the Colonel's. Good news, Tonio! The Colonel wants to start a baking business and I'm going to be his partner. I'll be doing all the baking. We'll be selling only exotic, fancy confections. My talent is being wasted on cookies. That's what the Colonel thinks."

Tonio leaned close to her and whispered in her ear. "I think so, too."

She ignored the pleasing innuendo in his tone. "He thinks he can sell them to fancy restaurants and rich people as far away as Spokane. The Colonel has connections." She sighed. "Connections I don't have on my own."

"Does this mean you won't be up at the mine selling them anymore?"

"I hope not as often. I don't like the mines." She took his arm playfully. "Come, Tonio. Let me buy you a cup of coffee to celebrate. You look like you could use some warming up."

"Indeed I could, Angel. But I have a better idea. Why don't I take you out to dinner this evening? That would be a real celebration."

"I'd love that, Tonio." His offer sent her heart pattering. "But why not do both?"

"I have business to attend to right now. I'll be back at the house around seven to pick you up."

"Are you courting me then?"

He looked at her oddly. "Courting so soon after being widowed? I thought you were turning down all suitors."

"I'm being selective."

"Well then, if you can survive the scandal, yes, I am courting."

"See you at seven, Tonio." She patted his arm, and turned towards home, giving her skirt a flirtatious flip as she did so.

The dining room of the Fuller House twinkled with candlelight and white linen tablecloths. The dim elec-

tric lights created an intimate atmosphere. Tonio and
Angelina were led to a quiet table away from the kitch-
en. Tonio held her chair as she was seated. "Two glasses of wine. Something dry and light," he instructed the
waiter.

Bright red tulips closed in tight bud decorated each
table. Angelina set her small purse on the chair next to
her. She wore her green day suit, hoping to impress
Tonio.

"Wine?" she said. "Shall I dare be so scandalous? An
American woman wouldn't."

"But it would be perfectly acceptable for an Italian
girl."

"Is that what I am, Tonio? I don't feel like I am so
much anymore."

He reached out and took her hand across the table.
"I'd say you weren't a girl anymore at all."

She smiled. "You know, we could eat May's food at
home."

He put a finger to his lips. "Shh. This is a celebration. The Fuller is the nicest place in town. Someday
I'll take you to Spokane and we can eat in real splendor."

The waiter arrived to take their order and disappeared quietly. They exchanged pleasantries and chatted about her new partnership with the Colonel, but
Angelina had the sense that his thoughts were elsewhere, his attention diverted. He sat opposite the door,
a position that allowed him to scrutinize people as they
came and went and his gaze never strayed far from it.

He acted different than usual. She felt that he studied her, looking for something, weighing his words carefully, as if he wanted to make a confession. They had finished their dinner and were being served dessert when a friend of Tonio's interrupted them.

"Isn't this a cozy setting?"

"Hello, Nokes," Tonio said.

Nokes moved around the table to look at Angelina. "So nice to see you again, *Signora* Allessandro."

Charley Nokes was a regular at the Fuller House. Charley frequently hung out by the kitchen, watching her work and snitching samples. She supposed he could be described as handsome in a pale way. Charley liked to flirt with her, with anyone. She enjoyed sparring with him but nothing more. He sometimes complained to her that Tonio had claimed her before he'd even had a chance with her. She'd told him that he was not her type of man, which did not seem to dampen his spirits greatly.

Uninvited, Charley pulled up a chair and sat down next to her. "I hear this dog has taken up residence with the Halls, the same home that you are staying in *Signora.*"

"It was his home first, Mr. Nokes. It is I who intruded on his territory."

"Nokes thinks he saw you first, Angelina."

"Mr. Nokes, Tonio and I are old friends. We met in New York."

Nokes smiled. "The lady defends you."

"She has good taste."

Nokes summoned the waiter. "I think I'll join you and have dessert."

He was about to order when Angelina interrupted him. "Mr. Nokes would like coffee and sweet biscuits, the currant studded ones that I made this afternoon," she said. "They are the very best ones." She winked at Nokes. "I know they are your favorite so I saved you a few."

Nokes returned her wink. "You see how she looks out for me, Tonio? You better watch yourself or I might just steal her away yet."

They chatted for a moment until Nokes' dessert arrived.

"I hear there's going to be a big union meeting the twenty fifth," Nokes said. "They'll probably call a strike. They're asking all the union brothers to go to the Bunker in a show of support."

Angelina interrupted before Tonio could respond. "If you men are about to talk mining, I will have to insist that Tonio take me home now. I am in no mood to hear another word about mining difficulties. This is a celebration, Mr. Nokes."

Something in the distance caught Tonio's attention. Angelina turned to look but saw nothing. He rose and pulled her chair out for her.

"Come, Angelina. I think you're right. It's time to take you home." Confused, she stood up.

Tonio looked at Nokes as he rose. "You have a winning way with the ladies, Nokes." He threw some money on the table. "Angelina, wait for me at the cloakroom. I need to talk to Nokes."

Tonio joined her just minutes after she retrieved her cloak. They walked back to the Halls' in silence, taking a circuitous route that led them under every streetlight in town. Tonio seemed uneasy and on guard. Neither spoke. Finally, as they arrived at the front walk, Angelina couldn't stand the silence. "Thank you for dinner, Tonio."

"Yes, very nice. Poor old Charley, he needs to go home and marry a socialite who'll keep him in his place. He's just play mining out here." He hardly seemed aware of her as he spoke. He'd been distracted since Mr. Nokes had interrupted them.

They stopped in front of the door. As Angelina reached for the knob, Tonio grabbed her hand to stop her. "I'm not going in, Angelina."

She looked at him, puzzled. "Don't tell me you have more mysterious business to attend to at this time of night."

"No, I'm heading back to Burke."

"Now? This late in the evening? It can't wait until morning?"

"No."

She stared at him. "Tonio, are you in trouble? Please tell me." She reached up and stroked his face. A stiff stubble met her fingertips. She wanted to run her hands over his entire body. "Tonio, please! You can trust me."

"Women! You like to imagine the worst." He took her chin in his hand. "Angel, I'm fine. I've neglected the Hole and I need to get back to work. That's all."

His eyes were dark, unreadable. She closed her eyes for a moment and looked down trying to steady her emotions. He was hiding something. When she looked back up he was studying her intently. Without thinking she reached up and kissed him, throwing her arms around him and pressing tightly against him. He kissed her back deeply and fully, but for the first time he was gentlemanly and respectful. His hands didn't wander. He pulled back.

"Tonio, I—"

"Angelina, right now you can't afford to be involved with me. I was careless in taking you out in public tonight."

"I knew it! You're lying! You are involved in something!"

"Yes, I'm involved in something that you don't understand and the less you know about it the better. It doesn't concern you. I've foolishly put you in danger. I didn't realize how much until tonight. If certain people believe we care for each other—"

"But I do care for you, Tonio! And you care for me, you must!"

"Angelina, I want you to go into the house and lock the door behind you. Do you understand me?"

She nodded.

"Then go straight to bed. Grab my stiletto and keep it beside you. I should have thought ahead and taught you to shoot."

She stared at him. "Tonio, what is—"

"I'm going to Burke immediately to guard the Hole. Damn that weasel Clell! He knows I can't be in two places at once."

"Tonio?" Tonio's cautious attitude frightened her.

He grabbed her by the shoulders. "Listen, Angelina, I don't want to leave you, but I have to get back to the Hole and warn Gus to post guards. The union's planning trouble any day now. Baker's mad as hell. He wanted me—" He stopped himself.

"Clell, Baker's goon, you remember him from the train?"

She nodded affirmation.

"He's been following me all day. He showed up while we were at the Fuller tonight and sent a very clear message. He wanted me to know he was there.

"Clell has a vendetta against me. For too long I was more in Baker's favor than he was. Call it a kind of rivalry.

"Angelina, I don't want you to go anywhere near that asshole. He's had his eye on you since he first saw you on the train. If I flinch in this game we're playing, he'll have all the excuse he needs to go after you. And believe me, he's dangerous. The ladies at the Lux don't even..."

Although she tried to look brave, she must have looked scared.

"I did something this morning that set him off. Now he's forcing me to choose which front I'm going to protect. I'm betting he'll follow me if I head to the Hole. He'll see where he thinks my priority is and leave you alone. You should be safe with May and Al."

"How long will you be there? When will you be back?"

"I don't know. Angelina, promise me that until I return you won't go near the mines. Any of them. I don't want you near the railroad either. And no going out after dark. Not unless Al and May are with you." He grabbed her by both arms. "Promise!"

"I promise."

He looked relieved. "Truthfully?"

"Yes. I have no reason to go either place now."

"Will you consider going back to New York?"

"No! Tonio, what's going on?"

"I'm leaving now, Angel." Suddenly he pulled her close, burying his face in the top of her hair. He let her go and opened the door, guiding her in by her arm.

"Tonio, whatever it is, be careful."

"Goodnight, Angel."

Once inside Angelina leaned against the door, shaking uncontrollably. "Tonio, what have you done?" She listened as his footfalls receded into the distance.

On April 25th, the Western Federation of Miners held a secret session at the heart of its camp in Wardner. At five thirty, the men filed out three abreast. Headed by President Baker, the 400 men formed a winding line nearly 1000 feet long. They wound their way up the hill to the Bunker Hill Mine where they demanded a chance to talk to the workers. Superintendent Burch complied. Cheers resounded each time a Bunker employee walked over to join the union.

Tensions escalated on the twenty-sixth, and shots were fired. After an all-night initiation session the union leaders decided to meet the Bunker dayshift as they came off duty. Enroute up the hill they stopped a quarter of a mile below the mine at the Last Chance Mill where they encountered a group of nightshift workers on their way to work. Baker encouraged them to join the union, but not one would. Several of the men tried to push through the union crowd but were turned back after members told them that the union did not mean for them to work.

T.S. Murray, a young smooth-faced union leader, emerged from the crowd. "Walk down this hill inside of four minutes or go down some other way!" He drew his watch and looked at the second hand. President Baker had his hand on a pistol but did not draw it. The men retreated.

In a futile attempt to defuse the tension, the Bunker Hill management capitulated and agreed to raise wages to union scale, but they held firm in their refusal to recognize the union. The union called a full-fledged strike.

In retaliation, the Bunker Hill posted no trespassing signs on their property and armed a small contingency of loyal employees as guards. Sheriff Young was summoned from Wallace to Wardner. Local officials hoped that the presence of the local law enforcement would discourage any illegal or violent activity.

May read aloud from the newspaper as she and Angelina prepared to leave for work.

"*It is absolutely and finally settled that the Bunker Hill and Sullivan Company will never recognize the miner's union, Frederick Burbidge, resident manager of the company, said upon his return from Spokane.*

"*Armed union men have even stopped butchers' and grocers' wagons, preventing them from taking supplies for the men and their families. Teams hauling freight have been stopped and those having goods for the Bunker Hill have been turned back by the strikers and ordered out of town. Despite all this we are keeping right at work, and we shall tie up the mine rather than recognize the union.*"

"What difference do the Bunker's troubles make to us, May? Everyone is so concerned about them, but the Bunker's miles away. It's not our fight." Angelina tied a scarf over her head to keep her hair in place for the walk to the hotel. May shot her a look that said she didn't know what she didn't know.

"Miners are miners and they all belong to the same union. You can bet our boys here in Wallace will be involved in helping their brothers out. There'll be trouble and it'll affect us. If it comes to blows, and it will if the Bunker doesn't recognize the union, our economy will be affected as well. The men will strike in the local mines and without money they won't be coming to the Fuller House."

"The Colonel can weather the tide." Angelina felt confident of the Colonel's business skill. "We're going to be doing a lot of business in Spokane. Anyway, why worry personally, May? Al works for the railroad and

Tonio is up at the Hole. You've said it before that it won't affect the Hole, even if our men walk out."

She wanted reassurance. Tonio had her looking over her shoulder.

"I wouldn't be too sure."

"You're worried about Tonio, too." Angelina studied her closely.

"Maybe, but Tonio can take care of himself."

"May, what's going on? No one will tell me anything."

"Maybe that's because you've got no need to know. Now, come on. We'll be late, and the Colonel won't like that. The breakfast crowd will be waiting."

Angelina grabbed her spring jacket on the way out the door. She was going to find out. They could be sure of that.

For two days it was quiet in the Silver Valley. Not a single incident of violence erupted. Work at the Bunker went on with a limited crew. Some attributed it to Sheriff Young's presence in Wardner, others thought the union had given up, but the majority believed that it was the calm before the blow up. The union was up to something, something big that took time to plan.

Angelina felt the uneasiness in town as keenly as anyone. The men who came to the Fuller House were quiet and subdued. They didn't joke and flirt as usual. People were cautious and exceedingly polite, as if a misplaced word would set the violence in motion again. Angelina overheard snatches of conversation on the street and at the hotel. Tonio's name was mentioned in hushed tones. Many times she walked up on a conversation only to have the participants still abruptly and look embarrassed or cover by suddenly being very interested in the weather.

Finally she could take it no longer. There was trouble coming and Tonio was directly involved. Whatever he was up to, she had to stop him. She had the sinking feeling that it had something to do with blowing something up. More than once she'd heard the men mention explosives. She remembered clearly the excited look in his eyes the day he'd set the charge in the Hole. She could almost still feel his heart thumping as he'd pressed her against him. She had to stop him. She prayed she'd be in time.

Angelina rose early the morning of the twenty-ninth, pacing and planning. She dressed with care and primped before the mirror. Her heart fluttered. She looked pretty but confident. Like a person to be taken seriously or at least she hoped. She wasn't sure whether to charm Tonio out of his plans with feminine wiles or to try and meet him as an equal and use reason on him. She was at a disadvantage not knowing exactly what his plans were. Should she bluff?

Al was scheduled to take the train to Burke and she intended to go with him. She would have to think on her feet when she met up with Tonio. May was already at work at the hotel by the time Angelina came downstairs and approached Al. May would never have permitted her to go to Burke, but Al was a soft touch. He readily agreed to take her along.

"I'm running a passenger car today, Angelina."

"That's nice, Al."

"So, you going to see your beau?"

"Al, you're a sentimental fool," she teased. The quiet man just smiled.

"May won't like me taking you."

"I'm worried about him, Al."

He nodded. "Might be you've got reason. Get your things and let's be gone."

She grabbed her purse and jacket. "I'm ready now, Al." She was halfway to the door when she stopped and turned back. "One minute. I've forgotten something."

In the bedroom she opened the bottom bureau drawer and reaching beneath the clothing she pulled out the small leather sheath with a strap. She pulled Tonio's stiletto from its holder and stared at it, shivering. She hated knives. Then she holstered it, and hiking up her skirts, strapped it to her thigh before rejoining Al.

Angelina fumed as the train steamed toward Burke. Al rode up ahead in the engine. She found herself alone in the passenger car with only a dark sense of foreboding for a companion. The town was too quiet. Why weren't there any other passengers?

Al's engine toted a passenger car and nine boxcars. Al let loose with his familiar whistle as they steamed past crossings. The trip to Burke should be quick and uneventful. She stared out the window, unseeing. The day outside was clear and beautiful.

As had been normal for the last few weeks, she felt like an outsider. Something was about to happen, something that she was not privy to. "Hurry, Al, hurry!" she silently willed. "Don't let me be too late!"

Al and his assistant Joe chatted about nothing as the train chugged along towards Burke. Both were experienced men who had run this route hundreds of times before. On a day like this the worst that could be expected would be that an animal would find its way onto the tracks. The tracks were clear and the day looked fine. As they approached Burke and the head of Canyon Creek, Al blew his distinctive whistle call, warning the local merchants to lift their awnings to let the train by. Their whistle was an unintentional battle call. Suddenly, out of nowhere the tracks ahead streamed with masked men wearing white armbands. Joe threw the brakes. "Shit!" he said.

"Looks like we're in for trouble," Al replied calmly. "Joe, go back and see to the safety of our passenger."

In the back Angelina bounced forward as the train lurched to a stop. Before she could grasp the situation, throngs of armed masked men boarded the train. She held back a scream. Everywhere she looked more men scrambled onboard, hundreds of angry unruly men.

"Al!" She rose, prepared to run for the engine.

A man from the crowd blocked her path. "What have we got here? Looks like a sweet little piece to me."

She recognized the insulting voice before she even turned to look at his masked face. *Clell!* Her hope fell.

"Of all the luck! Seems our meeting is inevitable, Angel."

She wanted to slap him for using Tonio's name for her, but he had a gun rammed into her ribs. "I think you'd better come with me."

Tonio heard Al's whistle and headed toward the depot. He needed to talk to his old friend. He'd been worried about Angelina since the night he'd seen Clell looking at her at the Fuller House. He was sure it had been Clell who had followed them home that night. He was stepping out of the stand of trees on the hill where he'd been waiting when he saw the mob. From his vantage point he could see directly into the engine. They had Al at gunpoint. Tonio untied the Hole's work horse from the tree where he'd left him and took off for Wallace. He knew a shortcut that avoided the railroad. He had to tell May about Al and find some way to help.

Clell took Angelina to the engine. Relief washed over her when she saw that Al was safe. His eyes conveyed the same. The apparent leaders of the operation were giving Al instructions.

"You do what we say and no one gets hurt. Not you or the lady. Any sign of resistance and I can't speak for the actions of my men. They're a determined bunch. We've got a mission to accomplish. Are the boxcars empty?"

"Yes," Al replied.

"Good, we were counting on that. You're going to take us to Wardner where we're going to take care of a few business matters. But first we'll be making a few stops to pick up reinforcements and supplies. The plan is nice and simple. When I tell you to, you stop. We'll be running past the Frisco to pick up some powder. Now, let's be on our way, shall we?"

Clell ran the barrel of his pistol along Angelina's cheek in a perverted caress and whispered in her ear. "I don't mind using force to get what I want."

The leader looked their way. "We should put her off."

"She's Tonio's," Clell replied. "I guess we can teach him a thing or two about cooperation."

Tonio took the front steps of the Hall home in one bound. "Angelina! May! Are you home?"

May met him at the door. "Tonio? What are you doing here? The Colonel sent me home when he heard there was trouble brewing. You need to get out of town before you find yourself deep in it."

Tonio shook his head. "Too late for that. The union men hijacked Al's train. I came to warn you. They're headed for the Bunker. I'm on my way there now to help Al."

"How many men, Tonio?" Her face went sheet white.

"Hundreds."

"They have Al and his train?" May sank into a chair. "I had no idea."

"Listen to me. Lock the doors and windows. Stay in the house at all costs." Tonio looked around for Angelina. "Where's Angelina? Angel!" he called to her.

"Angelina isn't here." May's voice was flat, shocked.

"Where is she?"

"With Al. He left me a note. Said he was taking her with him on the train to Burke. She wanted to see you. She was worried."

Tonio's pulse raced with fear and anger. "Damn that woman! I told her to stay away from the railroad."

"She went because of you. You should have told her."

"Close the curtains. Stay put, May. Hear me?" He ran out the door, mounted his horse, and rode hard for the Bunker.

Al argued calmly with the gang leader. "I can't jump off the OR&N tracks onto the Northern Pacific's. We don't know what trains are scheduled. We could meet one head on."

"It's the only way to get to the Bunker. Proceed." His eyes reminded Angelina of steel, hard and unyielding.

"Ordinarily a cornfield meet is bad enough," Al continued. "But after our little detour to the Frisco we're a rolling powder keg. How much powder did we take on?"

"Nearly three thousand pounds." The leader laughed.

"Look I'm responsible for OR&N property and the lives of my crew and passengers. You've loaded me up with upwards of a thousand men."

They'd made several unscheduled stops and at each one they took on several hundred unpaid male passengers.

"We meet a train," Al continued, "and they could all go up."

"We'll chance it." The leader thrust his gun more firmly into Al's ribs. "Take the tracks."

Clell had Angelina on his lap. She looked straight ahead out the window, silently praying and trying to think of other things to stifle the revulsion that his touch stirred up. He stroked her skin with his fingers and ran the gun barrel along her bustline.

"How do you like the feel of cold steel? Wouldn't the feel of a man be so much better? It's time to warm up to me, don't you think?"

She didn't reply. She concentrated on the faces of the people in the streets of the towns they passed. Everywhere she saw looks of horror and shock. Women gathered children and ran screaming for cover. The men onboard the train were angry and menacing, and with their mob mentality, out of control. They yelled and shouted and leered and fired their guns in the air for effect. Other people were hurriedly packing and preparing to leave town. Perhaps to the safety of Spokane or other parts of the Inland Empire.

Clell unbuttoned the top buttons of her dress and smiled at the sight of the top of her soft cleavage. She didn't try to stop him but steeled herself trying to remember how Tonio wielded his knife. Tonio's warning became all the more clear now. She had no doubt as to Clell's intentions. She wouldn't let this disgusting little man violate her. His hand ran the length of her thigh and she stiffened. He mustn't find the knife. It was her only defense. The leader looked over and admonished him just before he reached it.

"Leave the lady alone. I don't need you raping her in front of me. We have a job to do."

Her captor dropped his hand from her leg but whispered for only her to hear, "What'll Tonio do when he finds out I've had his woman?"

Al stared straight ahead, concentrating on the tracks.

"You have the misguided impression that Tonio will care. He won't but I will. I'll kill you if you touch me, you filthy thing."

The man laughed. "Is that any way to talk to an admirer?"

A wave of revulsion washed over her as she thought about the gifts and the notes with their allusions to her becoming his mistress.

"Didn't I warn you I always get what I want?" He stroked her cheek.

Angelina imagined the knife in her hand. She would have to wait for the right opportunity. She couldn't possibly take on all of the armed men present, even the few in the engine. But if the beast got her in private, she could. With her inexperience and his greater strength, it would be a tough battle, but she had the element of surprise on her side. She flexed and relaxed her hand, praying that she would recognize her opportunity to escape.

CHAPTER FIFTEEN

Tonio arrived just before the train to find the mine depot deserted. The Bunker had evidently been warned and the staff had retreated without a fight. Wise men. To try to fight the mob would have been futile.

Tonio scanned the train, hoping Angelina had gotten off before the men boarded in Burke. Then he saw her. The green of her dress stood out like a bright spring bud against the drab colors of the men. Clell held her captive in the engine along with Al. Before the train had slowed to a stop, a contingency of men streamed off and up the hill.

One of them grabbed Tonio's arm and pulled him along. "Tonio! You're here! Good news. The explosion's sure to be a success now."

Tonio nodded. "Where are you headed?"

The man looked confused. Probably wondering why Tonio didn't know the plan.

"We're being sent ahead as pickets to see if the mine is abandoned." He tossed Tonio a white piece of cloth. "You forgot your arm band, and shouldn't you of all people be masked?"

"What difference would a mask make?" Tonio coolly played along as he tied his armband on. "My reputation is well spread."

The man laughed. "I bet you can hardly wait for the excitement to begin."

"Hardly," Tonio repeated.

"Join us and have the further honor of securing the mine."

The tide of pickets being sent ahead swept Tonio along. For one brief moment as the tide pushed him off the depot platform, he was able to turn back and look into the engine in time to see Angelina. She turned away before seeing him. He had no choice but to play along and head up the hill with the scouts. Her safety depended on it.

Tonio knew the sequence of events to follow. They were going to blow up the pride of the Bunker Hill Company, its $250,000 concentrator. Without his expertise, they were forced to do it in broad daylight and with brute force. There would be no finesse today. Baker was right. It was war. A war with nearly a thousand angry, riled men. There was no stopping them from their course of action.

He climbed the hill with the pickets with an exuberance he did not feel. When they reached the mine, his suspicions were confirmed. The Bunker people had indeed been warned and had retreated. The mine was a ghost town. He scanned the surrounding hills, wondering whether the roughly two hundred remaining faithful workers were hiding there, armed and ready to defend the mine, their livelihood.

"The place's deserted! Them cussed scabs deserted!" The man next to him yelled. Without warning he drew his gun and raised it into the air, firing a shot to signal all clear before Tonio could stop him.

"Fool!" Tonio reached for the man's gun arm. "The mob doesn't know—"

Before Tonio could finish his sentence, a volley of gunfire erupted. As Tonio had feared, the mob below wrongly interpreted the shot, thinking that the pickets were under attack. In their frenzy, they fired ahead into the mine area at their own men. The panicked pickets shot back, fueling the battle. Tonio was completely without cover.

As he ducked for the meager cover of a stack of wooden crates, a bullet struck him. His left shoulder seared with burning pain. He fell to the hard packed dirt, cupping his shoulder and suppressing a groan. The first few drops of blood soaked his shirt and wicked out. He cursed beneath his breath. The bleeding wasn't overly heavily. He flexed his arm and wiggled his fingers. *Flesh wound.*

The volley continued. A man Tonio recognized fell to the ground dead. Stupid devil! Tonio couldn't chance running out into the line of fire to recover the body.

The mob streamed up the hill. As suddenly as it had begun, the volley halted. It were as if the mob had recognized its mistake all at once, and acted with one mind. Tonio watched as a group of men carted the dead man down the hill. Tonio struggled to his feet and made it to the shade of a nearby building. He collapsed on the ground and leaned back against the building, clutching his shoulder to stem the bleeding. He didn't want to be discovered and packed off to the hospital. Somehow he had to get back to the depot and help Angelina.

The blood pounded in Angelina's head as she watched a select group of the mob detrain and race up the hill. They whooped and hollered what could only be described as a war cry. The look in the eyes of the men all around her and those that streamed by frightened her beyond measure. Brown, blue, green, or hazel, each eye blazed with the same insanity. They were part of an uncontrollable, unstoppable presence, a force of a magnitude not often seen. The power of their unity was an opiate in which the sanity and reason of the individual was lost.

Moments later she heard what she thought was a blast of dynamite. Almost simultaneously, Al pushed her to the floor and whispered in her ear. "Gunfire. Keep low."

The volley that followed lasted only minutes, but the terror it wrought in her reverberated on and on like an unstoppable echo.

Men streamed off the train in a tide of black and flowed up the hill. Minutes later they carried a bloody corpse back down. The man's eyes were blank, the violent glint absent, and his mouth hung open, slack and limp.

She watched frantically, but no more bodies were retrieved.

The union men worked with feverish enthusiasm unloading the crates of blasting powder stolen from the Frisco. They unloaded carton after carton and shuttled them up the hill with no more concern for the contents than if the explosive powder had been powdered sugar.

Angelina shuddered, remembering the dissertation Tonio had once given her on explosives. One errant spark and they could all be blown up. She didn't know enough about the workings of a mine to know exactly what would cause the most damage to the mine's operations. The crowd she was among would know and would go after it.

What were these men thinking? Surely the law would eventually catch and punish the perpetrators.

A hard, cold gun barrel in her ribs brought her back to reality. "Time to lock you up while we finish our work here," Clell said.

"Swine!"

He dug the barrel deeper into her ribs. "Move."

He grabbed her arm and thrust her out the engine door. Al went for his gun arm but two men pinned him

immediately. Angelina heard the heavy thud of a fist
hitting flesh behind her, then she stumbled onto the
gravel next to the tracks. Clell pulled her to her feet,
then he shoved her toward an abandoned rail car.

Tonio leaned against the wall, clutching his shoulder and breathing deeply to stave off the pain. He had
to act quickly to free Angelina. Soon the shock would
wear off and his shoulder would stiffen. But before he
could act, he needed to stop the bleeding. At dirty towel lay a few feet away next to an overturned toolbox. He
winced, more from the thought of the filth next to his
open wound than from physical pain, as he retrieved it
and wound it around his bleeding shoulder. Then he
stood slowly and made his way down the hill.

The abandoned car smelled of stale hay and live-
stock. Bits of straw clung to her hair as she lay on her
side on the floor where the Clell had thrown her. Her
ears rang and her vision blurred from the beating her
head had taken when she hit the floor. She fought to
stay conscious as the vile man bent over her and tore at
her camisole in an effort to free her breasts. She needed to reach her knife but it was impossibly pinned underneath her. He suddenly knelt back, and confident
that she was too weak to fight back, tossed his gun
aside. She rolled to the other side and shoved her narrow skirt up in an effort to reach the knife holstered
against her thigh.

The man looked surprised and pleased. "Never seen a woman so anxious for it! Don't worry; I'll give it to you nice and hard in a minute."

Hoping to divert his attention away from the knife, she screamed as she looked toward the door, hoping he would think someone was coming. The moment he turned she'd grab the knife. But the ugly beast only laughed as he pulled her face around to him. "Scream all you like, lady. No one's gonna hear, and if they do, they aren't going to care."

"Care to bet on it?" Tonio stood in the doorway.

Angelina tried to roll away from the Clell. He caught her and pinned her beneath him.

Silhouetted in the doorway, Tonio looked calm and in control, almost casual, as if he were addressing a man in a card game, but his eyes were deadly.

"This is none of your business."

"I think it is. It's not really the lady you want, is it Clell? You want revenge on me. Come fight me like a man and leave her alone."

"Oh, I want her badly enough." Clell reached for his discarded gun.

Anticipating his action, Angelina kicked it just out of his reach. She meant to kick it to Tonio, but it spun and slid short of him.

"How do I know it would be a fair fight? How do I know you haven't got a weapon concealed somewhere?"

Tonio held both hands out in front of him in a show of good faith. It may have been a trick of the shadows, but Angelina could've have sworn he was favoring his left shoulder. From her position, she couldn't get a good look at him except to see that his shirt was stained. Something was amiss, but her panicked mind could not process what it saw.

Tonio clenched his teeth and spoke through them, adding to the menace in his voice. "I'm not wearing a holster."

Clell grabbed Angelina's neck in a choke hold. "Too bad. Take a step closer and I strangle her." He spoke to Angelina, "You're going to get me my gun."

Angelina could barely breathe as he tightened his grip. Surely he didn't expect her to move when she felt about to pass out.

Tonio sprung on Clell from the door in a single bound. Startled, Clell momentarily released his grip on her neck. Gagging and gasping for air, Angelina tried to roll away, but she was pinned beneath the wiry little man and now Tonio as well. As she struggled to get free, she brushed up against Tonio and realized that his shirt was crusted with blood.

Clell saw the wound in nearly the same instant and rammed Tonio's wounded shoulder. Angelina rolled up on her left side, exposing her right side from her hip down. Tonio reached to hold his wounded shoulder, but caught a glint of silver from Angelina's movement. A thin shaft of light illuminated the holstered stiletto. He pulled it from the sheath on her thigh.

As Angelina watched, Tonio stabbed Clell in the shoulder with a single, fluid motion. Clell screamed and rolled off Angelina. She scrambled to her feet.

Clell cursed and swore as he clutched his shoulder. As Angelina watched, his blood spurted up through his shirt.

Tonio stood over Clell, his knife poised for another attack. "Angelina, hand me the bastard's revolver!"

She couldn't keep her hands from trembling as she handed it to him.

Tonio pulled back the trigger and took aim, then eyed Angelina coolly as he spoke in soft Italian. "Shall I finish him?"

"No more violence, Tonio. Please."

He turned back to Clell. "The lady requests mercy on your behalf." He pulled Clell to his feet and shoved him toward the door. "Come near her again and I make you this promise—I will kill you. No mercy." He shoved Clell out of the door.

Angelina stood back from the doorway, pressed against the wall, listening to the heavy crunch of his footfalls as he retreated. Tonio stood guard, his revolver cocked and aimed at Clell's back until the man stumbled out of sight.

Then he slumped against the rail car wall.

"Tonio, are you all right?" Fresh blood soaked his shirt. "How did Clell manage to wound you?" Angelina couldn't think. Her head pounded from the impact with the floor, but no louder than her terrified pulse.

"He didn't."

She paid no attention to his answer. "We must get you to the doctor." She bent over him unsteadily in an effort to examine his wound. His eyes were riveted on her, but not on her face. She traced his gaze to her ex-

posed bosom. The heat of her blush surpassed the
warmth of the late April day. She was exposed from her
neck to her waist, her beautiful dress torn beyond re-
pair, her camisole ripped, holding together any modesty by mere threads. Below her waist, her smart green
skirt hung chastely, as if it hadn't been part of the earlier violence.

"Nice to see that your senses aren't all dulled," she
said.

He stood unsteadily, his breathing heavy and pained.
"Don't fall apart now, Angel."

He stripped off his shirt. "Put this on. I wouldn't ordinarily offer a lady a shirt in such condition, but the
situation being what it is..."

She took it and slid her arms into it. As she had finished buttoning it, she saw the small round hole in the
center of the reddish brown stain of his undershirt and
comprehension dawned on her. "Tonio, you've been
shot!"

"Yes." He stood and hefted his stiletto reverently.
"Good woman, carrying my knife with you." There was
no mockery or anger in his words.

He pressed the knife back into her hand. "We have
to get out of here. I'll carry the gun. You take the knife
for defense."

She stared at the blood-covered stiletto in her trembling hand. She couldn't draw her eyes away from the
darkening blood. Her hand shook so violently she barely maintained her hold. Another human's blood—

Tonio's hand covered her in a tight grip. "Don't look
at it. Don't think about it. I've nothing to clean it with

now," he said. "If we hurry, we can escape before the grand finale the union has planned. My horse is tethered just the other side of the depot. The problem is you; you're out of place here."

He quickly outlined his plan. "Don't say anything. Let me do the talking. Stay on my left and cover me. Anyone comes too close, cut him."

Outside the rail car, the sun shone bright and high in the midafternoon sky. It took a moment for her eyes to adjust. Tonio led the way, walking confidently toward the depot with his left arm draped loosely around Angelina's waist. He held her close and slightly in front of him, hiding his wound from those they approached. He laughed and looked lustily at her. The place was nearly deserted; the majority of the men were up on the hill at the mine works.

Only one man called out to them and that was to voice his approval. "Good idea, bringing a woman along to pass the time until the big fireworks."

Angelina turned to the voice. The man was tall, blond, and stocky, as so many of the Scandinavian miners were. His hair receded to the middle of his head and where his original hairline should have been a large, irregular scar protruded, standing out from his forehead in vivid purple. Even in her panicked state, she felt sorry for him. If only he'd kept his hair, he would have been an attractive man, but the scar was all one noticed on first impression. Tonio nudged her along.

"There's plenty more of them down at the Lux my friend," Tonio called back good naturedly.

They had nearly reached the depot when the first charge went off. It thundered down the valley like the wrath of God. The earth reverberated, the air clapped, the windows in the nearby buildings shook and shattered with the force. Angelina screamed. Tonio cursed as he pulled her under the eaves of a nearby building and crushed her against himself, shielding her with his body. She covered her ears, certain her eardrums had burst, unable to stand any further noise.

A second blast rocked the valley, followed closely by a third and fourth, possibly a fifth. Angelina lost track in her terror. Her ears rang until she could no longer distinguish individual sounds. The sky rained kindling and toothpicks, pieces of wood of various sizes, and razor sharp nails, bits of hot metal. The window above them showered the yard with shards of glass. For a moment there was stillness, nothing but Tonio's strong arms around her, the steady beating of his heart and the dull roar in her ears left by the explosion.

Tonio released her and stepped back to stare up the hill. She huddled against him like a child seeking comfort and noticed with horror that the backs of his arms were freckled with hundreds of small cuts. In his eyes was none of the excitement she expected to find there; something else was there instead, something she couldn't name.

Reflexively, she brushed at her skirt. They were both covered with soot and dust. Tonio didn't seem to notice. Her eyes followed his stare up the hill to the main body of the mine.

The mighty Bunker Hill concentrator was a pile of rubble. Tongues of orange and angry red flames leapt at the sky where the boarding house had stood only moments before. The fire so fresh that its plume had only begun to stretch to the sky and curl towards the valley.

Angelina released her grip on Tonio and stepped out from beneath the eaves into the rail yard. Odd personal belongings littered the area, blown thousands of feet away from the boarding house. Yet many were still intact and looked as if they'd been set carefully in place.

Everywhere buildings were reduced to piles of lumber, yet a single power pole stood untouched near the center of the tumult, rising ridiculously over the disaster to hold smoldering lines rendered incapable of carrying a single watt of power to the plant. For a few seconds all was quiet in awe of the show of power just demonstrated.

The distinctive blast of Al's train whistle shattered the silence. As if on cue, a current of miners left their posts and rushed down the hillside to board the train. They appeared from every direction, heading for the train in an unstoppable wave of humanity, whooping and screaming a victory cry.

"We've done it!"

"We've won!"

"The second Battle of Bunker Hill is a success!"

Their voices blended in a cacophony of human sound and victorious emotion.

Tonio was beside her again with his good arm around her. And then they were swept away toward the train with the black tide of miners.

The ride home on the train was a nightmare she couldn't forget. Through some miracle Tonio had been able to keep them from being separated. She rode home on his lap in a fetid, cramped rail car meant for hauling freight, not people, with a group of men so raunchy and drunk she feared for her safety and her immortal soul for witnessing their foul language and behavior.

Flasks of whiskey and rum circulated freely from man to man. Tonio drank liberally from each one that passed his way. She couldn't condemn him. He drank to deaden the increasing pain of his gunshot wound, but she worried about his ability to protect her. She clutched his stiletto with such passion that her knuckles turned white and the feeling in her fingers faded, but she would not weaken her grip. Tonio acted casual, joking and laughing with the men as he refused their lewd offers for Angelina. Still, his hand was never far from his revolver.

The train made stop after stop. At each tiny town, at every mine, men piled off, many returning to work the shifts in the mines that they had abandoned hours before, acting as though nothing out of the ordinary had transpired. Wallace was nearly the last stop. Somehow they got off the train and made their way to the Hall home with Angelina supporting Tonio.

The shock had long since worn off and Angelina could only imagine the pain each step caused him. The alcohol numbed his senses some, but unfortunately it had numbed his balance as well. They wove and threaded their way across the sidewalk until they reached home. May met them at the door and the two women shuttled Tonio into the second floor bedroom that Angelina occupied. Angelina's shoulders ached from his weight as she watched May guide Tonio the last few feet to the bed.

"Drop the knife, Angelina. You're home," May commanded.

Angelina wasn't aware she still clutched it. She stood in the doorway too stunned to respond.

In the end, May pried it from her hand. "Don't fall apart now, Angelina. Tonio needs help, quickly. Let's get him to bed and see to his wound."

Angelina helped May undress him. May moved with rapid precision. Angelina fumbled in a haze. They pulled off his boots and pants. May cut off his undershirt and untied the dirty towel to inspect the bullet wound.

"Couldn't find anything cleaner," he mumbled seeing the disgust May displayed as she dropped it to the floor.

She ordered Angelina to bring a basin and fresh towels and sheets to use as bandages. She was about to help him lie down gently on his back when he cried out. "My back, May. Clean my back first. I can't lie on it."

Angelina returned with the basin of water, soap, and rags. May wet a cloth to wipe clean the blood. Tonio cried out in pain. Confused by his reaction to her gentle wipes, May took a closer look. In the light from the window hundreds of tiny slivers of glass glinted viciously, piercing the skin of his shoulders and arms.

"Angelina, get the tweezers," May said.

"A window blew out above me." Tonio spoke through his teeth in great pain. "Should've known better."

When Angelina came back into the room May was asking Tonio a question and oddly Tonio seemed to be comforting her. Angelina heard only muffled parts of their conversation.

"He's all right, May. They didn't hurt him. He was driving when we pulled into Wallace."

May mumbled something and Tonio replied. "He'll be home anytime. You should be proud."

May realized Angelina was back. "The bullet's still in. Angelina, go for the doctor. Get old Foster. He'll come. And be quiet about it."

As Angelina left, May was gently and meticulously tweezing the glass from Tonio's upper body.

Finding Dr. Foster had not proved an easy task, probably made more difficult by her tired mind and the confusion and hysteria in town. May had finished the job by the time Angelina returned. Tonio was lying on his back, nearly unconscious, his wound neatly scrubbed, but oozing a clear looking fluid. May bathed his forehead with cool water. Doc Foster sent Angelina out, though she protested. May stayed to assist him. When they were finished, the bullet was out and the wound dressed and Tonio was ordered confined to his bed for at least a week.

Al didn't return until late that night. He was exhausted and refused to say much about what had gone on during the abduction. May didn't press. She was too happy that he was home safely to care about the details. She didn't even condemn him for letting Angelina go along.

For days the story of the explosion dominated every aspect of life: the newspapers, conversation, peoples' thoughts. Everyone had an opinion, an anecdote, a fear.

For three uneasily quiet days, euphoria reigned in the Valley. Many of the mines shut down. Most notably the Bunker but other smaller ones as well, those that depended on the Bunker's power plant for energy to operate. Nearly eight hundred mining jobs were at stake, but it didn't dampen the sense of victory the men felt. They drank and partied and bragged of their victory while their leaders quietly packed and left town without anyone bothering to question their conspicuous absence.

Governor Steunenberg had been wired immediately, but no action had been taken. Many felt none would be despite the governor's promise to "punish and totally eradicate from this community a class of criminals who for years have been committing murders and other crimes in open violation of law."

After all, what could the governor do? The Idaho State militia was away in the Philippines cleaning up the aftermath of the Spanish-American War. Angelina heard one young miner predict, "You can't steal railroad trains, dynamite mines, and burn villages without some reaction." Personally, she agreed with him.

Angelina spent the first day after the explosion never more than shouting distance from Tonio's bedside. Doc Foster claimed his injury was not life threatening, but that did not prevent nearly twenty-four hours of fever-induced delirium and pain.

Angelina sponged and sponged him again as he sweated and toiled to break the fever. Maybe she imagined it, but he seemed to desire, and even demand her presence in his room. He called her name over and over again. All the while she reassured him of her presence, his safety, her safety. On the second day, the fever broke and he sat up in bed drinking warm broth. On the third day she caught him sitting up on the edge of the bed pulling on his boots.

"Pull those things off and lie back down!" She watched him from the doorway. "What on earth are you doing trying to get up?"

He looked at her calmly. "I'm preparing to leave the state. Be a dear and pack me a bag."

She thought he was joking until she saw the serious glint in his eyes. "You're not teasing."

"Of course I'm not teasing, Angelina. This is a serious matter. Now find me a jacket, I've lost my black leather one. And find me a duffel of some sort, anything will do. I need you to run to the bank for me and make a withdrawal." He ticked off an impressive list of preparations for Angelina to make.

"Where are you planning on going? And why?" She had no intention of helping him move.

"We're going. Pack some things for yourself and grab any cash you have; we'll need it. It may be a while before we can return."

"I'm so happy you're including me in your plans, but we aren't going anywhere." She walked over and eased him back onto the bed. He didn't have the strength of a buttercup. "You're in no condition to travel if you can't defend yourself against me."

"Such a nice girl. I'd leave you behind in an instant, but you're an accessory now and I'd hate to see what they'd do to your pretty hide in jail." He leaned up on his elbow.

"What jail?"

"The jail where the officials will surely pen up as many miners as they can round up and charge with blowing up the concentrator. Haven't you read the papers lately?"

"What are you talking about?"

"Our fine governor has declared Shoshone County is in a state of insurrection and rebellion and asked for federal troops. It's only a matter of time before they arrive. When they do, it'll be '92 all over again. They'll round up every miner in sight and throw them into a makeshift bullpen, and then they'll make an example of one or two of them.

"I don't plan on being around when that happens. The Montana border is fewer than ninety miles away. With luck, we'll reach it before the troops arrive."

"That won't happen, Tonio. Men who are directly implicated are calmly awaiting their fate. So many can't be wrong."

"They're fools. Do you see Ed Baker or any of the other leaders hanging around?"

"We aren't going anywhere until you're well enough to travel. And then only when I say so. You've lost too much blood and there's still danger of an infection." She stood over him, trembling with fear and wondering whether she should heed his warning and get them out of town.

Tonio lay back in the bed looking pale and drained.

She bit her lip. Maybe Tonio was right. "I'll pack the things you asked for on the slim chance you're right and have to escape quickly. Now you need to rest. You can't possibly travel today."

"Tomorrow may be too late," he replied weakly. "You will come with me. I won't leave you behind."

She looked down so that he couldn't see her eyes and the desperate plea for his love they held. She could never veil her eyes the way he could. "Tonio, there is no need to leave, is there? Not if you're innocent?"

He didn't answer but instead closed his eyes. "I'm tired, Angelina. Please leave me alone now."

She covered him with a light blanket and walked to the door.

Tonio saw her hesitate, watching him for a moment before departing. Her doubt permeated the room. He could have reassured her, but he wanted her faith in him to be her own. What had he expected? That she would jump at the opportunity to flee with him? That she would tell him she believed in him? That she would love him at all costs?

Yes, that's exactly what he'd expected. He lay back and fell into a fitful sleep as she set about the errands he had sent her on, unaware of the damage she had caused.

CHAPTER SIXTEEN

Tonio's dire prediction became reality less than twenty-four hours later. Early on the morning of May third a special train carrying close to eight hundred African American blue-jacketed federal reserve troops rolled into the Silver Valley. Brigadier General H.C. Merriam, a tough man without a sense of humor concerning military matters and violation of law, headed the troops. With a precise efficiency known to very few outside of the military, he conducted his assignment as if he were planning a battle. Within hours of arriving, his men had secured arrest warrants for over fifty men.

They blockaded the rail lines and major thorough-fares, and took up office in local government offices. The troops arrested Sheriff Young and his deputies

and declared Shoshone County under martial law. He
made an official announcement to the newspapers and
posted signs in every town.

As the day progressed and it became obvious that
many men were trying to escape, the General ordered
troops not to bother securing warrants but to arrest
anyone that could be identified as being at the Bunker
on the day of the violence.

General Merriam commandeered a barn near Wardner and dispatched a group of troops to begin con-
structing a makeshift jail. Barbed wire fences went up
within a span of hours. Tents were erected. Another
dispatch of troops was sent to monitor the surrounding
hills and arrest any miners trying to escape. They ap-
prehended many miners as they sought refuge in the
hills. The unfamiliar sight of an African American soldier charging after them with rifle in hand was usually
enough to cause even the bravest man to surrender.
Lined up two abreast and closely guarded, the captives
were marched in groups of twenty to thirty men back
to the prison camp—the bullpen as it was soon to be
known.

Locals panicked as their men sought to escape. Horror stories quickly surfaced of miners being arrested as
they got off shift, still in their digging clothes. Dripping wet and foul, they were herded into boxcars and
shuttled into the prison camp, their families left to
wonder what had become of them.

Soldiers rammed in doors and ransacked houses as
they searched for hideaways. They smashed furniture
and insulted and roughly tossed aside women who tried

to protect their men. Tensions and fear were further amplified by the predominately white population's distrust of the African American troops sent to quell the labor rebellion.

The regular Idaho militia was fighting the Spanish American war with Teddy Roosevelt. Idaho Governor Steunenberg had been forced to ask the federal government for help. The feds had sent the African American militia. Anti-government sentiment ran high.

Truth and fiction escalated and commingled as the hours ticked by and tensions rose, until it became impossible to discern between them. Two things were certain—the Valley was in a panic and no one was safe.

Angelina was at the hotel when she heard the news. She ran for home without pausing to think out a plan. Out of breath and winded, she burst into the upstairs bedroom where Tonio rested, her words barely coherent, her thoughts wild and jumbled. She grabbed Tonio's boots and shoved them at him, then flew around the room, throwing odd items into the empty duffel she'd dragged out the day before.

"Tonio! Get up! They've arrested Al! Got him when he reported for work this morning. May's in a tizzy. Said to make sure you escape. Why are you sitting there! Hurry! They'll be here soon!"

Tonio lay back calmly on the bed watching her with mild amusement. "Who is they?"

"The troops, who else? They arrived in Wardner this morning, nearly a thousand of them. Mostly African American men. The General's declared martial law." She didn't slow from her frenzied task. "They're arresting everyone."

"I see. And what are we going to do?"

"Escape, of course!"

He laughed, a loud cynical laugh tinged with genuine amusement.

"Why are you laughing?"

"I'm laughing at you, planning to escape. We're a day late, my dear. You should have listened to me yesterday."

"It's not too late! They haven't gotten to Wallace yet. If we hurry—"

"You have a plan, I assume."

"No, I haven't had time to think." She paused for a moment. "We'll take a train."

"A train? You think the General is so stupid as to allow the trains to run, happily loaded with fugitives headed for Montana or Canada?"

"Perhaps not. What about the horses we use at the Hole?"

"We'd have to get to Burke. And I lost the only one that could run worth a damn at the Bunker. Angelina, by now I guarantee you, the hills are blue with troops. I've been in the military. I can guess the way the General is thinking. This is a battle to him. He'll have fortified the area. There is no escape."

"Then we'll hide."

"Where? Under the bed? In the root cellar? You don't think they'll search those places? Tell me, Angel, why are you so concerned? They won't arrest the innocent. You said so yourself, or do you doubt?"

She didn't understand his hard look. "They're arresting everyone who was seen at the mine that day. Everyone! We were there!"

"Are you so worried about yourself?"

"I'm worried about you." She couldn't tell him how much.

He leaned back against his pillow. "Sit back and relax. Destiny will be. We can't change it now."

The day passed in a slow, nervous tedium. Try as hard as she might, Angelina could not think up a plan of either escape or alibi. Tonio spent the morning quietly thinking or playing solitaire. She hoped he was concocting a plan, but his face was a mask, unreadable. Whatever he was thinking he refused to comment on. Late in the afternoon the troops stormed Wallace like an enemy attacker. She couldn't believe this was their own government.

The blue coated troopers marched up Pine Street in precise military formation. She watched in silent horror from the upstairs bedroom as they forcibly entered the house across the street. Then their neighbor to the right. She counted a contingency of nearly thirty troops guarding as many local men in the street as they stormed home after home. She winced every time one walked past their gate. At last it was over. They marched the men towards the rail depot, inexplicably ignoring 221 Pine.

"Tonio, they've gone! We're safe! All this worry over nothing!" She clapped her hands in a girlish expression of glee and then danced to the bed singing. "We're

free! We're safe! We're free!" The look on Tonio's face
as she bent to hug him froze her in place.

"Pack our things, Angel. We're leaving tonight as
soon as it's dark."

"Why? We're not suspect."

"We've been given a reprieve. They didn't stop here
because they already have Al. They expect to find me in
Burke. When they don't find me there, they'll come
back here."

"Where will we go?"

"To Harrison and the shack you own."

"How will we get there?" He had said that they
couldn't take the train and they had no horse.

"We'll walk."

"In the dark? The whole way! Oh, Tonio! I can't. I
don't know the way. We'd have to follow the tracks."

"They'll be watching the tracks for trains, not people. We can do it if we're careful. The problem will be
getting out of town."

May came home nearly an hour before dusk, fuming
and stewing over the treatment Al had received at the
army's hands. "Jackasses, all of them! They're claiming
Al is a part of all this, that he willingly participated. Al
was taken hostage at gunpoint! That constitutes will-
ingness? I suppose he should've let the holdup men
shoot him. Jackasses!"

She briefly outlined the condition at the bullpen.
"And the men don't have any food or blankets. And the
guards give you the worst kind of abuse when you try
to take some in."

"May, calm down. We need your help." Tonio told her his plan.

"They've imposed a curfew at dark, Tonio," she said when he'd finished.

"I expected as much. Just before dark Angelina and I will head to the Lux. I'm going to pretend to be escorting her home after treating a working lady to dinner. Once we're inside the Lux, we'll wait until nightfall and sneak out the back. The Lux is the last building in town before the depot. The tracks are no more than forty feet from the back of the building."

"This is craziness, Tonio. Those woods out back of there are as dense as they come. You lose your way and you're sunk."

"I won't, May. Now help us out. We don't have much time. I don't suppose you have anything racy for Angelina to wear?"

They set out at promptly at eight o'clock. The days were long in early May in North Idaho. There was still daylight. Angelina painted her face with rouge and lipstick so that she took on the hard appearance of one of the ladies who worked at the Lux. Her shirtwaist was unbuttoned and pulled apart to show a good deal of cleavage. She was conscious of the spring breeze across her bosom as they stepped out the door.

She padded her skirt with the money she'd withdrawn the day before. She tried to appear saucy and confident as she hung on Tonio's arm flirting animatedly. Her heart pounded with fear.

Tonio held her coat draped across his arm to conceal his revolver. He walked along calmly with a confidence Angelina hoped he felt. The daylight was nearly completely faded as they walked the last block to the Lux.

As expected the streets were heavily patrolled. Angelina picked up many admiring stares as they walked along. Just before they reached the Lux, a tall African American soldier stopped them. He and Tonio looked eye to eye.

"There's a curfew imposed." The soldier's voice was stern.

"So I've heard and that's why I'm escorting the lady home. We've just been out for a bite of dinner."

"I'll bet," the trooper said. "I hope you're prepared to spend the night in that place. By my reckoning dark has fallen."

"It won't be a hardship, I assure you." Tonio winked.

The soldier motioned him on. Angelina took a deep breath and squeezed Tonio's hand in victory. They walked up the entrance to the building just as the door opened before them and Nokes stepped out more than slightly drunk.

"Domani!" he called out in a too loud voice. Before Tonio could warn him off Nokes slugged him playfully in the left shoulder. Tonio winced in pain while struggling to appear normal. It was all over in a moment. Two troopers stepped up beside him and wrestled him to the ground. Nokes was flung back. The revolver went flying across the boardwalk as Angelina screamed.

"Is that Antonio Domani?" a white soldier wearing officer insignia appeared and questioned Nokes.

"Yes." Stupid Nokes—too drunk to cover for Tonio.

The officer motioned to his fellow soldiers. "Lock him up in the local jail tonight. We'll transport him tomorrow. We got ourselves a big one, fellows!" He kicked Tonio with his boot. Then the other two men pulled the struggling Tonio to his feet. "Get a good look at our famous bomber, men. Take him away." He turned to the stunned Angelina and opened the door to the Lux Building courteously. "You'd better go inside, ma'am."

She looked back at Tonio and mouthed, "I'm sorry." He nodded toward the building, motioning for her to continue the scam. She watched them haul him away.

"Ma'am," the officer said.

She stormed haughtily through the door. He grabbed her arm as she entered. "I'm off duty soon; perhaps I'll come back and give you a little business."

"I'm closed for business tonight." She shrugged off his hand and with head high marched up the stairs to the second floor without a thought as to where she was going. When she reached the top, she shivered and burying her head in hands, began to cry.

"You spent the night at the whorehouse?" May asked, incredulous.

"Yes, and they were very nice to me. They gave me a bed to sleep in and breakfast this morning."

"I hope you slept on the floor. Who knows what a woman might pick up just looking at one of those filthy beds."

"At that point I didn't care."

"You're a brave girl, Angelina."

"Yes." She smiled for the first time. "I am. Now how are we going to get Al and Tonio out of jail?"

"That's a good question," May said. "They could use a lawyer. Not that those cursed blue coats are offering anyone due process."

Angelina's eyes lit up. "John, John Lawlor. He's a prominent Spokane attorney. He surely has friends who can help us. Why didn't we think of him before?"

May didn't look encouraged. "Right now we can use all the help we can get."

"I'll telegraph him immediately. I don't know why I didn't think of it sooner." Angelina leapt to her feet and out the door before May could warn her to be careful. She didn't need another warning to add to her worries. The streets were full of desperate people and rowdy, power-swelled troops.

Angelina returned to the house less than an hour later looking disheveled and disgruntled. May had one basket loaded with food for the prisoners and was loading a second when Angelina came in, the porch door slamming behind her. "How'd it go? Your lawyer friend going to help us?"

"I don't know! They're *porco canes*, May, every last one of them. The troops have taken over the telegraph office and closed the post office. There's no way to get a message out. They're holding us hostage. We're out of communication."

She plopped heavily into a chair. "I've been man-handled, fondled, propositioned, and a few things I don't even care to name. The troops treat every woman like a lady from the Lux and act as if it's their right."

May shook her head. "It appears you'd better stay put for a bit. So we can't get through to John."

"I didn't say that." She smiled mysteriously.

"Well? Are you going to keep me in suspense?"

"They're letting some folks leave town, those they've deemed innocent. Nokes evidently decided it was time for him to return to help in his father's banking business. He threw his name around and they let him leave, but not before I begged him to take a message to John."

"Good work, Angelina. We'll see; we'll have to wait and see."

Though she went every day, May would not let Angelina near the bullpen, no matter how much Angelina pleaded.

"The men, the guards and military folk, are a rough crew, Angelina. They're hostile and obscene, even to a plain woman like me. I hate to think what they'd do to a pretty woman like you. The prisoners aren't so much better themselves, but they like me." She winked. "After all, I bring them food and supply them with blankets."

"They'd like you anyway, May."

"The bullpen is no place for a lady, Angelina. I've seen life at its worst. It doesn't shock me. But you've led a sheltered life. It'd be too much."

"How can you still believe in my naiveté and innocence, May? I was nearly raped in an abandoned rail car less than a week ago. I spent an entire night in a whorehouse. I'm no longer a cloistered Italian girl."

May remained resolute. "That captain that arrested Tonio still thinks you're a whore. Heard that he's been to the Lux several times asking for you."

"How would you know a thing like that?"

"I have my sources. The captain was quite taken by you. It only adds to your mystery and reputation that it's rumored you were at the mine at the time of the explosion. On Tonio's arm."

Since Tonio's arrest Angelina had waited for the warrant to be issued for her own arrest. After nearly four days of waiting, she'd concluded that no one had mentioned her presence there that day. "Where did you hear that?" She was alarmed.

"Some of the miners at the pen. They say that Clell identified you, but the Feds aren't interested in what a lady might have been doing there."

"Clell!" She could barely say his name. It tasted like venom on her lips. "I'm sure he turned Tonio in. Who else would have? May, if there's any justice—"

"I know, honey, I know. After what he did to you he ought to be the one put away for good. The Feds don't quite trust him, but they're depending on his testimony against Tonio."

"Tonio didn't ignite the charge, May. I was with him! If I went to the General and told him, they'd have to let him go."

"It wouldn't matter. It'd be your word against Clell's. They have plenty of witnesses that claim they saw a man wearing a black leather fringed jacket set off the charge."

"That doesn't make any sense. Why would Tonio be wearing his jacket on such a warm day? I haven't seen him in it for weeks. And I know I didn't see it on him that day. They must be mistaken. I'll tell my story anyway."

May grabbed her arm. "No, you won't. Next time you encounter the captain he won't be put off so easily. Besides, they have other evidence against Tonio. They found his black jacket at the site, Angelina, and they have record of his meetings with Ed Baker. I don't believe it for a minute, but the Feds think Tonio planned the whole operation and set the charges. It won't matter to them that he didn't light the fuse. In their opinion, he's still responsible for the rest of it."

"You don't believe he did it?"

"No."

Angelina looked away, not wanting May to see her doubt. She wished she had May's faith in him. May noticed her reaction but didn't comment on it.

"The captain is not a problem. He has nothing he can prove against me," Angelina said.

"What about helping a fugitive escape?"

"He has no proof Tonio was trying to escape. We were out for a walk. He was escorting me home. If we

were near the Lux building and the captain assumed I
worked there, it is his misconception. What's the real
reason you won't let me go to the pen?" Angelina
stared at May.

"Tonio doesn't want you there," May said.

"Since when have I lived and breathed on what Tonio wanted!"

For ten days Angelina didn't mention the bullpen.
She worked side by side with the rest of the women of
the community arranging aid for the families of the
imprisoned miners. These women and children depended on the daily wages their providers brought
home; without it many were destitute.

A few miners began to trickle out of the pen. The
governor issued an order requiring any miner seeking
employment in the Valley be required to obtain a red
card work permit. The card could only be obtained by
swearing an anti-union plea before the county coroner.
But even for those who were able to obtain a card, work
was scarce. The Bunker and several other mines would
not be operational until power could be restored and
the concentrator rebuilt. The reconstruction could take
months. Families packed and left the Valley. Grim described the general mood around town.

On the fourteenth day following his arrest, they released Al. May had finally convinced his fellow Masons
to help and he was let out. It was common men, and not
her fancy attorney that secured his release. Angelina
hadn't heard a word from John. She feared that Nokes
had gone back on his word and not contacted him. She

waited hours in line on the first day the telegraph office was reopened to send him a message, but she received no response. The General had reopened the railways and limited, carefully scrutinized routes ran. Families of imprisoned miners were finally able to make the journey between Wallace and Wardner by rail.

Conditions for the Halls remained grim despite Al's release. The railroad refused to reinstate Al, claiming that he was "a willing tool of the rioters." With no job to go to, Al resorted to working the Hole full time. Tonio remained in prison.

On the day of Al's release May was happily distracted. Angelina saw her opportunity and after stopping by the hotel to fill a basket with baked goods, she headed for the depot to catch a train to Wardner and the bullpen.

Bullpen was an apt name, Angelina thought as she approached the compound where the miners were being held. A hastily constructed fence of chicken and barbed wire surrounded a sea of tents and several weathered board buildings. Blue-coated troops swarmed throughout the compound yard, supervising their weary prisoners in a variety of tasks, most of them aimed at keeping the area clean and the prisoners occupied and dispirited.

Angelina stepped carefully around the recently formed puddles in the dirt road that led to the post gates. The spring sky was as gray as the camp and its sullen prisoners, but patches of blue were beginning to appear, lifting Angelina's spirits and adding to her optimism. The day would soon turn warm and humid. She was stopped at the bullpen entrance by a short, solid African American man.

"I am here to see a prisoner." She was not accustomed to African American people. Italy and Idaho had so very few. She smiled tentatively.

"Which one?"

"Antonio Domani."

The man laughed. "The demolitioner?"

"The *accused* demolitioner."

"You'll need to see the captain to get clearance to see that one."

"Where is the captain's office?"

The man pointed to a large building in the center of the compound. He grabbed her arm as she started through the gate toward the building. "We're under orders to search anyone coming in."

Angelina stood indignantly still as the man ran his hands familiarly over her bodice and skirt. He took liberty and pleasure with his assignment.

"The basket."

She lifted the lid. The guard smiled at the sight of the goodies inside. "These are too good for a demolitioner." He reached in and pulled out a plate of cookies.

"Help yourself." She didn't bother hiding her sarcasm.

The guard laughed as he motioned her through.

The captain's secretary showed her into his office, which was as small and stale as the man who occupied it. The set of his face as he looked up from his paperwork turned quickly from disinterested irritation to surprised recognition. Her heart sank. Surely a company of soldiers as large as the one stationed here had more than one captain, but it had to be her lot to meet up with the very one she was hoping to avoid.

"Sir," she said formally.

He rose and quickly closed the door to his office. "This is a wonderful surprise. I've been to the Lux looking for you ever since the first night of our occupation."

"How unflattering, *signor.*"

"I'd hoped that you would take it as a compliment."

"You seem to be under the misconception that I am associated with the Lux. Of course a woman of my upstanding reputation and purity would be insulted at such insinuation. I am here to see *Signor* Domani. If you will give your permission—"

"Mr. Domani is hardly the kind of man a woman of innocence would be seeking to visit. What relationship do you claim with him?"

Her eyes snapped. "Claim? I state the truth. He is my cousin and appointed chaperone here in Idaho. Don't tell me you don't see the family resemblance?"

The captain laughed. "Perhaps your family should be more discriminating in their choice of chaperones for such a beautiful young woman. He seemed friendly for a man tasked with protecting your honor, and then there's this matter of the explosion."

"I came also to make a statement about the day of the violence. He was with me when the explosion occurred."

The captain listened patiently and took notes as she recounted her story. "So you see, Clell has a, what is the word?"

"Vendetta?"

"*Si*, such a nice Italian word, that."

The captain smiled. "You would be willing to swear to this statement?"

She nodded.

"It's your word against our witness. And pardon me, ma'am, but it would seem that you're biased where the defendant is concerned, him being a relative. Besides which, it doesn't mean he didn't plant the charges. You need someone to corroborate your version of the facts. That will at least help your case."

"I don't understand 'corroborate.'"

"Verify. You need someone who saw you with Domani and would be willing to testify. Ideally this should be someone impartial. Do you understand?"

She nodded.

The captain was silent for a moment. "I'd be willing to discuss this further, over dinner tonight. You choose the location."

Angelina considered for a moment. "The Fuller House in Wallace. But not tonight, tomorrow night. And of course, I must have *Signor* Domani's approval before I can commit to such an invitation."

"Private Wilson!" the captain called out. His secretary appeared at the door. "Take the lady to visit the Italian." He turned to her. "Fifteen minutes, no more. And I like to know the names of the women I call on."

"Angel."

"That's all?"

"That's enough." She intended to keep her date only if necessary. He spoke again as she turned to leave.

"What's in the basket?"

"Italian sweets."

"Leave them. I have a sweet tooth."

"Lucky for you. These are but an outward extension of my sweet nature." She set the basket down on his desk and followed Wilson from the room.

CHAPTER SEVENTEEN

The maximum-security area was located in a small building next to the captain's office. A single dim corridor ran the length of the narrow building. Occupied cells lined either side. Her quick glimpses of the occupants stunned her. These couldn't be the same vibrant men that had frightened her with their mob mentality and violent thirst for power only weeks before. These were ordinary men, the kind she saw every day on the streets of Wallace. Individually, locked alone without the support of their peers, they looked defeated and tired and powerless.

Private Wilson stopped before a door with a small barred window. He spoke to her as he unlocked it. "Captain gave orders. No more than fifteen minutes. If you wish to leave before that call for the guard and he'll let you out."

The door swung open. She hesitated on the jamb.

"Domani, you have a visitor!" Private Wilson called out roughly.

She stepped inside

"Good day, ma'am." Wilson locked the door behind her.

It took a minute for her eyes to adjust to the dimness of the cell. Tonio sat on a cot next to the wall, one leg bent on the bed, the other on the floor. He stared straight ahead at the wall in front of him, not looking at his visitor even when the door clanged shut and the private departed.

"Tonio, you might at least acknowledge me after all the trouble I've gone to, to get here."

"Angelina?"

Her heart leapt at the sound of his voice, but she thought he stiffened.

"I told May I didn't want to see you."

"I don't live by what you want."

"Apparently not." He didn't sound happy. "Speak to me in Italian, Angelina, but be careful what you say. This is a dangerous place to talk." He stood slowly and faced her. "How did you get in here? They're restricting my visitors."

"I told the captain we're cousins. I don't think he fully believed me. I had to throw in my basket of *paste* and dinner tomorrow night to get this time."

"Stay the hell away from the captain!" His words exploded into the room. Then his tone softened. "For our own good, Angelina. Think about why he'd let you in to see me when he's denied so many others. Wouldn't a social setting be the perfect place to seduce information from you?"

"Tonio!" She flew across the room and threw her arms around him in an emotional embrace that he did not return. I'm scared." She took a step back, grabbed him by the arms, and looked up at him imploringly. "The papers are calling this bombing a capital crime. Whoever's convicted will hang. They're saying you set the charge.

"I gave my statement to the captain, swearing that you were with me when it went off. But it's my word against the union henchman Clell, and who are they going to believe?"

His arms tensed beneath her grip. "Damn! What else did you tell him?"

She didn't understand his fear. "Nothing."

"You shouldn't have talked to him. I don't want you involved. You've put yourself at risk."

She ignored him and looked at the floor, afraid of the question she had to ask. "Tonio, you aren't involved are you? They're saying that you're tied up with Baker, that you're the mastermind. I don't mean to doubt, but there were those late night meetings with Baker. Your uncle and Gambino were concerned about your association with—"

He clamped his hand over her mouth and looked past her out the cell door window. Footsteps came down the hall and stopped just short of the door.

"I'm innocent, Angelina." The sound of footsteps moved on. Tonio dropped his hand from her mouth. "Whose side are you on? They're listening to everything we say. I want you to leave now."

"No! Tonio, I'm sorry, I believe you. I had to hear from you is all. I've sent for John Lawlor. He'll represent you."

"I don't want his help."

"You need his help! Whatever evidence they have against you must be convincing. They released Al already even though they accused him of being a willing accomplice and stealing the train to help the union."

"Go." He tried to spin her toward the door.

She resisted. "Tonio, they'll hang you if they can."

"They won't hang me. That's not what this is about. Both sides are playing a game and I'm caught the middle. You don't understand, and I can't take a chance explaining it to you here. I want you to leave now and get as far—

"I'm not leaving until I've said what I came to say." Her heart raced. Her eyes misted. She barely got the words out. "I love you."

She watched his reaction closely. He didn't move, no light leapt to his eyes. He remained unreadable. Despite their weight, her words hung in the still air unanswered.

When he spoke, it was not a declaration of love. "You and half the other women in Wallace. There's nothing as romantic as a tragic hero." He raised his voice and his tone was suddenly falsely teasing.

She couldn't believe his words. He made light of her declaration. Perhaps he didn't understand. "I'm serious, I—"

His hand went over her mouth again and she thought he shook his head in warning, but the movement was nearly imperceptible. He whispered so softly into her ear that she had to strain to hear him. "Loving me is a dangerous game. One I can't let you play."

He dropped his hand from her mouth and pushed her away from him. Aloud he said, "I want you as far away from me as possible. Italy wouldn't be far enough."

"I don't know what game you're playing, Tonio, but I'll have to trust you." She called for the guard to let her out.

There was a white envelope waiting for her on her bed when she returned. It was from John, written on his official letterhead, with a bank draft tucked inside. She didn't bother to look at the amount it was written for. Her eyes scanned the letter quickly. So quickly that she had to read it through twice before the message sunk in.

Yes, he would represent Tonio and he was pleased to send her a draft for the timber money.

The bank draft! She scooped it from the bed. Her eyes grew wide when she read the amount.

May walked into the maelstrom unprepared. Angelina whirled about the room packing bags and stuffing clothes into suitcases with such fury and determination that for a brief moment the usually boisterous May was taken aback and left speechless. "You taking a trip, Angelina?"

Angelina jumped and put a hand to her heart. "Oh, goodness, May! You scared me."

"I've been standing here a minute, but you were so involved with your task that you didn't notice. When did all this come about?" She nodded toward Angelina's packing.

"This afternoon. I went to see Tonio and tried to help get him out of jail. I gave a statement to the captain. Tonio was with me when the concentrator exploded.

"But Tonio wasn't happy that I had done it. He wants me to leave the Valley. Because of the guards, he couldn't explain. But I think it is because he loves me. He has a plan. I must trust him in this, even though it goes against everything logical." Her voice cracked.

"Where are you going?"

"Where Tonio told me to go—as far away as possible. New York." She held up her bank draft. "My money came. I can do as I please.

"I don't understand all this. Why am I always the one on the outside? Everyone knows something I don't and I'm left guessing." Angelina folded a skirt and stuffed it in her bag.

"If you thought about what's going on, you'd know, too."

"I'm tired of trying. I'm going to visit Nonna Gia. I can't stay here and see him hang if his plan goes awry."

"He's not going to hang." May looked exasperated, but Angelina ignored it. "He's going to stay in jail until he tells the feds everything he knows about Baker's operation, including who set the charge. That's all they want from him.

"In the meantime the union boys are afraid that he does know something. We're all being watched. We're all under suspicion. Tonio wants you out of the fray. He hasn't forgotten that Clell's still on the loose and as long as he is, you're in danger."

"I hope you are right, both of you." Angelina snapped her bag closed.

"Give me this Nonna's address. As soon as things are safe here, Tonio will want you to come back."

Several days later, Angelina sat in Nonna Gia's small apartment, restless and worried though she had just arrived.

"Thank you for letting me stay with you, Nonna Gia. Cousin Mario was upset about me not going back under his roof, but I think Lucia was relieved. They are crowded enough as it is." Angelina mindlessly toyed with Nonna's small sugar bowl as she sat at the table with a cold cup of coffee in front of her.

"But what of you, Angelina?"

"What do you mean, Nonna?" She let the sugar bowl go.

"When are you going to come back?"

"I am back."

"In body, perhaps. I mean, where is the old Angelina? Someone seems to have replaced her with a shell. I expected you to come back full of life, not beaten."

"And I'm by no means beaten. Just worried. They still have not released Tonio."

"Angelina, I must confess something to you. I didn't just happen to pick Tonio as an escort for you. I was playing matchmaker. Tonio is like a son to me, always has been. I know you both well. Tonio and you belong together. I knew that before you even met.

"I was disappointed when I heard you intended to go through with your marriage to that old man and had turned down the young handsome one I had offered. Yet, I see now that I was not wrong. There is something between you. You must tell me, every detail."

It was a relief to confess to a sympathetic ear. When she was finished Nonna Gia spoke. "He loves you, Angelina. And he is smart. Tonio will not hang. Let me ask you this, do you want Tonio?"

"Yes, of course I do!"

"Then stop acting like a frightened little Italian girl. Act like the American woman you've become. It is time to stop moping around and prepare for when Tonio sends for you."

It was the last thing Angelina expected Nonna Gia to say. She sounded more like May Hall. "What?"

"In Italy," Nonna Gia said, "The woman must let her parents arrange a marriage. The good Italian girl bows to her parents' wishes, as you have done once, and marries the man of their choice. Here in the Italian community the process is little changed. Ah, but the truly American woman, she makes her own choice!"

"What are you saying, Nonna Gia? I can't arrange my own marriage and Tonio is never going to ask me. What am I supposed to do, ask him myself?"

Nonna Gia shrugged noncommittally. "You have said it, not me. All I can say is that if I were a young woman, I would head for Idaho the moment he is free. He's much too handsome to lose." Then she stood.

Angelina followed suit.

Nonna Gia put her arm around Angelina and led her gently to the little guestroom. "Get some rest now, little one. You're still worn out by your long trip. When you have rested, listen to the voice of the American woman you have become; she will know what to do."

Over the next few days, Angelina found herself alone much of the time. One afternoon when Nonna Gia and Papa Joe were both out, Angelina paced the small apartment listlessly. She opened the only window in the apartment and climbed out onto the small iron balcony where Nonna Gia had an herb garden planted in old crates. Voices rose from the street below. Variously accented Italian drifted her way, but she longed to hear English.

Life in Little Italy seemed little altered from only a few months ago. She felt restricted then, she felt doubly so now. In Idaho she was free. She got up and wandered back into the apartment.

Back in the guestroom she rummaged through the few possessions she'd brought with her. She grabbed her coat. She needed a walk to sort out her thoughts.

She'd barely rounded the corner onto Mulberry Street when a commotion near the *farmacia* caught her attention. Ten or so men were shouting and handing out handbills to any man that walked by. Many of the takers filed into the bar next door, where the local Italian fraternal order usually met on Wednesday nights to drink *vino*. Intrigued by the stir the handbillers caused, Angelina strolled forward and stuck out her hand to receive a flyer.

"Sorry, these are for men only."

"Why is that?"

"There's a judge in there." He nodded toward the bar. "He's naturalizing immigrants."

"Women have naturalization rights, same as men."

"Yeah, but they can't vote." His smug demeanor irritated her.

"What's that got to do with it?"

He shrugged and laughed, as if he shouldn't have to explain.

She yanked a billet out of the man's hand and scanned it. "This isn't legal."

The man shrugged again good-naturedly. "It looks legal enough to the authorities."

"So it does," she replied. She headed toward the crowd at the bar door.

"Wait! You can't go in there," the handbiller called after her.

She didn't break her stride, but threw a parting comment over her shoulder. "I'm from Idaho. I can vote."

She threaded her way through the line and into the bar where she was greeted by the bouncer. He looked amused as she strutted up to him. "You here to become a citizen?"

When she nodded, he let her pass.

Twenty minutes later she walked back out onto Mulberry Street an American citizen, naturalization papers in hand. She was an American woman! The one Tonio had wanted all along!

When she got back to the apartment, she found an envelope stuffed under the door. A telegram. She opened it without thinking.

Angelina

I am free. Shall I come for you? If yes I will catch the next train East. Please reply.

Tonio

He was free and he wanted her! Her heart raced as she clutched the paper to her bosom and danced around the room. The danger must be past. Tonio was free. And so was she. Why should he come to her? They both belonged in Idaho.

"This time I'm taking charge," she said aloud. Then she laughed a joyous tinkling laugh. She had to go uptown. There was shopping to be done. And she needed to send a telegram to May.

Nonna returned to find Angelina joyfully packing.

"Where are you going? Didn't you just arrive?"

"Tonio sent a telegram. He's free. He wants to know if I'm here; if so he'll come East. He's expecting your reply."

"That's wonderful! We shall telegraph him first thing in the morning. I can feel it—a marriage is imminent."

"I hope so. That's why we'll telegraph him in the morning, and tell him that I have left town."

"Left town!"

"Yes, and it will be the truth. I leave for Idaho tomorrow and when I get there I intend to arrange a marriage—my own. No more dishonesty. And this time, I intend to have the upper hand."

CHAPTER EIGHTEEN

"You're going to the ball at the Fuller House, Tonio, and that's that." May left no room for argument as she and Tonio sat at the kitchen table having coffee.

"You know how hard we women have worked on this fundraising event. I'm not going to let one of my own ruin it by not attending. You'll be there charming the ladies, dancing and smiling as if there were no place else you'd rather be. I've already let it be known that you're going. You draw a crowd. Everyone's still wondering how you got pardoned and if you really could've done it."

"Of course I could have done it, but I didn't. And I wasn't pardoned. I was exonerated. There's a big difference—pardoned implies guilt."

"My, my! We've certainly gotten surly these last few weeks. One would think you have good reason to be happy. You're a free man. Or was the bullpen so much better? And fortunately for you, you don't need to go begging for one of those cussed mining work permits to get work."

"What's the difference? We own a worthless mine, May."

"Tonio, I'm surprised at you—doubting the Hole. I've never seen you this morose."

"I'm not in a social mood." He rose and strode toward the kitchen door.

"I'll see your sorry hide at the ball tonight decked out in your finest. You hear me, Tonio?"

He waved acknowledgment back at her behind his head, not turning back or breaking his stride. May turned back to the kitchen chuckling to herself. "Believe me, Tonio. This is an event you don't want to miss."

Brilliant white linens graced the tables in the Fuller's main banquet room, each one topped by a bouquet of homegrown flowers. Volunteers and kitchen staff dressed in white were bringing out the buffet. Guests would begin arriving within the hour. The Colonel inspected the food as it was brought out. Cold salads sat in buckets of ice to keep the lettuce and fresh dandelion greens crisp. Silver ladles lay next to crystal bowls filled with May's homemade salad dressings.

May had planned the menu herself. She included every favorite dish she had cooked for the Fuller House.

The entrees were to be tasty and elegantly arranged but not fancy. Miners liked simple food. A commotion at the dessert table nearby caught the Colonel's attention as three women struggled to assemble a great, tiered cake.

May Hall saw the potential disaster looming and hustled through the swinging doors from the kitchen.

"Careful ladies! That's our crowning centerpiece. We don't want it dropped." May directed the women until the cake stood regally assembled in the center of the dessert table. A heavenly chocolate concoction with marzipan icing, someone had spent meticulous hours decorating it with intricate chocolate scroll. Candied roses and violets, and chocolate leaves cascaded over the top and along the sides, trailing into fresh flowers at the base.

"Good Heavens, May! What kind of cake have you created this time?" The Colonel's delight was evident in his tone.

"It's not a cake, it's a torte."

"Cake, torte, who can tell the difference? I thought only Angelina made such desserts. And here I was worried that we'd never be able to replace her with someone of equal talent. I see I was mistaken."

"Maybe you were and maybe you weren't," she said cryptically. "Now do me a favor. Go next door and help the band set up. I have my hands full in the kitchen."

She watched the Colonel disappear into the ballroom and then headed for the door to the street, tossing her apron on a nearby chair as she went. "Ladies, you can take it from here," she called over her shoulder.

"I have to get home. I have some prettying up to do before the guests arrive."

May's fellow volunteers shrugged as she left. May wasn't usually so concerned with her appearance, and as she topped the scale at over two hundred pounds and had a large, plain face, there wasn't much the poor dear could do. But since she'd spent all day cooking, they were unanimous in their opinion that she deserved some time to fix up. Every woman wanted to look her best tonight. The ball was the poshest event that had ever been held in Wallace.

May hurried nervously up the walk to her house and disappeared in the side door without being noticed. She lifted her skirts and took the stairs two at a time.

"Angelina, it's May," she whispered loudly at the closed guestroom door.

"Come on in, May. We're alone." Angelina leaned over the dressing table, peering seriously into the oval mirror as she inserted a gold fobbed, tear shaped garnet earring into her left ear. She turned to smile at May as she entered the room.

"Oh, honey!" May exclaimed. "Aren't you the vision! I've never seen anyone look so beautiful in my entire life, and I'm not making that up. Darling, you'll pop the eyes right out of that boy's head, out of every boy's head!"

Angelina wore a velvet evening gown in a deep shade of garnet that matched her earrings to perfection and set off her dark looks and creamy skin as no other color could. The bodice was low cut and sleeveless. Angelina intended it to catch Tonio's eye.

At each shoulder, one narrow velvet strap ended in a small tassel and lapped over the sides of her bust. Another narrow, lace covered ruffled strap hung beneath the first, capping each softly contoured shoulder. An oversized velvet bow at the front of the dress underlined her cleavage spilling provocatively over the top of the bodice. Her waist was encircled by a narrow band of garnet satin ribbon, beneath which her skirt clung suggestively to her hips before flaring to slightly more fullness and ending in two elegant velvet ruffles that kissed the floor and whispered as she walked.

Angelina had pulled her hair into an elegant creation that she had copied with studied determination from the New York society pages. Softly waved, then pulled into a lustrous bun of curls that ran from the top of her head to the nape of her neck where a few soft wisps escaped to curl airily. A few similar wisps adorned her forehead. Gone was the painfully foreign peasant girl she had been and in her place was a beautiful American woman.

"I hope so, May."

"You'd better take a shawl tonight or you'll surely freeze in that dress."

"Now you sound like my mama." She pulled on a pair of garnet velvet gloves that reached well above her elbows.

"Would your mama let you out of the house in a dress like that?"

"Certainly not, May! Not in hundred years!"

"So then, I'm certainly not your mama, aiding and abetting you like I am. To tell the truth, what I am is envious. Oh, to be young and beautiful! I was young once, but I was never beautiful."

"May, you've always been beautiful. On the inside where most people are ugly. Only a beautiful person would've gone to all this trouble for me. Tonio doesn't suspect, does he?"

"Angelina, that man is out of his head thinking you've gone back to Italy."

"Good. You'll send word when he arrives at the ball? I can't arrive before he does, it would ruin everything."

"I'll send word the moment he shows up. You're really going to go through with this?"

Angelina smiled. "You mean proposing to him? Yes."

"It's not traditional."

"I suppose not, but what did traditional get me? An arranged marriage to a man twice my age who died before I could meet him. I want Tonio. I won't lose him again."

May gave Angelina a little hug of support and turned to leave the room. "I'll send word when he arrives."

"Excellent!" Angelina sprayed herself with a heady perfume as May left the room and walked down the hall. *This perfume should send his senses reeling*, Angelina thought.

Tonio leaned on the bar, eyeing the crowd dispassionately. Several women gave him flirtatious looks, willing him to leave his post and ask them to the adjoining ballroom for a dance. He was fully aware of their appeals and just as fully disinterested. He dressed in a starched white shirt, white satin vest and bow tie, and tails which May had forced him into. He'd just as soon be in his black fringed jacket and jeans. A plate of appetizers sat on the counter in front of him. Harry Scott lounged to his left.

"You seem immune to the ladies' charms tonight, Tonio. Several attractive ones have been eyeing you for some time. Perhaps it's the monkey suit. You seem to be the only man in the place so attired."

"More than half of them are whores from the Lux. What's wrong with May, planning an event like this in a town where the men outnumber the women in such quantity? The Lux ladies will end up with more money by morning than the benefit collected, mark my words. Miners who can't find enough to feed themselves can always scrounge up enough for a good time with one of the willing women. They're probably charging two bits just for a dance. And what's wrong with the rest of you? I was told this was a formal occasion."

"Where does the ordinary man get a tuxedo, Tonio? Not being wealthy Italians, we must settle for ordinary suits."

Tonio laughed. "Why don't you go ask one of the ladies to dance, Harry?"

"Helen hasn't arrived yet and she'd be furious if she caught me dancing with someone else. I prefer to stay here in your uplifting company."

"There's no accounting for taste," Tonio said. "You sure picked a helluva a time to come home from Boise, Harry. How did the Senate session go? In what little space they're not devoting to the bombing, the papers are saying it was frivolous and an utter waste of time."

"We did better than the House. We at least ended the session with gentlemanly handshakes. The House ended by throwing paper wads dipped in ink and stealing every wastebasket, inkstand, and jar of paste in sight."

"The Senate's behavior can be credited to your able leadership. You evidently succeeded where their mothers had failed; you taught them manners. Not bad for a bunch of grown men."

"I wasn't entirely successful. Did I tell you about the man who stabbed his fellow legislator? I can't remember what their disagreement was. Stabbed him in the arm. It was only a superficial wound. Claimed he'd opened his pocket knife to sharpen his pencil and the guy fell into it—bad timing."

Tonio laughed. "Bad timing, like our little insurrection here. Sounds like our politicians in Boise are living up to their unsavory reputation. I can see how you'd be glad to be back working with us civilized Hole folk. To think that both suspected bombers, Orchard and myself, have at times owned the same mining shares. Ironic, isn't it?"

"Can't say I'm not happy that Orchard sold out to you and Cardoner. I never doubted your innocence, Tonio. I was happy to go to bat for you in Boise. As for Orchard, they'll catch him, sooner or later."

"Can't tell you how much I appreciate what you did for me, Harry."

"Anything for a partner." Harry nodded toward the banquet tables. "Looks like they're stocking the buffet. Shall we give it a try?"

A volunteer in a white apron busily set out trays of small sweets meant to serve as appetizers until the grand cake was served. Tonio grabbed a small plate. If he was going to drink heavily tonight he might as well fill his stomach. He didn't want to get drunk too fast. May had made it clear he was required to make more than a cursory appearance.

As he reached to fill his plate with mints and cookies, he stopped. In front of him was an elegant tray of *Piemontese paste*, tiny cream puffs filled with buttercream and custards and delicate individual *profiterole*. Angelina was the only one who knew how to make such things.

He looked up and scanned the room as if he expected to find her. If she wanted her necklace back, she'd have to come back and face him. He had no intention of mailing it back to her. She wouldn't leave the country without it, he was certain of that. May breezed by. He caught her by the arm. "May, where is she?"

May looked confused.

"Who made these?" He pointed to the *paste*.

"Oh, those? An old Italian woman in Kellogg. Why do you ask?" May's puzzlement seemed genuine. He let her arm go.

Angelina made her grand entrance. She walked in with head held high, drawing the attention of the male crowd, fully aware of the impact she made. Take a deep breath, she reminded herself. Enhance the presentation of the bustline and calm the nerves. Tonio, where are you?

Tonio heard the heightened buzz of the crowd and turned to see who'd come in. Their eyes locked immediately. She was a lovely vision, a dark beautiful Angel. He'd been done over by May and Angelina, but he didn't care.

He was in a tunnel and Angelina was at the other end with the entire crowd separating them. He pushed his way through the throng, determined to take her in his arms. He wasn't going to lose her this time.

She saw him making his way toward her and smiled in encouragement. The look on his face told her that she was not wrong in coming. He didn't mince words when he reached her.

"Angelina, we need to talk." There was a plea to the hard edge of his voice.

"Yes, Tonio. Someplace private. We have unfinished business."

"The Colonel's office?"

"Wherever you like."

CHAPTER NINETEEN

The Colonel's office reflected its masculine owner. Furnished with heavy wood and leather, the
thin walls allowed music from the dance band
to drift in. Tonio closed and locked the door.

"No interruptions." He stood straight-backed and
solemn. A month ago she would have found his stance
intimidating.

"No interruptions," she repeated dumbly. Now in his
presence, she was suddenly at a loss. "You're looking
handsome tonight, Tonio. You've recovered well from
your stay in the bullpen. Harry did a good job of getting you out."

"Harry Scott is the best friend a man could have. He
used his influence as a state senator and convinced

Governor Steunenberg that I didn't know any more than I'd already told them."

He stepped forward, so close that she longed to touch him. "Angelina, as long as I was in the bullpen and not talking, I was at a stalemate with both sides. I felt that we were both pretty safe. Your visit nearly tipped the balance.

"The guards had orders to listen in on every visit I had and the captain was smart enough to post Italian-speaking watchdogs. Maybe I was paranoid, but I half-imagined them with a cup to the wall trying to hear us. You came in talking about my meetings with Baker..."

"I'm sorry."

"Me, too. You almost gave them the fodder they needed to charge me as an accessory and you put yourself in danger. I was concerned that Clell would get wind of your visit and come after you, thinking that you knew something. Or that he'd realize how much you meant to me and use you as a union hostage to keep me from talking.

"Hell, I was just worried about you. Telling you to leave was one of the hardest things I've done."

"You're much too good with a poker face, Tonio. I almost believed your ruse. Did you know more about the union's activities?"

He broke into a crooked smile. "What do you think?"

Angelina returned the smile. "What about the union, Tonio? Are we safe now?"

"Harry and Baker are friends. Baker is courting Harry's sister Eleanor. Harry convinced him that I wouldn't talk. They know I'll never divulge what I know unless subpoenaed.

"To be honest, Baker never concerned me, it was Clell. Rumor is he ran to Canada. If that bastard ever steps foot in North Idaho again..."

He didn't need to finish, his meaning was clear. Hatred for the man filled his eyes.

"I suppose you've come back for your necklace," he said. "You had me doubting my ability to judge character, Angelina. When Nonna Gia telegraphed that you'd left New York, I thought I'd misjudged how much you valued it.

"Do you remember—you told me once that you would never leave the country without it? When I thought you had left, I held onto those words. If you were really going back to Italy, you would have asked for it back. Now I see that I was right and you didn't lie."

He paused. "I could have told you where it was that day in the bullpen, but I thought that as long as I had it you wouldn't go far."

"I came back for you."

The raw look that she could never explain before was back in his eyes as he stared across at her. He watched her as closely as he would the fuse on a stick of dynamite. This time she hoped she read it correctly.

She pulled a folded document from the small velvet purse that hung from her wrist and held it out for him to see. "Citizenship papers."

He pulled it from her hand to get a better look. She watched as a tiny frown turned the corners of his mouth and a barely perceptible crease wrinkled his brow. "This isn't legal."

"Legal enough to fool the authorities, or so I was told. I was sworn in by a certified judge of the United States of America and all I had to do was swear that I could vote."

"Damn, Angelina! You charmed your way into a naturalization mill!" He was clearly amused.

Angelina bit her lip. Her hands wouldn't stop shaking. She didn't know how to go about making a marriage proposal. She didn't suppose many women did. Even men seemed to have a tough time with it.

She took a deep breath, hoping her voice would stay steady. "I had a little speech planned, but it escapes me now so I'll just plunge ahead. Tonio, I may not be the blond American woman that you've always wanted—"

"Blond woman?"

"Maria told me that you've always liked blondes."

"What does she know about what I prefer?"

"Please, let me continue before I lose my nerve. I may not be blond, but I am an American now." She stepped close to him and looked up at him, grabbing him lightly by both arms. "Let's be the ultimate partners. Marry me, Tonio."

He stood perfectly still long enough for her to grow nervous and drop her gaze. Her hands fell to her side. When at last he spoke his voice was low and solemn. "Why do you want to marry me?"

She answered in a strong confident voice. "Because I love you."

"Good. And no, I won't marry you."

She froze. Before she could respond he sunk to one knee and grabbed her hand. "You may be a modern American woman now, but I'm still enough of an Italian male to want to do the asking. You may as well know that I was on the verge of chasing you to New York to do just that."

A tear slid down her cheek, this time one of joy. "Yes."

"I haven't asked yet. Will you let me make an honest proposal?"

She nodded and wiped the tear away.

"*Ti voglio bene. Sei il mio tesoro d'oro e ti amo con tutto il cuore—*"

"I'm your golden treasure?" She laughed. "If I can't be blonde, I may as well be golden."

"Please, no interruptions, I'm in the middle of a proposal." His tone turned serious. He squeezed her hand. "Marry me, Angelina. Marry me tonight, here at this ball."

"Tonight?"

"We're dressed for it, aren't we? I saw the judge out there." He nodded toward the party. "I'm sure we can convince him to perform the ceremony."

"Yes!"

In a fluid motion he was on his feet and she was in his arms locked in a kiss.

Half an hour later Tonio carried her across the threshold of the suite the Colonel had given them with his compliments. In the ballroom on the floor below several hundred miners drank to the new couple's health. Their laughter and the tinkling of their music filtered through the floor into the bridal suite. But the reminder of the crowd below and their ribald, joking threats to crash in on the new couple didn't deter Tonio. He would have his bride this night.

He didn't set her down until he'd let them in and locked the door. He set her gently on the bed, then moved the only chair in the room so that it was braced snugly beneath the doorknob. "To discourage visitors."

He walked to the bed, pulled her to her feet and hard against him wrapping one arm around her waist, using the other to hold the back of her head and guide her mouth upward to his. She leaned into him and stroked his hair as his tongue in her mouth sent shivers that ran to the tips of her toes. The shadow of his beard scrubbed at the corners of her mouth, but the masculine reminder only caused her to lean harder into him.

He smelled clean, of good cologne, of heaven. The excitement that coursed through her was nearly unbearable. She didn't want to let him go even as he pulled away to shed his jacket. She loosened his tie and unbuttoned his vest and shirt and ran her hands over the strong line of his shoulders.

His shirt hung open revealing hard muscles and a flat abdomen covered thickly with curling black hair. She stroked him lightly, running her fingers over his nipples then bending to suck them gently. He pulled her away and spun her around. His eyes sparkled with the heady excitement she'd seen in the mine the day they set the charge and her heart raced with the knowledge that the excitement there was for her that day, and this.

She presented her back to him. He nibbled her neck leaving warm circles of moisture on her flushed skin as he unbuttoned the dozens of tiny velvet buttons that lined the back of her bodice. She backed up against the warm bulge of his manhood as he expertly released the buttons from their velvet loops. She slipped off her shoes.

The gown dropped to the floor followed by her underskirt and hose until she was left standing in only her strapless gartered chemise. She heard his shirt fall to the floor and felt the hard warmth of his bare chest against her back. He circled her with his arms and massaged her breasts until she felt as if the titillation of his touch was almost too much. Then he turned her back around until she faced him again, and slowly untied her chemise until it pulled free and joined his shirt on the floor.

She kissed the perimeter of his lips as he pulled the pins from her hair and ran his fingers through it until it fell cascading in raven waves over her shoulders.

"Beautiful," he murmured. She ran her hand over the coarse hair of his abdomen as he released his pants to join the pile of clothes on the floor. He stood wonderfully naked before her.

"Beautiful," she whispered in reply.

He pulled her to the bed, where he lay down and stretched out before her, confident and aroused. Then he pulled her on top of him. She positioned herself on him so that she could feel his hard manhood. As she bent to kiss him her hair curtained their faces. Her hands stroked and caressed his body in an expression of

months' worth of fantasies. He shuddered in pleasure at
her touch, reaching to fondle her full breasts that fell
like ripe peaches above him. Then, with a motion as
fluid and smooth as a choreographed dance, he rolled
them over. He poised on his elbows above her and entered her moist, welcoming body and the two became
one. Their shadows melded together against the pale
wall behind them, the fading light filtering through the
curtain enough to cast a shadow of passion and ecstasy.

Angelina opened her eyes long enough to look into
the face of the man she loved and see the consumed
look of passion on his face above her. As the surroundings faded away, and she was aware of nothing more
than the two of them, and the passion that built inside
her, she reached up and coiled the tiny lock of hair
above his eye around her finger. With a final thrust
they shuddered in completion and she uttered a cry of
love perfected. He collapsed on top of her.

She encircled his moist, warm body with her arms
and traced the firm outline of his back with her fingers.
"I love you," she said very softly. Without thinking she
reached to finger her necklace in a gesture of happiness
and found only bare skin. She still expected it to be
there, even after its long absence. Her instinctive action
was not lost on Tonio.

"I almost forgot. I have a something that belongs to
you." He rolled off her to the side of the bed and leaned
over to fumble in the pile of clothing on the floor. He
rolled back next to her and leaned up on his left elbow.
He opened the fingers of his right hand. She caught the
glisten of gold as he dropped a chain and caught it be-

tween two fingers. Her necklace bobbed from his fingers.

She reached out for it. "Please put it on me."

"Tomorrow." He reached over her and hung it on the bedpost behind her. "Tonight I want nothing but the feel of you."

He settled back down beside her. They lay in silence as she lightly traced his chest with her fingers, listening as his breathing became slow and regular and she was certain he was asleep.

A tiny shaft of moonlight filtered in through a crack in the curtain. As she followed it with her eye she caught a glint of gold. *I'm an American woman now. Even you can't tell me what I can do, Tonio.*

She reached up and pulled her necklace down from the bedpost and over her head until it lay softly between her naked breasts. Then she lay back down beside him and drifted off to sleep with one arm curled over him and a lock of his hair wrapped around her finger.

ABOUT THE AUTHOR

Gina Robinson lives in the Pacific Northwest with her husband and children. She loves humor, romance, suspense, and spies. Not necessarily in that order. She writes contemporary romance, humorous thrillers, historical romance and women's fiction.

Most days she writes while wearing slippers, flip-flops, or tennis shoes, depending on the season. But she loves a great, sexy heel and has a closet full for special occasions.

She belongs to Romance Writers of America and International Thriller Writers. To find out more about Gina, visit her website at www.ginarobinson.com